COUNTERFEIT PAWN

"You know, I'm not sure that he is the right man . . . This blighter can think . . . We might be better off with someone who—"

"The Germans have to believe him," Ross said. "And they will when he finally tells them what they want to know. The mission *must* be a success. The real show is for June the sixth and Normandy is the target. Tagget will get the right date but the wrong place. The Germans must believe that we will invade the coast of Brittany."

"I would much rather see us use a regular army type."

Ross shook his head. "Every bit of information the Germans get out of him, they will have to beat out. He will not crack easy."

Fleming nodded and pounded out his cigarette. "I would not like to meet him after the war."

"Little chance of that happening, even if we scratched him from this operation and sent him back. His unit is scheduled to go in on D-Day. An air drop behind the lines . . . statistically, the entire unit has been written off."

TAGGET

BY
Irving A. Greenfield

BALLANTINE BOOKS • NEW YORK

To the memory of my good friend Herb Hirsh,
who was always there to lend a helping hand
when it was needed

Library of Congress Catalog Card Number: 78-72920

ISBN 0-345-28802-5

This edition published by arrangement with Arbor House

Manufactured in the United States of America

First Ballantine Books Edition: August 1981

JOHN TAGGET awoke with a start. He could hear his heart pounding in the stillness of his room and he was perspiring profusely. At the same time he felt so cold he couldn't stop himself from trembling.

Tagget was not the trembling type. He was tall, distinguished looking with pepper and salt hair, an open, almost boyishly innocent face and green eyes tthat seemed to turn slate gray when he was angry. He was fifty-five, widowed three years and worth a million and a half dollars. All of his money came from fees he earned as a microelectronics consultant and from the royalties on the twenty patents that had been assigned to him. Now he had the time and money to enjoy himself.

He glanced at the glowing green numbers of the digital clock on the night table, 3:15:8. Even as he was looking at it, the time changed to 3:16:1. His eyes went to the window. It was opened slightly more than a crack despite the falling snow that had formed a white barrier between the window ledge and the bottom of the sash.

Manhattan traffic noise from twenty-two floors below was muffled by the snow, but there were other sounds besides the drumming of his heart: the moaning of the wind, the scratching of granular snow as it whipped against the window pane, and the almost mournful hoot of a ship's fog horn somewhere on the East River.

1

His eyes moved back to the digital clock. 3:16:6. Nothing changed.

His heart was still pounding. For a moment he worried that he might be having a heart attack, but he did not have the slightest twinge of pain. Besides, at his annual physical three days ago the doctor had pronounced him fit. Fit as any man of fifty-five could hope to be who had sustained a neurological injury during WWII that had left him with a slightly game left leg and the inability to raise his left arm more than a few inches away from his side.

He ruled out heart failure. Maybe it was just indigestion.

He had dined with Claudia Harris at the Café des Sports and had eaten nothing more than filet of sole, three glasses of wine and an espresso. Nothing in that fare that would have upset his system . . .

Tagget pushed himself up into a sitting position. He threw back the blanket and reached for his woolen bathrobe. He padded out of the bedroom and into the living room, where he switched on the light. He went to the wagon bar, poured himself a double shot of twenty-five-year-old scotch and drank it in two gulps. He felt it move down his throat and into his stomach, warming him.

"Better," he said aloud. But despite the warmth of the scotch he was still not himself. Something was bothering him, an—uneasiness. His heart was still banging away. What the hell was happening?

He began to pace, dragging his left leg slightly as he walked. He stopped in front of the sliding door that led to the terrace. Snow had built up along the base of the glass. On one side of the terrace the wind had sculpted a series of hollows and intersecting curves which caught the light from the living room.

He returned to the wagon bar, poured himself a second drink of scotch, and looked toward the telephone. He could call Claudia . . . But what could he say to her at three in the morning? Come over and hold his hand because he had a severe attack of the frights? He shook his head.

He considered phoning his son, David, in San Francisco. It was only just after midnight there. David, if he was home, would probably be up to his eyeballs in his novel, or since it was Friday night—or rather very early Saturday morning—with some girl. He didn't want to interrupt his son in either situation.

Tagget turned away from the phone. He no longer felt the pounding of his heart, but the feeling of agitation was still with him.

He went into the small room that served as his den. The light from the living room cut a wide white swath into the room across the portion of his desk where the color photograph of his wife stood, shortly before Helen was told that she had cancer of the bone. She had been a beautiful woman, with rich red hair, green eyes, and a svelte body . . . until the cancer. Tagget had loved her and though he had a comfortable relationship with Claudia, and was even considering marrying her, he still loved Helen in a way. He had met her shortly after he had been discharged from the army and had been sent home after two years in the William Beaumont Army Hospital outside of El Paso, Texas.

He had been a very different man then than he was now. The war had just about wrecked him, and Helen had put him together again. She had seen him through his master's degree in electronics and had stood by him when he quit his job to become a consultant. They had made a good life together and he regretted that she had not lived to see and enjoy the wealth he had accumulated in the last two years.

He stood in the doorway and looked at the photo of Helen, remembering how in the early days of their marriage she would hold him in her arms for most of the night if he had an attack of the shakes, or felt, as he was feeling now, so awfully uneasy. These episodes had been particularly violent after his quarterly visit to the VA hospital. But as the years passed his reaction to the hospital visits had smoothed out.

Tagget switched off the light and went back into the bedroom. The time was 3:30:8. He slipped off his robe, dropped it over the chair and went to the window. He couldn't tell whether the snow was still coming down or whether the wind was just blowing it against the pane.

He padded back to bed and lay down, pulling up the blanket and closing his eyes. But after several minutes he sat up. His heart had begun to pound again. Suddenly he knew he was experiencing the after-effects of some dream he could not remember.

"A nightmare about something," he mumbled.

He leaned over and switched on the night-table lamp, fluffed up his pillow and leaned back against it.

Years ago when he had been in the army hospital and afterward for the first few years of his marriage to Helen, he always had dreams he could not remember. The doctors had told him that the injury he had suffered prevented him from remembering his dreams or the things that had happened to him between the spring of 1944 and March 1945, when the British liberated a concentration camp and found him along with a few hundred other surviving prisoners. It had taken the British a while to identify him as Captain John Tagget, 0-6895642, of the Fifth Ranger Battalion. The official records had listed him as missing in action three days after D-Day, June 6, 1944, but he remembered nothing about the invasion or what had followed it. He had good recall of everything prior to April 1944, when he had served with the Fifth Ranger Battalion in Africa, Sicily and Italy. Today he had a remarkable memory. It was almost photographic, except for this gap . . .

That the dreams might be starting again was in itself enough to make him apprehensive. For years now he had thought he had done with them. They belonged to a lost piece of his life, to the war, and he wanted no part of it. The war was a battle his mind had stopped fighting. There was no hope of his ever recalling the part he had played in it. Moreover, he had since become antiwar and held to the idea that the one he'd been in had been a manifestation of mass insanity that had somehow managed to pass itself off as a conflict of good against evil.

He shook his head and decided not to think about it any more. The best thing to do was to divert himself. He reached over to the night table and picked up the new autobiography of Sir William Enright, who like himself was an antiquarian. The difference between them was that Sir William was a professional and he was an amateur, though a good one. Enright had been with the British MI-6 during the war and had devoted a short chapter to his activities with the Intelligence group. Tagget opened the book and reread the paragraph he had been reading when he fell asleep.

"Of all the one-, two and three-man teams sent into Europe prior to Overlord, none were more successful than those directed from 29 Russell Square. Though much of the information about this joint American and British intelligence operation is still sensitive, one of their teams was certainly responsible for drawing German armour away from the invasion beaches and toward the city of Brest."

He stared at the paragraph, rereading it silently and then aloud, stopping at "29 Russell Square." His heart was pounding again. It was the address all right, he thought. Somehow, I had something to do with this place and I've got to find out what it was . . .

He closed his eyes and lay very still. For the first time since March of 1945, when he had found himself in a British hospital, there might be a hope of knowing how he had gotten there. He wanted to know what he had done from April 1944 to the day when a British Tommy had said, "It's alright, mate . . . Just lean on my shoulder," and he had managed to say thank you before the world went blank.

He put the book back on the night table. Switching off the light, he slid down on the bed. He was still uneasy. . . .

London, April 10, 1944

John Tagget walked rapidly past the British Museum, crossed Montague Street and went toward Russell Square.

Though it was almost the middle of April, it was still cold enough for his breath to steam in the air. A heavy overcast of gray clouds brought a premature twilight to the city and with it the threat of a sodden evening.

Halfway to the square, the wind suddenly picked up. He bent his body into it and thrust his hands deeper into a U.S. Army field jacket stained from hard use. The bottoms of his trousers were bloused into the tops of battered jump boots. He wore captain's bars on his overseas cap but no distinctive unit identification patches.

He turned onto Russell Square and looked up at the number 29 on the first building. He went straight to the door and knocked twice with the heavy bronze clapper.

As with most of the buildings in the city, the lower walls were sandbagged. From what he saw above the barrier, it was very old, made of red brick with a steep roof.

A buzzer sounded and he opened the outside door into a dimly lit hallway.

"One flight up," a distinctly British voice called out.

There were two men in the room at the top of the stairs. One of them was behind the door. Tagget did not even see him until he was three steps inside and glanced over his shoulder.

The man was as tall as himself, but thinner, with

a long, horselike face. His lips drew back in the hint of a smile. He wore a gray civilian suit.

The second man was seated behind a large oaken desk, his ruddy face bathed in the light of a desk lamp. He was barrel chested and a pair of crutches rested against the right side of the desk. Behind him a window was partially hidden by dark purple drapes. He too wore a gray civilian suit, looking as if he had been sleeping in it.

The walls were paneled and there were floor-to-ceiling shelves of leather-bound books. A large fire in the hearth made the room uncomfortably warm for him after the cold outside.

The door closed and locked, and the crackling of the fire became the loudest sound in the room.

He finally saluted. "Captain John Tagget reporting as ordered, sir," he said.

"No need for that sort of thing here, Tagget," the crippled man said with a wave.

Tagget brought his hand down.

"My name is Harry Ross . . . My colleague, George Fleming."

Tagget made a half turn to the right.

Fleming was standing with his back to the door, arms folded across his chest. A broad smile revealed a gap between his front teeth.

Ross gestured toward a leather armchair and told Tagget to sit down, then studied him for several moments. Well built, twenty-two, according to the records. Brown eyes and hair. The leanness of a young panther, right. The kind of man who would be able to withstand an enormous amount of physical punishment before cracking. The kind of man the Germans might believe . . .

Ross moved his eyes from Tagget to his colleague.

"If he's as good as his record says he is," Fleming spoke up, "I jolly well think he'll fit our needs."

"Sir?" Tagget asked, looking back at Fleming.

Ross shuffled some papers on his desk and read Tagget's name, rank and serial number from the papers in front of him, his voice never going above a stage whisper. "Silver star with four oak leaf clusters; a recommendation for the Congressional Medal of Honor; action in North Africa, Sicily and Italy—"

"May I know what this assignment is about?" Tagget asked.

"How is the weather in Italy?" Ross said pleasantly.

"It's spring."

"Spring," Ross echoed almost wistfully. "Though it's April, we won't really see spring until June of this year."

Tagget shrugged. So far Ross and Fleming were some kind of weird comedy team. Ross, despite his susurrant voice, was evidently American.

"What do you know about why you're here?" Ross asked.

"Orders came down from HQ. The next thing I knew I was pulled out of the field and was on my way."

"And when you arrived in London you went straight to the American HQ and were directed here."

"Yes."

"Then obviously we're the reason why you're here, captain," Ross told him. "The three of us in this room," he explained with a catlike smile, "will soon hold the fate of millions of Allied soldiers in our hands, so to speak."

"It's as Mr. Ross says," the Englishman put in.

"Today is the tenth of the month," Ross said. "On the night of the fifteenth you'll be in France."

"France?"

"France. Your mission will be outlined to you in detail at our next meeting."

Tagget frowned at the way he was being treated; Ross and Fleming were playing it too close to the vest. "If I'm going on this mission," he told them, "I'd like to know more about it—"

Ross waved him silent. "I have a few questions first. For one thing, captain, would you be so good as to tell us why you volunteered for the Rangers?"

"Lately I've been wondering about that myself. Action, I suppose, or maybe I was suffering from a touch of insanity."

"You speak French," Fleming said.

"Fluently, as well as Spanish, German and Italian. But all that's on my record. I was a graduate student in linguistics at the Sorbonne before the war and—"

"You met and fell in love with a young Polish Jewess named Leah Wolinsky," Ross said, reading from a folder. "After the fall of Paris she was taken by the Gestapo and sent to service German officers at a recreation center. She was given the option of becoming a prostitute or being sent to a concentration camp . . . She chose the former—"

Tagget started out of his chair. Fleming's surprisingly strong hands gripped him by his shoulders and forced him down.

"Three months after she arrived at the center," Ross continued to read, "she committed suicide."

Tagget went limp. "I didn't know," he murmured. "I had heard through our friends in Paris that she had been taken to a concentration camp. . . . I didn't know . . ." His voice cracked.

The Englishman released his hold. "Mr. Ross and I are with the Special Projects Office. . . . Our operation is a joint effort of MI-6 and your OSS and is under direct supervision of General Donovan. It is one of many such operations, each one vital to the successful invasion of Europe. You were chosen for this particular mission because of your outstanding combat record and your ability to speak French. You of course have the right to refuse the assignment."

Tagget said nothing and Ross picked up the thread. "Good, then. You have the next twenty-four hours to yourself," Ross said. "There is a room in your name at the Hotel Bedford Corner, on Bayley Street. That's just on the other side of the Museum. You will find clean clothes in the room. The ID you're to use while you're in London are in this packet." Ross handed him a used wallet. "I want you back here by fifteen hundred tomorrow to start your briefing."

"Any questions?" Fleming asked.

"Not now," Tagget answered. "But I will need some money."

Ross gave him a fifty-pound note. "Enjoy yourself. You have a difficult time ahead of you."

Fleming came back into the room after he saw Tagget safely out of the house. He sat down in the chair next to the desk and lit a cigarette. "Harry, I was not in the least bit prepared for that bit about the girl. . . . Any truth to it?"

"Only that she was taken by the Germans," Ross said with a smile. "He wasn't going for it so I thought it best to make him very angry."

"Oh, that he was." Fleming laughed. "I was having the devil of a time holding him down. . . . I think he would have torn your head off if he could have."

"Let's hope he does as well over there."

"You know, I'm not sure he is the right man. . . . This blighter can think. . . . We might be a lot better off with someone who—"

"The Germans have to believe him," Ross said. "And they will when he finally tells them what they want to know. This mission *must* be a success. The real show is set for June the sixth and Normandy is the target. Tagget'll have the right date but the wrong place. The Germans must believe we will invade the coast of Brittany."

"I would much rather see us use a regular army type."

Ross shook his head. "Every bit of information the Germans get out of him, they will have to beat out. He will not crack easy."

Fleming nodded and pounded out the cigarette. "I would not want to meet him after the war."

"Little chance of that happening, even if we scratched him from this op and sent him back. His unit is scheduled to go in on D-Day. An air drop behind the lines . . . Statistically the entire unit has been written off."

Fleming sighed but said nothing.

Ross reached for his crutches and pulled himself up. "Better have someone watch him until he reports back here."

TAGGET SLEPT late and was awakened by the persistent ring of the phone. He had to rub his eyes before he could find the phone by his bed.

"Yes," he said in a voice still gravelly with sleep.

"You sound terrible," Claudia told him.

He cleared his throat. It was 11:10:6. "I was still asleep when the phone rang."

"Anything wrong?"

He remembered the attack of anxiety in the middle of the night and hesitated.

"John, are you all right?"

"Just sleepy. I . . . I stayed awake reading too long."

She asked him if he had forgotten his one o'clock luncheon with Donald Hicks.

He had in fact put it on his calendar but in the wake of what had occurred in the early hours of the morning it was hardly in the forefront of his thoughts.

"John, are you sure you're all right?" This time the inflection of her voice showed her concern. "Usually you're the one who's up and ready to go at the crack of dawn."

"Sign of old age finally getting hold of me." She was only thirty-five and he always made fun of the discrepancy between their ages.

She gave a lascivious chuckle. "I don't remember you being in the grip of old age the night before last . . . In fact you were quite youthful in everything you did."

"That's why this morning old age has gotten hold of me . . . I overextended myself, so to speak . . ."

They both laughed.

"I'll see you about ten of one in the lobby of the Plaza," he told her. "By the way, is it still snowing?"

"Now, yes. But the forecaster said there would be intermittent flurries all day . . . See you, love."

He hung up and padded into the bathroom, where he shaved and showered. In less than a half hour he was dressed in a white turtleneck, black slacks and a dark red sports jacket. He went into the small kitchen and used his old fashioned dripolator to make himself a pot of strong black coffee.

The phone rang again. He picked up the wall extension.

"Are you sure you want me along?" Claudia asked without preamble. "I mean, it's going to be a sort of a business conference."

"Would I have asked you to come if I didn't want you there?"

"No."

"I'll meet you as planned. And now I have to go . . . my coffee is ready." He hung up and poured himself a mug of coffee. It was hot and strong, the way he liked it.

Carrying the mug, he went into his den. He quickly found the folder with the correspondence to Mr. Hicks, who lived in London and was here on his yearly buying and selling trip.

Tagget had never met him. They were just never in the same place at the same time. When Tagget was in London, Hicks was in Paris; the last time Hicks had been in New York, Tagget had been in Mexico City. Still, they had done several thousand dollars worth of business together. Tagget bought quite a few books from Hicks, who in turn purchased often from Tagget.

Now Hicks claimed to have a manuscript—actually a diary—of an M. Bigot, an English spy at Yorktown during the Revolutionary War who had later ar-ranged, during the French Revolution, for the abduction of the Dauphin from the Temple, saving the male heir to the throne of France.

Ordinarily, Tagget would not have been interested in Bigot. But he had come across the name in a letter written by a Captain Jean Audubon who had been with the French forces in America during the Revolutionary War. Bigot and indeed Audubon had been shadowy figures on the fringes of some highly celebrated historical events. If the diary would be authenticated as having been written by Bigot, it would easily be worth five thousand dollars and probably more. Tagget had decided he would be willing to pay up to six thousand.

In his last letter, Hicks wrote he had documents that would support the authenticity of the diary, including the opinion of a British handwriting analyst who had compared the writing in a letter known to have been written by Bigot to the writing in the diary.

Tagget slipped the folder of correspondence into a leather attaché case, took his shearling lined three-quarter coat from the hall closet and left the apartment. He had decided to walk from his building on York Avenue to the Plaza.

"Mean out there," the doorman commented when he saw Tagget. "Cold as a witch's tit."

Tagget smiled and walked through the open door.

York Avenue was deserted. A few abandoned cars stood in the street. On Sixty-ninth children were playing in the snow.

Tagget walked cautiously but was surprisingly sure-footed for a man with a game left leg. The cold was tolerable, but the wind cut.

Traffic moved slowly along Second and Third Avenues, and Park was completely tied up. Madison and Fifth were already filled with gray slush as he crossed them and walked toward the Plaza along Central Park, which the snow had turned into an extraordinarily beautiful scene.

He was directly across from the Hotel Pierre when he saw two teenagers standing along the stone fence separating the park from the street, eyeing him. One wore a pea coat and a broad-brimmed leather hat. The other had on a heavy brown woolen turtleneck sweater and a tan ski-cap.

Tagget shifted his attaché case to leave his right hand free.

The young man with the leather hat approached him. "Will you give me a dollar?" he asked.

Tagget shook his head and continued to walk.

"Listen, man," the leather-hatted one said, "all I'm askin' you for is a dollar." He came alongside Tagget and tried to step in front of him.

"No," Tagget told him.

"You old fuck!" he said, and grabbed Tagget's good arm.

Tagget stepped aside and at the same time slammed the edge of his hand against the bridge of the man's nose. The blow brought a sudden gush of blood and a howl of pain.

The second one came running to his friend's aid. Tagget waited until he was almost on top of him, then drove his fist into the young man's solar plexus. He dropped to the ground, gasping for breath.

"If either of you move," Tagget said evenly, "I'll have to break a few bones."

Neither one looked able to move. Tagget continued to walk down Fifth to the Plaza, wondering what the hell he would have done if one of the muggers had pulled a knife or a gun. He might have been killed. Still, it was not in him to be an easy mark for anyone.

By the time he reached the Plaza, Tagget was more angry with the two muggers than he had been when he had downed them. He paused on the steps and looked back toward Fifth Avenue, but there was no sign of them.

He entered the warm lobby and looked around for Claudia. She was sitting in a high-backed chair reading the *Times*. She wore a green pants suit that flattered the russet color of her hair. At thirty-five, she was indeed a beautiful woman with a good body and good features. Two years before, her husband had been killed in a freak plane crash; the plane had exploded on take-off. Though Tagget had never discussed money with her, he guessed that she had been left a considerable amount when her husband had died, or had perhaps inherited some from her parents. He was reasonably sure she was not financially attracted to him. Sometimes he found it hard to believe she would find him interesting for other reasons. Yet she did, and when they were in bed her passion pleased and flattered him.

As he started toward her, she looked up from the paper and came over to him.

"I didn't expect you for at least a quarter of an hour," she said.

He gave her a hug and said that he needed a drink.

She arched her eyebrows.

"I'll tell you about it," he said, leading her into the darkly paneled bar. They sat down in a booth and he put his coat on a nearby chair.

"Even in this light," Claudia told him, "now that I look at you, you don't look so good."

He summoned the waiter and asked Claudia what she wanted to drink.

"I'll pass," she answered.

Tagget ordered a double scotch, neat. He looked at his watch. "We still have about half an hour before we meet with Hicks."

She nodded and asked, "Now tell me what's wrong with you? You sounded awful when I called."

For the present, he decided to say nothing about the passage in Sir William Enright's autobiography and the unsettling feeling of its possible connection to his own life. Instead he told her about the attempt to mug him.

"You mean just now, on your way here?" she asked.

Tagget nodded. The waiter brought a scotch and he downed most of it in one gulp.

"Is that all?" Claudia said.

He finished the drink before he said, "That's what happened."

"You were mugged and you tell me, 'that's what happened.'" There was a note of exasperation in her voice.

"I decked the two of them," he said. "I wasn't about to give them anything. Two young punks tried to take me after I refused to give one of them a dollar."

"What if they'd had guns?"

"That was the reason for this," he said, lifting up the empty glass. "I thought about it afterwards, believe me."

She shook her head.

"I know it was a stupid thing to do," he said.

She reached across the table and took his hand. "If something happened to you—" Her eyes were watery and she couldn't go on. "What I have with you," she managed to say, "I want to hold on to."

"Thanks," he said quietly.

She removed a tissue from her bag and wiped her eyes. "And don't tell me I'm being foolish," she said.

"It's nice to know someone cares."

"If I didn't care," she laughed through her tears, "I would have never gone to bed with you. Now, some white wine would be nice."

Tagget signaled the waiter and she changed the subject. "How are we going to recognize Donald Hicks? You've never met him, have you?"

"When I talked to him on the phone, he told me that we would have no problem finding each other. Something like birds of a feather flock together, one antiquarian will find another."

London, April 11, 1944

Shortly before 1500 hours the phone on Ross's desk rang and Fleming picked it up. He listened for a moment and replaced the earpiece on its hook. "Tagget is on his way."

Ross came across the room from the hearth to the desk, dropped down into his chair and leaned his crutches against the wall. "From what you've already told me, not a terribly interesting night. I would have expected Tagget to bed down with some broad, or at least booze it up."

"Nothing more exciting than going to the Cheshire Cheese for dinner, then back to the hotel and up to his room. He did come down to the lobby several times during the night; he seems to be something of an insomniac."

Ross eased himself against the back of the chair. His lower body was again in the grip of the dull pain.

"He wrote one letter, addressed to his father," Fleming went on. "I took the precaution of having it intercepted . . . We will have it here shortly."

"I had considered telling him not to write to anyone, but that might have made him suspicious. This way we'll see what's on his mind. Anyway, I spoke to the chief last night about the operation," Ross said. "He wants the pilot taken out too."

Fleming waited for more.

"Captured or killed," Ross continued, "but I don't think we can be sure of either happening unless we attend to it ourselves . . . A bomb set to detonate, shortly after the plane leaves the drop zone, would take care of it."

"Or the Jerries might get him. I could set Gunner on to it . . . he could pass the word to the Luftwaffe."

"Can't risk it," Ross said, shaking his head. "Gunner will have enough of a problem handling our man. We don't want to give him something else to worry about . . . I want a bomb powerful enough to demolish the entire plane. When it comes down, I want it to be in bits and pieces."

"Then it will have to be two bombs wired to go off simultaneously. One in the tail section and the other in the nacelle of one of the engines. Gunner said that everything else is ready. His patrols will start sweeping the area tomorrow night."

"Excellent."

Fleming moved away from the desk and took a curved-step pipe from his pocket. He stood by the hearth to warm himself. "Gunner closed his message, 'We are all waiting.' If the Jerries believe Tagget's information, then when we go in for the real show we should be able to punch our way through most of France in a few weeks." He struck a match. "God, I hope this works."

"The chief says that with any luck, most of the German armor will be tied up in Brittany and our aircraft will keep it there. If we can isolate the panzer divisions, the path into Germany will be wide open . . . Hitler's generals will see that coming and try to stop him before he brings the ground war to their own soil."

Fleming puffed hard on his pipe. Their part of the overall plan might be worth an entire German field army and months of hard fighting if it came off. Whenever he thought of it in that light, the expenditure of a man or two seemed small, or at least outweighed by the lives of possibly tens of thousands of others . . .

There was a sharp rap on the clapper on the door downstairs. "On time," Ross said, pressing the buzzer.

Fleming tapped the tobacco out of his pipe, which he put back into his pocket. He went to the door and opened it as Tagget came pounding up the flight of steps, dressed in a dark blue civilian suit and a black trench coat. "It's raining," he said as he walked past Fleming into the room.

This time the door was closed and locked.

Fleming took Tagget's dripping coat and hat and placed them on a chair near the hearth.

"Have a good twenty-four hours?" Ross asked.

"I slept most of it."

"Pity. Despite the war, London still has a great many places where a man can have a good time."

"Chacun à son goût," Tagget responded testily. "My taste last night was for a bed with clean sheets."

Ross ignored him. He took hold of his crutches

and worked them under his arms; then, with considerable effort, he struggled into a standing position.

"This way," Fleming said, gesturing toward a door off to one side.

Tagget, feeling uncomfortable with these two, waited until Ross was out from behind the desk before he followed Fleming.

The second room was about half the size of the main office, windowless and painted a flat hospital green. A large lamp hung down from the ceiling over a table draped with a sheet.

"This is our briefing room," Ross said as Fleming removed the sheet from the table. "What you see is an authentic reproduction of the coastal city of Brest at the northwest tip of France. Here is the harbor, and here the surrounding terrain. Two inches, then, for every thousand yards. Your mission, quite simply, will be to make contact with François Cordez, the leader of a well-organized group of Maquis, and lead them into Brest, where on the early morning hours of June the sixth you will knock out the power plant—here." Ross picked up a pointer from the table and directed it to a small building on the south side of the harbor. "And then you will blow up the switch tracks in the rail yard next to the power plant."

"You see," Fleming said, "and this is of course most secret, the cross-Channel invasion will take place in the area between Tremazan and Lanildut northwest of the city by the Americans, here, and at Point de Pen Hir and Cape de la Cheevre to the south by the British, Canadian and Australian forces." He moved his right hand over the areas chosen for the landings.

Tagget took a deep breath and moved closer to the table. This was it, the invasion Europe had been waiting for. He had been privy to plenty of classified operations, but the enormity of the secrets he was hearing now made his heart race.

"By taking out the power house," Ross said, "you will neutralize most of the German communications and disrupt the railway system in and around the city.

Destruction of the switches will prevent them from moving any rolling stock out of the rail yards and will hinder the repositioning of armored units along the coast."

Tagget was impressed by what he was being told. The role he was expected to play in the invasion, and the risks he was supposed to run, were sobering. It was almost worth putting up with these two if he could get into the middle of this thing.

"You understand," Ross said, "that for the first few hours it will be damn rough going for you and your men."

"How many men will I have?"

"About a hundred."

"And weapons? Equipment?"

"We will make three separate drops to you once you've made contact with Cordez . . . here at Montfaucon, then north up here at Monteneuf and last at Ploundaniel, just outside Brest. These drops will be made on your command, by radio."

"And where will I be sent in?"

"Just west of a place called la Roche-sur-Yon," Fleming said.

Tagget smiled. He even knew the place. "I spent several days there with a friend of mine from the university. His family owns a farm west of the town. I'll probably land in his fields."

"What's your friend's name?"

"Claude Suret."

Ross gave Fleming a blank look as he said, "With your knowledge of the area we're already ahead of the game."

"You will be dropped at night from one thousand feet," Fleming said, "for minimum exposure. You'll be on the ground in a little under a minute."

"There is one other thing." Ross pointed to the harbor area of the city again. He had planned this touch. "About a mile from the power house there is a large ship repair yard. We would like to have as much of it held intact as possible. It is not heavily guarded and should, I think, be taken and held with no more than ten men."

"How long is my group supposed to hold the power house *and* the ship yard?"

"Advance elements of your own battalion will make a predawn jump outside the city," Ross answered. "They will make contact with you and from then on you will be back under the command of Colonel Swift."

Tagget nodded. The colonel had been his commanding officer for the past two years. "He's about as good as they come," he said.

The briefing continued until almost six o'clock in the evening. Ross told Tagget to develop alternate plans of attack for each of the three objectives and gave him a list of the weapons to be dropped in. Whatever additional equipment he needed, he would be given. Whatever he needed to hear they told him . . .

"You have about eighty hours to refine your plans," Fleming said. "Any information we have about enemy force dispositions is yours, and if they will be any help there are hundreds of reconnaissance photographs at your disposal, plus files in the other office."

"My suggestion," Ross added, "is to go at this a bit at a time. I wouldn't suggest spending whole nights at it . . . You're going to need your wits and your strength for the operation."

Tagget thanked him for his advice.

"Have you any specific questions now?" Fleming asked.

"Can my group count on being the only one operating in the sector, at least initially?"

"No . . . There are several like it. I can assure you that we have made sure there is adequate separation between them. There have to be multiple teams, because in an operation of this magnitude many vital objectives must be taken or destroyed simultaneously, before the enemy knows what is really taking place. I'll tell you this . . . enough will happen in and around Brest to make him think the world is coming apart."

Ross suggested that they meet at 0900 the following morning.

"Tonight," Tagget said, slipping into his coat, "I think I *will* go out and enjoy myself."

Ross stubbed out a cigarette. He was in a fury. "Listen," he shouted into the phone, "you tell me every time Tagget sneezes but you damn well didn't know he had visited la Roche sur Yon . . . Yes, it was *and is* important that we know that. He says he knows people in the area . . . Great, you'll add it to his record now. Foul-ups, that's what the whole damn bunch of you are!" He slammed the receiver down and put his hands on the edge of the desk to steady them.

"We have two ways to go," Fleming said. He had been standing on the far side of the room while Ross raked his information officer over the coals. He sat down in the chair next to the desk. "We can change the DZ, which might cause problems for Gunner. Or, we can find some reason to get Tagget out and a new man in. But it's a bit late to start over, and it might cause us some new problems."

With his hands still shaking, Ross managed to light another cigarette. "This is my baby," he said. "I conceived it and brought it full grown to the chief and I'm damned if some jerk in our Internal Security Group is going to abort it for me now."

"Suppose we do nothing?"

Ross took one deep drag on the cigarette and stubbed it out. "I don't like doing nothing about something like—"

"Wait a minute, old chap. Remember there is damn little chance of Tagget getting more than ten yards from where he lands, let alone to his chum's house . . . The dummy radio intercept will have a German patrol there to pick him up. He will have come and gone without his friend ever knowing he had been there."

"Yeah, I suppose we have to leave our bets on Gunner."

"I should think so. We've had enough success with him. He'll attend to his job."

Ross was trying hard to let himself be reassured. "What do you make of Tagget?"

"I would still much prefer a regular in there. But Tagget is what we have, and we'll use him to good effect, I assure you. He was quite overcome when he saw the mock-up, you know. Hears the victory bells already. We're letting him be the unsung hero he wants to be."

The clapper sounded. "That will be Tagget's letter to his dad," Fleming said. "Let's have a look."

III

TAGGET PAID for the drinks, draped the shearling coat over his shoulders like a cape and put on his broad-brimmed hat.

"You look like a cowboy with the boots and hat," Claudia said, taking his arm.

"It was either that or my Eskimo look."

The lobby was still fairly crowded. By the revolving door there was always a knot of people coming in from the street, stamping their feet and shaking snow from their coats.

"Do you see anyone remotely resembling an anti-quarian?" Claudia asked.

"As a matter of fact, I do. There, sitting next to that potted palm."

The man looked British enough in a dark business suit, white shirt and a gray tie. Three precise corners of a white handkerchief adorned the breast pocket of his jacket and he had an expensively tooled dark leather portfolio on his lap.

"He's staring at us," Claudia whispered. The man removed a pair of glasses from its case, put them on and smiled tentatively.

"Come on," Tagget told her, "and I'll introduce you to the other antiquarian in the lobby."

The man stood up and walked toward them. "What a pleasure to meet you, Mr. Tagget," he said, extending his hand. He smelled faintly of gin.

"The pleasure is mine, Mr. Hicks. This is Claudia Harris."

25

"I am charmed," he said, raising the back of her hand to his lips.

Claudia was unprepared for the courtly gesture. "How do you do," she said.

"Have you been waiting long?" Tagget asked.

"Not at all . . . I had just got settled when I saw the two of you looking my way . . . I had to put on my specs to be sure . . . Shall we go into the dining room? I've already arranged for a table."

Lunch was preceded by a round of drinks and Hicks offered a toast to a continuing and mutually profitable relationship between himself and Tagget. He asked if Claudia was interested in rare books.

"I'm afraid not," she answered. "I'm not much of a collector of anything. Maybe John will convert me. I can see how someone can get caught up in collecting anything from books to sea shells."

"I fall into that category," Hicks said. "I have a very strong acquisitive drive . . . Rare books are my passion, but I also collect coins, paintings, and when I can afford them, pre-Columbian figurines."

"Your wife must be a good sport," Claudia said.

"All my ex-wives eventually thought me more than slightly batty," he laughed, plucking the olive out of his martini.

Claudia blushed at her faux pas.

"It's all right," Hicks said. "I don't in the least regret my various marital experiences."

Tagget was amused that for all Hicks's volubility he really didn't reveal much about himself, other than that he collected things. Obviously women were among them; he was certainly open in his admiration for Claudia.

A waiter asked if they were ready to order. Hicks said he would like a second martini and opened the elaborate menu.

"May I call you John?" Hicks asked, focusing his attention on Tagget from across the table. "Because of our previous dealings and our correspondence, I

feel as though we have known one another for a while
—at least long enough to be on a first name basis."

"Please feel free," Tagget replied. "I'd much prefer
to be informal."

"I am just interested in when and how you became
one of us."

"You mean an antiquarian?"

"Of course. We are, you know, something rare ourselves." Hicks laughed and swirled his drink in his
glass.

"My accountant gave me a little talk about appre-
ciation and taxes."

Hicks looked crestfallen.

"From that venal beginning," Tagget laughed,
"everything else flowed."

"My own interest started during the war," Hicks
said as if he were answering a question. "I had the
good fortune to meet Sir William Enright, whose
friendship I still consider it a privilege to have. He got
me into rare books . . . Poor old chap just recently
suffered a stroke. He's not much more than a bloody
vegetable now."

Tagget leaned closer. His heart had skipped a beat
and was going like a trip hammer. He drank off the
remaining bit of whiskey and cleared his throat to be
sure of his voice. "I wasn't aware you knew Sir William
personally."

"I don't suppose I would have mentioned it in any
of my letters to you," Hicks said with a wave of his
hand. "Sir William Enright taught me everything I
know about rare books. You know he has written a
most informative autobiography."

"I'm reading it now," Tagget told him.

"Are you? Marvelous, isn't it? I thought—"

"You said you were with him during the war,"
Tagget interrupted.

"Well, not with him in the true sense of the words
. . . Rather I served in a subordinate position on his
staff."

"Then you were in Intelligence."

"Well, yes, MI-6. But I really did nothing more interesting—or hazardous for that matter—than drive a lorry, or carry papers from one office to another . . ."

Tagget felt himself perspiring. He was a little unsteady.

"John, are you all right?" Claudia asked.

He nodded but his voice was weak. "It'll pass . . . I'm okay." He picked up a glass of water, but he couldn't bring it to his mouth and it slipped from his hand as he slumped over.

"Oh, my God." Claudia was coming around behind him.

"Waiter," Hicks called, getting to his feet, "we need medical assistance immediately!"

Tagget was filled with a strange sensation—a dark vertigo in which he floated over a checkered landscape with a heavy bag of books on his back. Then he was hurtling toward the ground, while the air around him throbbed with the sound of engines. The wind tore at the mouth of the sack; books were tumbling out, their pages rattling in the rush of air. His fall was checked with a sudden snap. He was floating . . . no, he was moving away from the ground. The sound of the engines drifted away and his nose was filled with the sharp smell of ammonia. He shook his head and found himself looking down between his own legs. . . .

Someone was holding his head down and putting ammonia up to his nose.

"Okay," he said unsteadily. "I'm okay."

"Lift your head slowly," a man said.

Tagget came into an upright position and managed a weak smile. "Now for the classic question: what happened?"

"Too much excitement, from what Claudia told me about your encounter with those muggers," Hicks said. "That and perhaps a bit too much to drink."

Tagget sensed people at nearby tables looking in his direction. He had a giddy urge to wave to them.

"I think you should go home and rest." Claudia was pale and looked frightened.

"No, really, I'm fine now," he assured her. "If the waiter would change our table cloth and repair the mess I made, we'll just go on with our lunch."

"Are you sure, John?" Hicks asked.

"Yes. I want to hear about Bigot."

"Ah, Bigot. An astonishing fellow really." Hicks sounded relieved. He gathered up his portfolio as the waiter moved them to another table and began serving their entrees.

"I don't think you want wine after those scotches," Claudia said.

"I'm all right," Tagget said. He held his wine glass for the waiter to refill and turned to Hicks. "Listen, before we move to Bigot, I have one more question to ask about the war, or rather your experiences with MI-6. Did you ever visit number Twenty-nine Russell Square?"

Hicks blinked.

"Enright mentions it in the book," Tagget said. "I was just curious."

"Not at all likely," Hicks responded. "That was very high level, if you know what I mean. The book says practically nothing about it, as I recall."

"Did you know anything about it?"

"No."

"Must have been a very interesting place. . . ."

A few moments of awkward silence went by and Tagget sensed Hicks's uneasiness. He obviously knew more than he was telling and now probably regretted having mentioned the war and Sir William at all.

"To Bigot," Hicks said, holding up his glass of wine.

"Why not . . . to Bigot," Tagget responded, touching his glass to Hicks's.

Hicks rubbed his hands together. "Bigot," he began, "was most certainly in touch with Benjamin Franklin before the Revolutionary War and most probably during it. The diary seems to suggest that Franklin was paid various sums of money by Bigot . . . But these are just reflections on past events. The diary is

actually concerned with Bigot's association with the
Royalists and his association with Captain Audubon
to free the Dauphin."

"You said you have authentication of Bigot's handwriting?"

"Yes, indeed," Hicks said, peering into his portfolio. "Here are the papers drawn up and signed by
Howard Eggers, the chief handwriting analyst of the
British Museum, and here are two other expert opin-
ions on the subject of Bigot."

Tagget pretended to study the papers but he had
already made up his mind to buy the diary, if for no
other reason now than to get closer to Hicks and find
out what the man really knew about the operations at
29 Russell Square during the war.

"I'd like to have one of our experts here authenticate
the writing."

"Certainly, that would be wise."

"And you are still asking six thousand dollars?"

"Well, yes. It's worth considerably more."

"How long will you be in New York?"

"Until Wednesday . . . I suppose I could stay a day
longer if necessary."

"I'd very much like to have it. I'll have my lawyer
get in touch with you on Monday . . . It shouldn't
take more than a day to wrap this up."

"I shouldn't think so. Would you like to see the
diary?"

"I certainly would."

Once more Hicks dug into his portfolio and brought
out a small packet of pages wrapped in tissue and
held together by two tie-strings. "Notice the small
precise way the man formed his letters," he said,
addressing Claudia but handing the diary to Tagget.
"Bigot was a perfectionist."

Tagget untied the strings and began to peruse the
pages. At the moment he couldn't have been less
interested in the diary. But he made a small show of
enthusiasm as he went from page to page. When he
returned the packet to Hicks, he said, "Quite an

intriguer, Bigot. I get the feeling from these pages that a man like him would have fitted very easily into a more modern war. He could probably hold his own as a spy even today, don't you think?"

Hicks gave him a questioning look, then said, "He would have fitted very well indeed."

Their eyes met for a few seconds but neither of them spoke.

London, April 15, 1944

By the sunny morning of the fifteenth, Tagget had developed three alternative plans of operation. Each one of them was arranged according to a minute-by-minute schedule so that he and Cordez, the commander of the Maquis group, would know where their men were and what they were doing during each phase. The main action in any case would not last more than thirty minutes.

"If we don't have the power house and the drydock in our control at the end of that time," Tagget told Ross and Fleming, "we will have encountered heavier resistance than intelligence indicates we should. Then it becomes a holding action."

They were standing around the table, looking down at the model of Brest. He pointed down to a roadway. "From the reconnaissance photos we know that there is a good-sized ditch that runs parallel to the road from about this point in the city . . . to the power house, here. I'll put two squads of four men in it to keep the German reinforcements from reaching the power house during the action. I'll want two bazookas for them. Heavy ones. We'll have to count on them sending tanks, probably Tigers."

"I'll include the bazookas in your last drop at Ploundaniel," Ross assured him.

"Here, where the Germans have machine guns," Tagget pointed to three miniature weapons near the power house, "I'll try to take them out quickly without

any shooting . . . If I can't, then I'll use grenades.
But the attacks will be coordinated."

"How will you breach this fence?" Fleming asked.
Previous to his assignment in MI-6 he had been a
commando and had seen men shot to pieces after
getting hung up on the wire.

"We won't. We'll come in from the water side, two
rubber rafts with six men each . . . I'll want those in
the last drop too . . . There isn't any fence on the side
of the building that faces the harbor . . . My men will
be inside the power house before the main attack
actually starts."

"Timing will be touchy on a seaside approach,"
Ross said. "What if the boat group is delayed?"

"Then two assault teams will blow the fence with
bangalore torpedoes. . . ."

For three more hours, Tagget explained and de-
fended his ideas. He had given it the best he had and
he carried his points well. But his battle experience
had taught him that no matter how detailed the plan,
the unforeseen always cropped up during combat. It
was the extent to which the unforeseen could be overcome that determined the success or failure of the
mission.

Tagget said as much. He made no effort to keep
the irritation out of his voice. He thought the operation was in danger of being over-planned.

"Just one last question," Ross said.

"Shoot."

"How do you expect to move a hundred men and
all the supplies you'll need into the city without the
Germans becoming aware of it?"

"I will work that out with Cordez," Tagget answered. Without giving either of the men a chance to
interrupt him, he said, "I think he'll be in a better
position to know that than I am."

"You should go in with some plan of your own,"
Ross said. "The frogs have a way of making something
complicated out of something simple."

"Look, I do have a plan and I think I've shown you

what it is. It depends in part on Cordez, but it has to. Either you buy it the way I laid it out," he said without raising his voice, "or I don't jump tonight."

Ross's face was blank, but there was an unmistakable twinkle in Fleming's eyes. Tagget was sure the Englishman had seen action and equally certain Ross had not.

"I don't like it," Ross grumbled.

"It really doesn't make any difference what either of you thinks . . . I can't possibly give you details of the infiltration plan until I've discussed it with Cordez. For Christ's sake, he's your man, after all, and I haven't even seen him. And that reminds me, I think I should be shown what he looks like."

Tagget was given briefing photos and passwords, and the conversation turned to the terrain at the drop zone. Nothing more was said about the plan for moving men and supplies into the city of Brest. Ross knew he had nearly pressed the charade too far. "I don't imagine there is anything else," he said after a long silence. "Be here at twenty hundred. That will give us plenty of time to get out to the airfield and for you to get suited up . . . Anything special you want in the way of equipment?"

"A Schmeisser and all the ammo I can carry."

"Standard issue is a burp gun," Ross replied.

"Let him have it," Fleming said.

"One hundred eighty rounds enough?" Ross asked.

"Yes . . . For now." Tagget put on his coat and hat. "There is one other thing. If I catch one, I would appreciate it if someone took the time to explain to my father how it happened. I wrote to him, but of course he has no idea that I'm in London. He still thinks I'm in Italy."

Neither Ross or Fleming spoke.

"On second thought, never mind . . . It won't make a hell of a lot of difference to him where and how it happened."

"I should be happy to see that he gets word but I really think there's every chance . . ."

"Thanks . . . But really, it won't matter . . . In fact the less he knows, the better off he'll be . . . Civilians can't really imagine what it's like when the flak goes up . . ." Though he was speaking to Fleming, his eyes were on Ross.

"As you wish," Fleming told him.

"Thanks anyway," Tagget said, going out the door. He trotted down the dimly lit steps, opened the downstairs door and turned to Fleming on the stairs just above him. "I get the feeling that if Ross could replace me with someone else, he would."

"Oh, I hardly think—"

Tagget saved him the trouble. "I was just thinking out loud."

"If anyone would replace you," Fleming said with uncharacteristic feeling, "I would."

Tagget pondered that for a moment, then stepped into a clear spring day that made the war seem far, far away. . . .

Fleming returned to the office. He said, "He thinks you want to drop him. I told him that I would if I could." He filled his pipe, lit it and sat down next to the desk.

"You still would dump him?" Ross asked.

"Absolutely," Fleming answered, puffing hard on his pipe. "He's a thoroughbred and what we need is a dray horse."

"You think he'll crack too soon?"

"Not at all. He will take a great deal of punishment before he gives way . . . *if* he gives way. My worry is that he could die before he tells the Jerries what we want him to." He pointed with the stem of his pipe. "Tagget doesn't reveal much of himself, even in friendly circumstances, now does he? All you and I know about him, really, is what you have on those sheets of paper. My guess is that he doesn't know much more about himself. He's wound very, very tight. The war is something very special for him. Perhaps it's a game of sorts, but it's very special all the same. He is one of those strange men—I've come across one or two of them before—who are capable of pulling their roots out of the past, forgetting about the future and living for today . . . You picked up that bit about his father, right?"

"Yes, I did," Ross said. "He has a great deal of feeling for him."

"I know. But that in no way changes anything I have been telling you."

Ross lifted himself back into the chair. "So we'll go with what we have. There's no way I can go to the chief and tell him I've chosen the wrong man. And I think that would be wrong-headed at this point. Tagget will either serve our purpose or he will not. In either case he will be killed. If he talks, mission accomplished. If not, his presence in Brest will at least make the Germans wonder."

Fleming returned the pipe to his mouth. After a short silence, he said, "I am a natural pessimist."

"I've noticed that."

"That way I don't expect much, and when I get nothing I'm not in the least bit disappointed."

Ross picked himself up on his crutches. "Let's set this business aside for a while and go down for a drink."

IV

HICKS STOOD at the window of his hotel room holding a glass of gin. Below him Central Park was a swirling white fantasy. A few automobiles threaded their way through the snow-covered roadways and the tall buildings on either side of the park loomed out of the middle distance like phantom structures. Farther to the north were the towers of the George Washington Bridge, all but invisible through falling snow but marked by the intermittent flashing of the red aircraft warning lights at their tops.

Hicks had found his meeting with Tagget disturbing. In another set of circumstances he would have been pleased with the sale of the Bigot diary. Instead, Tagget had started probing around the MI-6 and the Russell Square ops and confronted him with some positively bizarre behavior which he could not let go unreported, as much as he would like to bow out of this sorry business once and for all. He sighed wearily and wondered if he should have read all the occasions on which he had been unable to connect with Tagget as a signal to avoid the man altogether.

The question was, what to do about this one? There was no doubt Tagget now felt he knew more than he was telling. Other than the cryptic mention in Enright's book, Hicks knew next to nothing about the operations out of 29 Russell Square. There had been all sorts of rumors which had floated around back channels for a while after the war, but nothing had ever come out in the open, even after Intrepid's BSC files were finally declassified in the Seventies. Though Hicks had been more than the office aide he had described to Tagget, he had never had access to any really high-level operations until much later, during the Berlin crisis, and had gotten out entirely—or almost entirely—soon after.

Hicks wracked his brain, trying to recall something about Tagget. As far as he could remember he had never heard the name until he had received the first letter from him, requesting some information about a biography of Francisco Sforza, an Italian condottiere who had become the Duke of Milan. . . .

Hicks moved away from the window and refilled his glass. He wanted to let the entire matter pass. But over the years, though he no longer had any operational standing with MI-6, he was sometimes quietly asked to obtain information for them. Once or twice he had put them on to things he thought they might be interested in. It had become a habit. For this service he never received or expected any financial recompense, but certain aspects of his life were made much easier, especially those connected with travel and customs. He considered himself to be a member of a very particular club.

His sense of loyalty made it impossible to disregard the Tagget matter. Hoping he was doing the right thing, he picked up the phone, dialed the number of the British consulate and asked for the senior staff member for Anglo-American cultural exchanges.

After a few moments, a man announced, "Bright here."

"The name is Donald Hicks. I was told you phoned my New York number but could not reach me."

"And what number was that?"

"212-884-3261," he said, giving Bright the authentication.

"Will you please wait, I have another call." Hicks walked back and forth holding the telephone while Bright checked his ID number against the inactive list.

When Bright came back on the line he asked, "What books do you have for sale?"

"One in particular," Hicks answered. "I would like to meet and tell you about it."

"Today?"

"Someone else may be interested in it."

"May I know the subject matter?"

"World War II."

There was a pause on the other end; then, "I can see you at Brentano's, downstairs in the paperback section. Against the far wall where the science fiction is displayed, at four. I will be carrying an old copy of Arthur C. Clarke's *Deep Range*."

"I will be there," Hicks said, putting the phone down.

It was snowing heavily as Claudia and Tagget walked down Fifth Avenue without speaking.

Claudia looked at him and recognized the familiar signs that he was angry, but this time she had no idea what had provoked him. He had come out fine on the diary. This new moodiness was a side of him she hadn't seen before. Though a passionate lover, he had always seemed fairly dispassionate and accepting about the events in his life, viewing them objectively, as they were, not as he would prefer them to be.

They were opposite Scribner's book store near Forty-eighth Street when he said, "I want to show you something." He turned and started across Fifth without even taking her arm. She picked her way through the slush and caught up to him halfway across the avenue. He went into the bookstore, walked to the desk and asked the clerk for a copy of the Enright book.

"It's on the tables under biography . . . The books are arranged alphabetically by subject."

He gave a curt thank you and went to the case marked BIOGRAPHY. He found the book and leafed through it quickly to the page where Sir William mentioned the covert operations that emanated from 29 Russell Square.

"Read this," he said, handing the book to Claudia. "The last paragraph on the bottom of this page."

She read it. "So? That's what you were talking about at lunch. I still don't get it."

Tagget put the book back on the shelf and started out of the store.

"Are we going anyplace in particular?" Claudia asked, following him out.

"I want to walk," he told her.

She waited a full block before she said, "John, will you at least tell me what is going on?"

"I don't know what's going on," he said, without looking at her, "I don't know what *went* on. But in some way I had something to do with number Twenty-nine Russell Square."

"You think from the way Hicks acted that he knows what your connection was?"

"I have a gut feeling I was involved in the mission that drew German armor away from Normandy to Brest."

"What do you mean 'gut feeling'? Don't you know where you were?" She knew his disability had been the result of something that had happened in the service, but he had never talked about it or anything else connected with the war, and up to now she had been happy enough not to ask.

"There's a place on Thirty-seventh Street where we can stop and have a drink," he said.

"You didn't answer my question."

"I knew where I was and what I did before April 1944."

"But—"

"The better part of a year after that is gone," he said. "In Germany, in a POW camp, I remember a Tommy telling me to lean on him. Then I woke up and found myself in a British hospital."

"Wounded?"

He shook his head. "Have you ever seen any scars on my body?"

"I thought you had a head wound or something."

"I don't have a steel plate in my skull, if that's what you mean. I had the limp and the damage to my arm when I woke up in the hospital. I had no idea what happened . . . The doctors guessed that I was struck on the head and that the blow precipitated some kind of nerve damage . . . But they didn't really know either. They've been looking at me a few times a year ever since, always talking about finding a cure but not getting anywhere."

"Hicks told us he never knew anything about what went on at this Russell Square place."

"He knows."

"Then it's funny he wouldn't just come out with it, to be helpful. He could see you wanted to know. He'd hardly need to be so evasive about something that happened thirty-five years ago. And you hardly need to obsess yourself about whatever happened."

"Well it happened to me," he said with an unfamiliar harshness in his voice, "and I'm entitled to know about that year of my life, if there's a chance to put the pieces together. I mean, where was I? The army had me missing in action in France three days after D-Day. I don't remember having been in *any* invasion. I don't even remember ever leaving Italy."

Claudia said nothing.

Tagget walked in silence until they were opposite the public library. "I know it's not easy to understand, but what would you do in my place? Suddenly, after so many years, you come across the merest opening that might allow you to slip through to the truth, to understand why you were left maimed without ever having sustained a wound."

She shook her head. "I can't honestly answer that. I guess I can understand it, though." She took his arm. "You know, I'd much rather have a cup of coffee than a drink."

They stopped at a luncheonette in the next block

and sat down at a small table where a gum-chewing waitress took their order.

"I'm going to find out," Tagget said. "There must be some explanation for what happened."

"Beyond what the army has already told you?"

"They told me what they wanted—or had—to tell me . . . But there's more to it. For one thing, there's Hicks. There's my reaction to Enright's account for another, the simple gut reaction."

Their coffee was banged down in front of them, saucers awash.

"I'm sorry," he said, reaching across the table for her hand, "that you had to sit through all of this. I didn't know about Hicks's former association with either Enright or MI-6."

"I'm frightened," she told him, "and I don't know why . . . I've got goose bumps all over me."

He gave her hand a squeeze and took up his cup of coffee. "I guess I am too, but something happened to me, Claudia, and it left me with a game leg and a bum arm . . . I just want to know what it was."

"Mr. Bright" was a tall, angular young man with a long face and small brown eyes. His real name was Sands and he had done errands like this for Bright before. Despite the weather, he had made do with a heavy turtleneck sweater and a wool watch cap and his only concession to the snow was a pair of brown lace-up boots. He stood in the science fiction section of Brentano's carrying a battered copy of *Deep Range* and a tote bag.

Hicks saw the book and approached him, saying, "Mr. Bright? I *am* sorry to have gotten you out on a day like this."

"Ah, Mr. Hicks? How do you do. Really, it's no trouble . . . I rather like being out in the snow. Let's go for a walk, shall we?" He dropped the book back into his tote bag and led Hicks out of the bookstore. There was slush in the gutters but the sidewalks were fairly clear.

"Suppose you just tell me what you think is the danger," he said, heading uptown again toward Central Park.

Hicks explained his meeting with Tagget and as much as he felt he had to about his relationship to MI-6 during WWII. "I don't know what Enright really knew about the operations out of Twenty-nine Russell Square," he said.

"Well, it's unlikely that anyone will now. . . . He recently had a severe stroke that left him paralyzed and speechless."

"Good heavens, I hadn't heard that," Hicks said. "When was this?"

"Not long ago at all. Happily it . . . I mean, it was fortunate for him that he was able to finish his book before it happened. But I still don't see the connection between Tagget and Enright."

Hicks took a deep breath and exhaled a cloud of mist. If a single characteristic distinguished the young men in MI-6, it was their impatience. They were forever in a hurry to get at the heart of the matter without ever digesting important background information.

"Your Mr. Tagget," Sands went on, "has no real reason for his interest, apart from curiosity, I should think. His name doesn't appear on our list here."

"Did you run a check with headquarters?" Hicks asked.

"Yes."

"Well, I don't really think he has any connection with Sir William Enright," Hicks answered. "I think Tagget's real interest is what went on at the Russell Square office. That is what I am reporting to you."

"That was thirty-five years ago—ancient history."

Hicks gave him a disapproving glance and said, "Much of what you refer to as ancient history is still considered sensitive. Tagget's reaction to being told of my involvement with MI-6 during the war was, to me at least, indicative of some very strong associations. And I don't mean merely psychological ones."

"Strong associations, or a couple of strong drinks?

You said he was drinking scotch?" Sands said. They've been going uptown since leaving Brentano's—had to be on Fifth all along.

"Look, once he was brought round," Hicks said, "he was perfectly fine and cold sober."

"Maybe he suffers from some form of epilepsy. It can come and go quite suddenly."

"I wouldn't know that," Hicks said, sorry now that he had ever called the consulate. The young man was succeeding at making him look absurd.

"What exactly was your specialty with MI-6?" Sands asked as they crossed into Central Park.

"During the war I served as an administrative assistant to Colonel Enright," Hicks answered. "But the title really meant nothing. I did everything from driving to courier work. During the cold war, I had agent status."

Sands did not press him for details. He seemed to be thinking of something else. Hicks was dumbfounded by the man's lack of concentration. It was a characteristic that complemented his lack of patience.

Hicks had no desire to be trudging through the park in his street shoes. The path was deserted and adrift with snow. He was cold and ready to return to the hotel bar for a brandy or two, then go up to his room for a nap. The meetings, first with Tagget and now with this Bright, had about done him in, but it was not in him to be rude, even if Bright was something of an idiot. He suggested that they cut across the corner of the park to the hotel where Bright could join him for a drink. The younger man agreed and they made their way down a snow-covered path that bordered on a pond.

To Hicks, the depths of the park seemed colder than the streets. For one thing, the snow was deeper, and it was very taxing to get through some of the drifts. The tall fellow seemed to be taking them in the direction of a stone bridge, and Hicks followed along as best he could. He recalled the view from his hotel room window and reflected that the park was not as pleasant to be in as to look at from a distance, which was no doubt why they were the only ones around on a day like this.

Sands stopped for a moment to allow the older man to catch up to him. Hicks paused to catch his breath; he could hear the wind as it blew through the bare trees. He was about to suggest that they retrace their steps and go around the park when Sands took what looked like a black collapsible umbrella out of the book bag and smashed it full force into Hicks's temple, knocking him to his knees. He brought the pipe down again on the back of Hicks's head, so hard that it stuck in the riven-in skull and almost slipped out of his hand as the body fell forward into the snow.

Sands pitched the pipe into the pond and turned Hicks over. He took Hicks's wallet, pocketed the money and credit cards, and threw everything else in a nearby bush. He left the park by way of the children's zoo, hailed a cab and told the driver to take him to Fiftieth and Third, a block from where the offices of the British Information Service were located. He used Hicks's money to pay for the ride.

France, April 15, 1944

There were perfunctory good-bys from Ross and Fleming at the door of the twin-engined Dakota as Tagget slung his gear inside. Ross reminded him once again to send his first radio message at 0200 the next morning and started his painful-looking hobble back to the staff car as a ground crewman pulled the chocks away from the wheels. From the look on Fleming's face, Tagget half expected him to try to climb in with him, but the Englishman turned and walked off with Ross. Tagget climbed aboard the plane and waved to the two men from the door. Inside, he switched on the intercom and told the pilot that he was ready to take off.

The engines sputtered, caught and finally roared steadily enough to sound airworthy. As the plane lumbered out to the runway, Tagget sat down on the bench opposite the open jump door and checked out his equipment for the third time, then closed the door as the pilot finished taxiing and turned into the wind.

The plane raced down the runway, swerving slightly as it put on speed. Finally it took an abrupt leap, the tail dropped frighteningly, and they were airborne. At an altitude of something under a thousand feet the plane turned to the southwest and leveled off.

Tagget made his way forward to the cockpit where a young first lieutenant sat at the pilot's controls. The co-pilot's position was vacant. He offered Tagget a cigarette and yelled, "A good clear night . . . Sometimes I fly through fog so thick I can't see if my own props are turning." He grinned at Tagget in the ear-numbing drone of the engines.

"Where's your co-pilot?" Tagget yelled back, slipping into the missing man's seat.

"Orders said only one pilot was needed for the job," he said. "It's really a nothing kind of mission . . . I mean for me, you know . . . In a few minutes we'll pick up our escort, two fighters to take care of any bogies that come around for an easy kill. But I can tell you, in my last ten flights, I've seen not a one."

"How long before we reach the drop zone?" Tagget asked.

"An hour, give or take ten minutes. Depends when the escorts get up here."

Tagget leaned back. He closed his eyes. The cigarette hung limply out of the right side of his mouth.

"I sure as hell don't envy you guys who go in like this," the pilot was saying. "You go in, you're there; I do my job and I go back to base. An hour and a half, two hours at the outside after you jump, I'll be bedding down with the loveliest blond piece of ass this side of the Atlantic."

"I'll be thinking of you," Tagget said.

"That should have been my line."

Tagget closed his eyes again and took a long drag on the cigarette.

A few moments later the radio began to crackle. The pilot answered and yelled out to his passenger, "The fighters have picked us up . . . They're behind us . . . One at five o'clock, the other at seven . . . Usually they stay about five hundred feet behind me."

The plane flew directly south over the island and Tagget guessed they were staying clear of the Portsmouth air defense area. Then they turned southwest over the Channel. When the plane made the transition to flight over water it bounced several times before settling down to level flight.

"We're going down to seven hundred feet," the pilot said, pushing the control yoke forward and cutting back the throttles. "The German radar, such as it is, won't be able to pick us up . . . There's no need to have them throw flak at us on a nice night like this."

Tagget snuffed out the cigarette against the metal side of the fuselage. A full white moon turned the water below to silver-crested dark swells, and for a while he could make out the surf along the blacked-out English coast to his right. In what seemed like a matter of minutes—he must have been dozing—England was gone and the coast of France came into view ahead of them and to the left.

"Some of the guys I've been dropping in," the pilot was saying, "wear civies. They're generally nervous as cats."

"I just have the regulation coverall over my civies," Tagget said as the pilot banked the plane into a more southerly course. "Listen, I've got to test-fire my weapon," Tagget said.

"Just don't put any new holes in this old crate," the lieutenant said. "I've grown kind of fond of her. And watch our fighters."

"I'll be careful." Tagget moved back through the fuselage, loaded up the Schmeisser and took off the safety. He slid the door open, pointed the muzzle of the gun down at the sea and fired a short burst.

"Hey, what the hell have you got back there?" the pilot shouted over the intercom.

"A German machine pistol," Tagget answered, putting the safety back. He sat down opposite the door. The sound of the wind was very loud, even over the constant throbbing of the plane's engines.

Tagget leaned back. The last few days had an unreal quality about them, traceable, he thought, to his relationship with Ross and Fleming. Despite what they were, Tagget had never really lost his image of the two top planners as some sort of comedy team, a bizarre troupe of which he was now a member . . . It occurred to him he might well be the oddest of the three, since he was the one going on the road, on his way to play out what the other two had dreamed up. . . .

The plane made a slight turn to the left.

Tagget checked his watch. Ten more minutes to go. He stood up and began to slip into his gear.

The pilot came on the intercom and told him, "Drop zone in approximately eight minutes . . . I'll start taking her up . . . You want out at a thousand, right?"

"Yeah."

The plane tilted slightly upward and then leveled off.

Tagget carried two regulation chutes. One would be opened by the static line when he left the plane. If it failed, he'd manually pull the rip cord on the auxiliary. In addition to the Schmeisser, he had a .45 revolver, a trench knife, two throwing knives hidden in the top part of his boots, a half-dozen grenades, a flashlight, a canteen of water, K-rations for three days and a first aid kit with some sulfa powder.

As soon as his chutes and shoulder bag were securely on, he tied the machine pistol across his chest and slipped the grenades into the pockets of his jumpsuit so that he wouldn't risk pulling a pin along with his rip cord. He strapped a jump helmet on his head and waited.

"You want me to circle the DZ once before you go in?" the pilot asked.

"Hell no, just get in there and get out," Tagget answered.

"Three minutes to go . . . watch for the red light on the forward bulkhead," the pilot said.

Tagget moved toward the door. He hooked on to the static line. The wind whistled past him and he had to brace himself in the door. The fighters were long gone and down below the ground was covered with moonlight. He couldn't manage to wet his lips in the slipstream. All of his previous jumps had been made with dozens of other men right behind him, it was a strange feeling to be doing this alone . . .

"Stand by for drop zone."

Tagget looked at the bulkhead. The red light was flashing. He swallowed hard, grabbed the outside of the open door and with his heart pounding pitched forward out of the plane.

Almost no sensation, except for the sound of the wind, the receding plane, and the loud rustle as the static line pulled the chute out of his pack. The chute quickly billowed out above him and checked his fall with a knee-jarring snap.

The wind was taking him somewhat to the south and he seemed to be going down very fast. He grabbed the shrouds and pulled hard to guide himself away from a clump of trees. He touched down, rolled and came up, already hauling in the shrouds of his chute to spill the air from it. As he worked, Tagget looked around him. The night was still except for the light breeze, and the moon was so bright he could see everything with startling clarity. He was relieved that the plane had disappeared and could no longer be heard. The chute was down and he slipped out of his harness, instinctively squatted down, freed the Schmeisser and clipped the grenades to his belt. Suddenly, far off behind him, there was a distant explosion—or perhaps two explosions very close together. The dull report boomed out over the silent countryside. He turned around to look in the direction of the sound and caught a burst of light in the sky that rapidly dimmed until it was no more than a red flicker miles off to the northeast, the general direction his plane had taken. He wondered if his pilot had seen what it was. . . .

After several minutes of hard digging, Tagget had buried his chute. According to the information from Ross, Cordez and several of his men would be waiting for him behind a stone wall at the edge of this large field, about a quarter of a mile to the east of the clump of trees he had avoided on the way down.

Tagget shouldered his bag. He held the Schmeisser ready with the safety off and his finger close to the trigger, moving in a crouch.

Between him and the trees was a small gully. He decided to use it and had just started down the side when there was a momentary glint of metal in the trees.

Tagget stopped and sucked in his breath. There was to be no one in the field, only on the other side of the stone wall. That had been very clear. He sat down and waited. Nothing. Then he slipped the shoulder bag off and took one of the grenades from his belt as he thought of the possibility that the op was already blown. His heart was beating very fast. The palms of his hands were sweaty and he had to wipe them on the legs of his coveralls. His movements were going to have to be well-timed. There was always the risk that the French had got their signals crossed and were out here to meet him. Well, it would be their risk, not his.

Tagget pulled the pin from the grenade, released the spoon and waited as long as he dared, then threw it toward the spot in the trees where he had seen the glint of metal. The instant the grenade exploded, he was up and firing his weapon, running for the copse.

There were screams and shouts from the woods, and they were German. He was in the trees before any fire was returned. As he dropped down and hugged the earth, he listened to what was being said.

"Two men are dead," a man told another. "And one wounded."

Tagget bellied his way in the direction of the voices. A lieutenant was ordering the rest of the patrol to search the woods.

Tagget took another grenade, pulled the pin and lobbed it toward the voices, hoping it would not strike a sapling and fall short.

One of the Germans must have spotted the grenade as it dropped to the ground. He shouted a warning that ended in mid-sentence as the blast filled the air with debris and the sharp stink of burnt cordite.

Tagget leaped to his feet as soon as the shrapnel from his grenade had gone by overhead. He ran through the clump of trees. As soon as he was clear of it, he headed for the stone wall. It was visible in the moonlight, as he knew he was too, and he ran as fast as he could, knowing that there were no doubt a hell of a lot more Germans around than the small position he had just hit. He reached the wall and vaulted over it, dropping down to the ground, expecting to see Cordez. No one was there.

Tagget took deep gulps of air. He wiped the sweat from his eyes. The Germans were shouting, looking for him. In another moment they would realize that he had left the trees, and when they saw the wall they would come for him, knowing he would make for it as the nearest cover.

"Well, Cordez," Tagget whispered to himself, "we'll have to find each other another time." He began to work his way along the wall. Now and then he looked over it. Back at the trees, he saw several trucks which had been driven out of the woods at the margin of the field. He could see the blue slits of their blackout lights.

The wall came to an abrupt end, leaving Tagget in the middle of an open field. He ran to the top of a small hill and looked around. On the far side there was another wall and beyond it more trees. He went toward the wall at a lope, jumped it, and was soon moving through a heavily wooded area.

He reached a clearing. He stopped and listened. He was just about to begin circling around it when a man told him in French to raise his hands over his head. He recognized the sound of a rifle bolt slamming home.

"Do not touch your Schmeisser," the man warned in French. "Do anything other than raise your hands over your head and I will blow your head off."

Tagget dropped his weapon and slowly lifted his hands. He was relieved, but cautious. He could not see the man who spoke and the voice was that of a man who would not hesitate to kill.

He felt a sharp jab in his back. He was told to walk.

"Follow the path to the left," the man said.

"My name is John Tagget—"

"Just walk," the man said. "And keep those hands on your head."

V

Sunday was bitter cold, and more snow was forecast for Monday.

Tagget read the *Times,* prowled around his apartment and made several calls to Hicks at the hotel, hoping to have dinner with him, draw him out, get the man in his cups again and perhaps learn something more about 29 Russell Square. Hicks wasn't answering and he finally gave up, leaving a message with the hotel operator.

Late in the afternoon Tagget was feeling restless, so he left his apartment and walked to the small park overlooking the East River. A strong northeast wind made the gray water choppy and except for a tug laboring upriver with sand barges close to the Astoria shoreline, nothing was moving in the channel. The cold made his eyes tear and his nose run.

He turned away from the river and started back to his apartment. He had been thinking about making some written inquiries to the Department of the Army and the Veterans' Administration to try one more time to get some facts about his whereabouts toward the end of the war. He had an unsettling sense that not everything the army knew had found its way into his records. Years ago, when he'd left the hospital in Texas, he had been willing to accept the promotion to major before they discharged him, and he had been willing to accept the double talk of the doctors and the succession of debriefing officers who seemed inordinately interested in his case but unable to find out anything more for him than he already knew about the blank period. Their long explanations had always gradually worked their way around to still more questions, and he recalled that he often simply fell asleep during the debriefings.

Now, thirty years later, he was waking up in the middle of the night. He wasn't a shell-shocked survivor any more, he had some clout and some important friends among the defense contractors who had bought licenses for his electronics components—men who could help him get some answers. There was the Freedom of Information Act. Most of the records of the British Security Coordination operations had been declassified. He could throw his weight around. He would talk to his attorney who had a partner in Washington, D.C., and apply some pressure. . . .

When Tagget opened the door to his apartment, the phone was ringing. He answered it in time, despite his limp.

"Hello."

"Hi, how are things in snowy old New York?" It was his son, David, calling from San Francisco.

"Wait and I'll tell you . . . I have to get my coat off."

"Okay, but remember, this is my nickel."

Tagget slipped off his coat, placed it over a chair and picked up the phone again. "We've had quite a snow, and right now it's freezing."

"I keep telling you to come out here."

"I do—now and then."

"I mean for good. . . . You could do what you're doing just as well here as there."

"I know . . . I think about it sometimes. . . . Tell me, how's the book coming?"

The downstairs bell sounded.

"That's why I called you," David began. "I wanted you to know it's been sold to—"

"Wait a minute, Dave," Tagget said, "there's someone ringing the bell in the lobby."

"Go ahead, I'll wait."

Tagget went to his security monitor and switched it on. Two men were looking at him from the TV screen. He pressed the button and asked who they were.

"Detective Alcantara and Detective Singer, New York Police Department . . . We would like to come up and ask you some questions." They held their shields up to the TV monitor.

Tagget buzzed them through and, returning to the phone, said, "Dave I have some . . . guests coming up. Let me phone you back in about an hour . . . Who'd you sell your book to?"

"Blakely House, for an advance of ten big ones."

"That's really great . . . Stay close to home . . . I'll get back in about an hour." Tagget replaced the phone in its cradle and went to the door.

The detectives identified themselves all over again. The one named Alcantara looked Mediterranean, with curly black hair and black eyes. His partner, Singer, was tall, thin and blond.

Tagget led them into the living room. He suggested that they sit down.

"Do you know a Donald Hicks?" Alcantara asked.

Tagget gave him a strange look. "I've been trying to reach him all day. He's a business acquaintance . . . I buy rare books from him."

"When did you last see him?" Alcantara asked.

"Yesterday afternoon . . . Why these questions?"

"Mr. Hicks was found dead in Central Park early this afternoon," Alcantara told him.

Tagget sank back in his chair.

"He looked to be the victim of a mugging," Alcantara said. "But we found your name and address among his belongings."

Tagget nodded. "Sure, I was going to buy a rare book from him. You say they killed him?" He told the two detectives about his run-in with muggers on his way to meet Hicks that day.

Alcantara looked at his partner. "Where did you learn to use your hands?"

"I was a Ranger during the war," Tagget answered. "Some things never leave a man. Anyway, you were saying it was a mugging."

"Or a murder made to look like mugging," Singer said.

Tagget shifted in his chair. He didn't like the direction of their questioning. Alcantara picked this up and said in a more conciliatory tone, "Neither one of us is saying anything but the obvious."

"Do you know of anyone who might have had a reason to kill him?" Singer questioned. "Would he have been carrying a lot of cash?"

"Yesterday afternoon was the first time we met, though we've corresponded with each other for three or four years. Everything is handled by check when we do business." They were playing him, volleying him back and forth between them.

"Did anyone else see you with Hicks?" Alcantara asked.

Tagget did not want to involve Claudia. "No, but you can—"

"Come on, we've already spoken to the waiter," Singer said. "We know there was a woman with you."

Tagget felt foolish. He made an open gesture with his hands.

"We have reason to believe that Mr. Hicks accompanied whoever killed him into the park," Alcantara said.

Tagget said nothing.

"You understand these questions are routine," Alcantara told him. "We might need you to identify the two muggers who tried to score off you, if we get lucky and pick them up."

"In other words, you want me to make myself available," Tagget said. "Not to leave town, as the expression goes."

"That's it."

"Tell me, does the NYPD always go through all this trouble when a mugging victim gets killed?"

"Hicks was not just an ordinary run-of-the-mill foreign businessman," Alcantara said. "He appears to have had some important connections."

"He did tell me that during the war, and I imagine

for some years afterward, he was with MI-6, the British equivalent of our CIA."

Again Alcantara gave his partner a look. "We know."

Tagget's heart started thumping again.

"We'll be in touch," Singer said as he and Alcantara stood up.

Tagget led them to the door, and as soon as it was closed behind them he went to the phone and dialed Claudia's number. "Listen," he said, the moment she picked up, "the police were here. Hicks—"

"I know," she told him. "They were here too. The waiter remembered me. For some reason Hicks had gone to the trouble of writing my name down . . . I was the third Claudia Harris they tried. There are about fifteen in the phone book. Do you think it could have been the same two who tried to mug you?" She had been speaking very fast and stopped to catch her breath.

"No," Tagget said simply.

"Then who and why—"

"If I were to make a guess," he said, "I would say it had something to do with number Twenty-nine Russell Square."

"But how could it? . . . That was so long ago."

"It's just a guess."

Neither of them spoke. He told her about the sale of David's book.

"That's wonderful."

Another silence.

"Why don't we have dinner together," he suggested. "We can drink to the success of my son's book."

"All right."

"I'll be at your place around seven," he said.

After he hung up, it took him almost a minute to remember his son's telephone number.

They got back into the car. Singer was at the wheel and Alcantara sat next to him.

"Peter, do you believe his story about the two

earlier muggers?" Singer asked as he guided the car away from the curb. "He only has full use of one hand and he sure as hell couldn't run or kick with that gimpy leg of his."

"I guess it's possible, if he surprised them and took them one at a time. Do you think the woman might have been the cause? Hicks had her down in his little black book. Maybe he was after her, Tagget gets pissed off . . ."

Singer shrugged. "It was one helluva day to go walking in the park."

"Did anyone come down to the morgue to make positive ID?"

"Eleven this morning, a little Britisher by the name of Bright showed up . . . He's some official at the consulate . . . Something to do with Anglo-American cultural programs. A real dapper little guy with a mustache and a bowler hat."

Singer turned onto Fifty-seventh Street and drove west. "I think it would be a good idea to go back to the hotel in the morning and check his things again."

"Okay, I'm game. You know it could be connected to his work with MI-6."

"I was thinking the same thing," Singer replied.

"Bright said Hicks was more or less inactive," Alcantara said. "But he didn't really explain what that meant . . . He was very polite, assured me that Hicks was not involved in anything with them. He told me not to press any questions about Hicks's operational status with MI-6. It would become unnecessarily awkward for everyone concerned, he said."

"Fine, but I'd still like to run a complete check on Tagget . . . He's probably clean. But I want to make sure. We'll put him through the teletype tonight and see what comes up."

Bright sat at his desk and pulled at his mustache. He was a pipe smoker and blew clouds of sweet-smelling smoke around him while he reviewed the events of the last twenty-four hours.

God, it was nasty business when someone had to be taken out. Most unpleasant when it was one of your own men. Not that Hicks had ever worked directly for him. He was a career man, while Hicks had never been considered anything but a stringer. But he had heard of him during the Fifties when he had supplied MI-6 with information on Russian industrial development. In recent years, Hicks had taken to drink, and drink—no matter who the man—sooner or later led to a loose tongue. Hicks's had become very loose, rather pathetically talking up a cloak of intrigue around his low-level errands for MI-6 which had called unwanted attention to some important operations higher up.

Bright would have preferred Hicks to have been taken out in someone else's territory. He hadn't enjoyed ordering him killed. But the man had stumbled into a situation that was way over his head and it was critical that he not meet with Tagget again. With Hicks dead, Tagget lost a potentially disruptive link with his past, a past which the CIA had very cooperatively devoted hundreds of thousands of dollars and its most advanced psychiatric techniques to wrest gently away from Tagget's grasp. It would not do to have this showcase achievement undone, to have Tagget go out of control after so much effort had been expended to save him from the consequences of his own background . . .

In any event, MI-6 was spared any further difficulties arising from Hicks's talkativeness. Everyone in the business knew that there were no such things as *former* connections to MI-6. Once a member—active or inactive—always a member. But Hicks's problems had apparently become too much for him of late. There were recent rumors that he had fallen in love with a woman young enough to be his daughter and had been foolish enough to divorce his wife of twenty years and marry the girl, only to discover that his bride was a lesbian. Some said he had her killed and afterward took to the bottle. The divorce, at least, was a matter of record, and the rest—well, the fact was, Bright had never had time to delve into it more deeply.

There was a knock on his door. Bright set his pipe down and glanced at the clock on his desk. It was going on six.

"Come in."

The door opened and the tall, angular young man with the long face walked in.

Bright gestured to the chair at the right side of the desk and said, "It was a good job, Sands . . . The police are treating it as a mugging . . . I've had some of our diplomatic people raise a fuss. I've even been down to the morgue myself."

"Do you expect Tagget to become a problem?" Sands asked, still standing.

Bright parried the question. "We'll have to wait and see. Shall we call it a day?"

"More like two days," said Sands. "More snow tomorrow," he said, looking toward the window.

Bright came out from behind his desk and walked to the door with Sands. It all seemed unreal. Here he was, going home to his wife, and Sands no doubt would also be in the company of some woman for at least part of the night. . . . He suppressed an urge to ask him what he was going to do with the rest of his weekend. It was better to keep their relationship on a strictly business level. It was better unreal.

They went down the elevator together and signed out at the door. Out in the street, they went their separate ways.

Tagget couldn't find a cab and was almost fifteen minutes late getting to Claudia's white brick apartment house on the corner of Houston and Sixth Avenue. When she came to her door, he told her to bundle up. "With the wind chill factor tonight," he said, "it's more like ten below than eighteen or nineteen above, or whatever it really is."

She put on a heavy woolen duffle coat and started winding on one of those six-foot-long scarfs. Her fur hat made her look Russian. "Those lined boots are a good idea," he said. "The streets are like Stalingrad in December."

While she went off looking for something he went to the window that faced onto Sixth Avenue. Not much traffic was moving except a few trailer trucks. They seemed to roll in any kind of weather.

"I just have to find my mittens," Claudia called from the bedroom, "and I'll be with you."

"No hurry," he answered. "I don't think we'll have any trouble getting a table." He turned away from the window. The apartment had a small but adequate kitchen, a dining area, a living room and a large bedroom. Every one of the rooms was exquisitely decorated. Claudia liked French Provincial and she had managed to make the pieces she had look at home here.

"Ready," she called, coming out of the bedroom.

Tagget put on his shearling and a fur-lined trooper hat. A few minutes later they were making their way toward Bleecker Street. She held onto his arm; it was almost too cold to talk. "Where are we going?" Claudia finally asked as they turned onto Bleecker.

"To Monte's, down the street on MacDougal," Tagget answered. "We haven't been there for a while and, my sweet, I feel like eating something that will give me a feeling of wellbeing."

"Italian food does that?" she laughed.

"Sure. For me it does," he said. "Anyway, I know everyone there."

Claudia pulled her scarf across her mouth. Here was another one of those things, the places from his past that intruded into their present. The first time he had brought her there he had let slip that he had often eaten there with his wife and son. She had accepted that one in silence, and she fell quiet now at his announcement that they were going back tonight. In some ways, she realized, he was more a creature of habit than he would be willing to admit. And so was she.

The restaurant was practically empty. Tagget got a warm greeting, first from Pete, one of the two brothers who had inherited the restaurant from their parents, then from Mike and the waiters. There was a rapid-fire exchange between them in Italian and everybody laughed as the couple was shown to a table. Mike told Claudia that he was happy to see her again and took Tagget's order for a bottle of Bardolino. He and Tagget spoke about the abominable weather in a combination of English and Italian.

When they had ordered, Claudia looked up from her wine glass and said, "We've been avoiding the late Mr. Hicks, though he's uppermost in both our minds."

"What can we say about him?"

"I don't really know," she answered with a shrug. "But it's an awfully peculiar feeling to lunch with a man one afternoon and the very next afternoon find out he has been killed."

Tagget didn't answer. Hicks's death couldn't be as significant to her as it had become to him. Had Hicks lived, he might have provided him with a way to get at the past, might have known others who had some knowledge of the activities at Russell Square . . .

"John, you don't feel peculiar about it?" she said.

"If you mean does it make me aware of my own mortality, then the answer is yes, of course. But if you mean do I have some feeling for the man, then I'd be less than truthful if I said yes. I am not sure I'm in shape to feel anything, other than a sense of my own frustration."

"You're a much harder man than I thought you were," she said as Mike brought the soup Tagget had ordered.

For the rest of dinner, they managed to avoid speaking about Hicks. They drank a second bottle of wine and Tagget mentioned his son's book again.

"What's it about again?" Claudia questioned.

"Some sort of East-West confrontation . . . one man holds the fate of the world in his hands. David hasn't really told me the details. He's too happy over the ten thousand dollars."

When they finished eating, they lingered over their espresso for a while and Pete sent over a drink, courtesy of the house. By the time Tagget signed the check it was past eleven.

They went back to her apartment and found that the radiators were all cold. They got into bed laughing and made love with the blankets pulled over their heads. They had drunk a good deal of wine and Claudia drifted off to sleep, with Tagget not far behind. For the first time in forty-eight hours he felt at ease with himself. He had let himself become obsessed by this thing, but being with Claudia helped. Maybe he should stop living alone . . . He closed his eyes—

Abruptly the name Cordez chimed in his mind and he was wide awake. He tried to think who Cordez was. Maybe that homicide cop—? No, that was Alcatraz or something like that. Cadiz, El Cortez. It was Cordez all right. He had once known someone with that name.

"Cordez."

"What?" Claudia lifted her head off the pillow, still more asleep than awake.

"Who is Cordez?" he was saying into the darkness.

"What's wrong?" She pushed herself up to turn on the lamp on the night table. "God, it's cold." She pulled the blanket back up over her breasts.

"I've remembered something, the name of a man."

"What man?" Claudia's eyes were shut tight in the glare of the lamp. "Who are you talking about?"

"Listen to me," Tagget said. "A man who had something to do with Twenty-nine Russell Square . . . a man I couldn't remember before . . . I was about to fall asleep when it came to me . . . A man named Cordez . . ."

"It happened just like that?"

"One minute I was thinking about nothing and the next minute Cordez was there . . . I tell you it was just as if it were waiting somewhere in my brain, ready to spring into the light, so to speak . . . Cordez, Charles Cordez . . . Charles was his first name, I'm sure of it." Naked, Tagget got out of bed and began to pace back and forth at the foot of the bed.

"Come back to bed," Claudia urged. "You'll wind up with one helluva cold."

He obediently got back into bed and pulled the covers around him while Claudia turned out the light. "You're cold as ice," she told him in a sleepy voice, holding him tightly.

"I've got a name," he said.

The snow started again at three in the morning— light at first, no more than a fine white powder. By dawn it had become heavy, snarling traffic and causing delays of up to an hour on the commuter trains coming into the city.

Detective Peter Alcantara lived in Little Neck, on the north shore of Long Island. His house was actually inside the city limits but it offered him and his family most of the advantages of suburban living. He especially enjoyed the proximity to Long Island Sound, where during the summer he sailed a reconditioned twenty-foot day-sailer. But the winters could be rough, especially when there was a heavy snow or an ice storm like today.

He was up an hour early and phoned Ralph Singer, who was recently divorced from his wife after five years of a difficult marriage to a woman who was an habitual gambler. Singer now maintained a bachelor pad on East Twenty-eighth Street, a few steps off Third Avenue.

A woman answered in a voice still heavy with sleep, and Alcantara had a moment of embarrassed confusion.

"Who is it?" Singer was on the line.

"Ralph, it's Pete . . . I'm going to be a little late. I'll see you at the hotel."

"Sure . . . No sweat."

That was all there was to the conversation. Alcantara put the phone down, got dressed in heavy clothing and went out the kitchen door to begin shoveling out his driveway.

He wondered what the woman with Singer was like. During his own ten years of marriage he had had two extended affairs. The first had been before he had been awarded his shield, with a woman who lived on his beat in the Murray Hill section of the city, an artist of sorts who painted illustrations for magazines and sometimes worked for the ad agencies. The other had been a society woman. . . .

Alcantara finished the driveway and went back inside the house to shave, shower and dress. When he left a half hour later, his wife Gene and his two sons were still asleep.

The Long Island Expressway was slow going, bumper to bumper in places, and the murder he and Singer were investigating wove in and out of Alcantara's thoughts. He could understand a mugging and then a killing, especially if the victim put up a struggle. But there were no signs of a struggle. And it was obvious from the footprints that Hicks had walked into the park with someone. Unless Hicks had been gay and had picked up someone—but even that possibility seemed absurd given the kind of day it had been. Besides, Hicks had a hotel available to him.

The more Alcantara had thought about the killing over the past few days, the more certain he had become that it had merely been made to look like a mugging. In fact, killing Hicks had been the reason the mugging had been staged . . .

Alcantara reached the hotel at ten o'clock. Singer had already been there for an hour.

"Sorry I woke you up," Alcantara said.

"She understood."

Over coffee they discussed the case. Singer agreed that it looked more and more like a set up, a planned hit.

They went out into the park. It was still snowing, but not as heavily as before. The area around the murder site was still cordoned off, but the new snow had obliterated the footprints that had been photographed the day before and neither man really knew what they were searching for—some angle, something that would give them a clue to who the killer might have been. They found nothing and returned to the hotel discouraged and cold.

The manager was waiting for them in the lobby. He was off to one side talking to a tall, dignified Asian man whom he led over to them. "This is Mr. Paul Kurokachi," the manager said. "These are detectives Alcantara and Singer. Mr. Kurokachi is here for the meeting of The Society of Photogrammetry, he wants to talk to you."

Alcantara and Singer shook hands with Kurokachi.

"I understand," Mr. Kurokachi said, "that one of the hotel guests was murdered in the park." His English was very good.

Alcantara frowned. The killing was supposed to have been kept out of the newspapers.

"This morning when I adjusted my equipment I saw the police barriers in the park," Kurokachi explained.

"Your equipment?" Alcantara said.

"If you'll be so kind as to come to my suite, I'll be happy to show you. I have cameras up there and I'd like you to see something."

On the way up to the sixteenth floor, Alcantara asked, "How did you learn about the murder?"

"Two of the bellboys from the restaurant were speaking about it, and I overheard them. I also understand Spanish." He smiled. "They said the man was an Englishman. Is that true?"

"Yes," Singer answered. The elevator door opened at the sixteenth floor. "To die far from one's home is a terrible thing," Kurokachi said, stepping out. "Even to be ill in a foreign country is frightening." He let them into his suite, where at the window, pointing down into the park, a tripod supported some sort of telescopic device.

With a smile, Kurokachi explained, "It is one of my inventions. It is specifically used for long-distance, time-lapse photography. Into the optical system of a telescope I built a camera and a strobe light that triggers at variable intervals for an extended period of time, up to forty-eight hours. The telescope has the apparent effect of bringing something five hundred yards away to within, say, twenty feet of the camera."

"Let me get this straight," Alcantara said, "are you telling me you've been photographing part of the park for the last forty-eight hours?"

"Not just the park, but the pond down there by the bridge. Birds come and go all through the day. Birds are my favorite subject, but even the changing weather itself makes a fascinating, panoramic drama when compressed into a few minutes of film."

"And you photographed the area where the police barriers are set up?" Alcantara asked.

Kurokachi nodded. "Yes. I was disappointed to find it in my field of view this morning; then I heard about the killing and immediately asked the manager to contact the police. Since Saturday morning, the film is all still here in this canister. It has not yet been developed."

"We'll develop it for you," Alcantara said. "We give quick service."

Two hours later Alcantara and Singer were in the projection room of the police photographic section. The time-lapse photographic effects of the birds were spectacular and gave the falling snow an awesomeness it did not ordinarily possess.

They ran the segment through twice before Singer spotted the two figures walking toward the bridge. The movement was speeded up significantly and the whole sequence covered only a few dozen frames. Still, one figure looked like Hicks. The other was a tall man, with something in his hand and some kind of hat pulled down over his ears.

The two figures in the film stopped for a split

second. The one in the turtleneck sweater made a complete three hundred and sixty degree turn. For a second, he faced the camera.

"Stop and go back to the face," Singer told the projectionist.

The figures on the film went backward and the face came into view.

"Hold it!" Alcantara said.

The film stopped.

"Not too clear," Singer commented. "A long face, that's all you can say."

"It's all we have," Alcantara said. "We want stills made of it. Have a sketch made and give the photograph and the sketch to the newspapers. Better not tell the press where we got the film."

The projector started again.

Alcantara and Singer watched the film several more times and pieced together, from fragments of action captured by the camera, the killing, and the killer going through the dead man's pockets. There was another full face of the killer as he left the scene of the murder in what looked on the screen like three giant steps. It was not any better than the first view of him.

"Okay," Alcantara said, "now we *know* that Hicks knew the man who took him out, but we keep that to ourselves for now. Set up a special number for the public to use . . . The official word is still to be that it was a random mugging. Have someone notify Kurokachi that we will have to keep part of his film." After a moment's pause, he said, "I guess this means Tagget isn't our man."

"It would have been a helluva lot easier if he had been."

Alcantara shrugged. "I don't want to let Tagget off the hook yet," he said. "Maybe there's some tie between him and the long-face guy."

"You think so?"

"I don't know . . . But it's worth a try."

The two men left the projection room and Singer

went to another part of the photo section to have the stills made and follow through with a sketch of the killer. Alcantara returned to his precinct and began to write the preliminary report of the investigation.

London, April 16, 1944

Ross drummed his fingers on the desk. His legs ached badly; a harbinger of rain. He looked across the room, where Fleming stood near the fireplace, then back to the decoded message on his desk.

"How could there have been a Maquis group in the vicinity? What kind of coordination is this?"

Fleming straightened his back. "The best answer I can get from Intelligence," he said, "was the usual one that the Maquis units move from place to place, they usually don't report to their London control when they're in transit . . . still, that doesn't account for why they were in place to pick up Tagget, unless it was pure coincidence."

"We're going to have to change our plans," Ross said.

Fleming approached the desk.

"When Tagget radios in," Ross said. "We're going to have to give him a rendezvous point with Cordez. One that will put him in German hands."

"What are we going to do with this unit he's with?"

"Nothing. It will have to take its chances. If they're in the wrong place at the wrong time, I can't do a damn thing about it. Their presence will just make Tagget look credible to the Germans. He'll have to explain it and won't be able to. Then they'll push him harder."

Fleming filled a pipe and began to smoke.

"If he stays free, he's going to become a nuisance," Ross added.

"I know. But I think we'll be able to button it up at the new rendezvous point."

"I thought that would be the situation *now*," Ross said. He crumpled the radio message and threw it

into the fire. "We can't afford another screw-up . . .
This time we were able to cover ourselves, or rather
the Maquis unit covered us . . . The next time we
won't have a ready-made excuse . . . Tell our friend
that."

"Most certainly."

"If the Krauts don't start shifting their armor toward
Brest by D-Day minus three . . . it will be too late."

Fleming held his tongue. He had been worried about
sending Tagget in from the beginning and regretted
not having made a louder noise about it. He might
have prevailed on Ross to change his mind, but he
doubted it. Ross was a compulsive planner, and it
made him a bit rigid, as he was being now.

"I just can't understand why nobody in this fucking
organization knew about the Maquis group," Ross
complained.

"Your troops have the name for it," Fleming answered. "SNAFU . . . situation normal, all fucked up."

"Not if I can help it," Ross said.

VI

THE PHONE on Alcantara's desk rang. The desk sergeant told him that a Mr. Smith wanted to speak with him.

"What about?"

He could hear the sergeant ask, and the man answered that it was a matter between himself and detective Alcantara, but a police matter. "I guess you caught that," the desk sergeant said.

"Yeah . . . Tell him I'll be down in a few minutes." He put the phone down and looked at the homicide report form in his typewriter. He spelled out the essential facts of Hicks's murder, and there were too damn few of them. He'd finish it when he returned.

Downstairs the desk sergeant gestured toward Smith, a man of average height who wore a loose tweed coat and a wide-brimmed hat. He looked prosperous but not from New York. Alcantara noticed that he held pigskin driving gloves in his left hand.

"Detective Peter Alcantara," he said, offering his hand. "What can I do for you, Mr. Smith?" He felt Smith's brown eyes taking his measure, and instinctively knew that they were in the same, or allied, professions.

They shook hands. "I'd like to speak with you in private," Smith said. "It's about John Tagget."

"My office is—"

Smith shook his head. "I'll tell you what, why don't you get your coat and I'll buy you a cup of coffee."

He was about to object; Smith wasn't asking, he

was telling him. But Smith gave him a knowing, almost conspiratorial look and he decided to go along. He needed any lead he could get.

"I'll get my coat."

"My car is down the street," Smith said as they left the precinct house.

"There's a coffee shop around the corner," Alcantara replied. He sure as hell wasn't going for a ride with this guy, whoever he was from.

Smith didn't push it and they wound up at a table in the rear of the luncheonette. The waitress, a frowsy young blonde, knew Alcantara and gave him a bosomy hug. "I haven't seen you around for a few days," she said, as if his absence meant more to her than a tip. Alcantara laughed and told her he was thinking about her all the time.

Smith cut in, all business. "I take my coffee black."

Diana served two coffees and two prune Danish. She stood close to the table and commented on the "lousy weather."

Smith looked unhappy so Alcantara told her, "We have something to talk about." She walked away, wiggling her behind.

"Okay," Alcantara said, "you can tell me what this is about."

Smith took a sip of coffee before he answered. "You recently requested information on a John Tagget."

Alcantara was about to bite into a piece of prune Danish. Instead he put the piece back on the plate. He and Singer had punched a query on Tagget into the FBI teletype the night before. They were still awaiting a reply, and already this guy shows up. Looking at Smith, he asked, "Who are you?" His voice was level.

"CIA," Smith answered. He took out an ID and held it across the table. The detective had seen them before.

"I wired the FBI, not the CIA," Alcantara said. "How come you guys got into the act?"

"We'd like to know why you're interested in Tagget."

"No, that's what I'm asking *you*," Alcantara said patiently.

"He came up red in the FBI computer."

"A commie, huh? I thought they had quit with all those surveillance lists."

"No, it's just a color code indicating that we have to be notified whenever there is a request for background information on the individual . . . Tagget is one of those who are not only coded red but also carry a numerical rating. That puts him in a special category."

Alcantara took a bite out of his Danish. Ever since Viet Nam, where he had first seen spooks in action up close, he had never had any use for them. They had committed more atrocities than people back home dreamed possible. Now they were numbering people back home with red codes. Alcantara looked at Smith and waited.

"Let's say that Tagget is a high interest item," Smith said. "That makes him a low interest item for you, after you tell me why you submitted the query."

"What's that supposed to mean?"

"Come on, it means we're interested," Smith told him with an engaging smile. "Look, even if you don't tell me, I'll find out . . . I just thought it would save a lot of time if I spoke to the man who made the request."

Alcantara took several sips of coffee. He decided to give Smith something; maybe he could trade on it in a minute. "It was routine," he said. "Tagget and his girlfriend happened to be with Hicks shortly before he was killed. We checked him out. But now we have photographs of the man who killed Hicks. Not very clear ones, but it's certainly not Tagget, and with a bit of luck, the picture may lead us to get the killer."

Smith nodded and ate his Danish. "So that was all there was to it?"

"That's all . . . Tagget is off the hook. And you're

the first to know; we haven't even told him officially yet." Alcantara smiled back.

"Why not?"

Alcantara shrugged. "This guy Hicks," he said, "had some connection with the British MI-6. We're just going slow."

Smith put down his Danish. " 'Had', like in the past, or 'had', like he was connected with them at the time he was killed?"

"I think both. The British are making noise and are asking us about results, asking at the same time that the investigation be kept quiet. I think he may still have been active."

"And Tagget knew about those connections?"

"Hicks was apparently evasive about that at lunch . . . Tagget got sick and passed out. He and his girl claim Hicks didn't tell them anything."

"Do you know why they were lunching together?" Smith asked.

"Hicks deals in rare books and Tagget does too, although he's not in the same league Hicks was. That checks out too. Hicks had correspondence in his room, and some old diary he was going to sell Tagget."

Smith frowned. "Tagget meets Hicks to buy a book. During the course of the conversation he discovers that Hicks was MI-6."

"Yes."

"And gets dizzy."

"Yes."

"What else? I mean what else was mentioned?"

"Some book—not a rare one, a recent one—and the two men seemed to know something about it. At one time, Hicks was close to Lord Enright, the man who wrote it. During World War II Hicks was apparently on Enright's staff."

Smith nodded, picked up his coffee and before he began to drink it, he said, "Tagget still might be your man . . . He could have hired the man you photographed."

"Possible . . . But not very probable . . . My guess is that if he had any killing to do, he'd be the type to do it himself."

Smith didn't answer. He looked worried, though, Alcantara thought.

Alcantara finished his Danish and coffee. "So am I ever going to get anything on Tagget from the Bureau?" he asked.

"No. Not when you have another suspect. No need to reply to the query now."

Alcantara signaled Diana to bring the check.

"I'll take it," Smith offered.

"Not on your life," Alcantara said, shaking his head. "I didn't get what I asked for, and I sure as hell don't want anything you got to offer."

"Suit yourself."

Alcantara didn't answer. He put a dollar on the table for Diana and told her he was giving her something for the days he'd missed. He paid the cashier and walked out of the coffee shop without looking back at Smith.

Tagget was impatient for the day to begin. He was up early. From Claudia's window, he could see that the snow had stopped and the sky was clear. He padded into the kitchen and started a pot on the electric coffee maker. He set two places at the table and when the toast was ready he called Claudia.

She came to the kitchen in a green negligee. Though her face was puffy from sleep, she was still beautiful. Few women, Tagget realized, would look this good this early in the morning.

He went up to her and kissed her on the neck. "Good morning . . . How would you like a cup of coffee and toast?"

"That wasn't exactly what I was dreaming about," she answered, "but I'll settle for it."

Tagget filled their cups and sat down opposite her. "I was up early," he said.

"You didn't happen to figure out who Cordez was?" she asked as she buttered her toast. .

Tagget shook his head. "Only that he had some connection with Twenty-nine Russell Square," he said, holding the coffee cup in his right hand. Even as he spoke, he found himself looking at her breasts, feeling a sudden flash of desire. He set the cup down on the saucer and reached across the table to take hold of her hand. "I want to apologize for the—"

"You don't have to," she told him. "I know you were upset."

He started to speak, checked himself and lapsed into silence.

"Go ahead and say what you want to."

"It's just that what I want to say doesn't come easily . . . You know, I loved my wife."

She nodded. She didn't mind his talking about it.

He was having difficulty finding the right words. "Once this is over, I mean once I find out what happened to me during the war, I want to marry you."

"I'll marry you now. Today, if that's what you want."

He shook his head. "I guess I knew that," he said in a low voice. "But will you wait?"

"I'll wait," she said, squeezing his hand. "I hoped you knew that too."

Smith returned to his office in the New York CIA station and immediately requested a meeting with Mr. Josiah Reynolds, the northeast area's chief.

Reynolds's office was done in walnut paneling and decorated with attractively framed prints of clipper ships. On a table, against the wall opposite his desk, was a scale model of the *Flying Cloud*. He sat behind a desk made of darkly stained oak. He was a tall, thin man with an "interesting" face, coal black eyes and black hair. He was an excellent listener and sat attentively while Smith told him about his meeting with Lieutenant Alcantara.

"Given the connection to MI-6," Smith said, wrapping up, "I thought you might want to have some follow-up on it."

Reynolds leaned forward and picked up an ivory-handled letter opener from the desk. "Did anything come down with the red tag from the Bureau?"

Smith shook his head.

"That's because if it had, it would make our life easier," Reynolds said with a frown, "and why should the Bureau want to do that?" He tapped the blade of the opener in his palm. "No matter, we'll do it ourselves . . . Something about Tagget and World War II, eh?"

"That seems to be it."

"And the police are sure that Tagget didn't do Hicks?"

"Lucky for them and lucky for Tagget."

Reynolds turned to the computer terminal. His fingers moved rapidly over the keys as he typed in his user ID number, then paused for the computer acceptance to show on the display board. Within moments READY came across the top of the screen in green letters. Quickly he typed Tagget's name, cross-referenced it to MI-6 operations originating from 29 Russell Square during WWII, and requested a resumé on Donald Hicks, a former member of MI-6. Then he also asked for a detailed report on Sir William Enright.

When he finished, Reynolds faced Smith and said, "The next generation of this kind of gismo will be voice actuated. Each operator will have a voiceprint on file for ID purposes. I can't wait to try it."

They spoke briefly about the weather; more cold on the way, they preferred rain to snow, especially in New York. . . . The flashing of a red warning signal on the upper left corner of the screen interrupted their conversation. The requested information was writing on the display.

TAGGET, JOHN 0-4566231, CAPT US ARMY 1942–1945. 5TH RANGER BTN. ACTION IN NO. AFRICA, SICILY, ITALY. AWARDED SILVER

STAR, TWO OAK LEAF CLUSTERS, PURPLE
HEART, MISSING IN ACTION 9 JUNE 1944.
FOUND IN GERMAN PRISON BY BR COM-
MANDOS. TWO YEARS WM BEAUMT ARMY
HOSP, EL PASO TEX. DISCHARGED 23 AUG
1947, 75% DISABIL.

Reynolds turned to Smith and said, "Nothing ex-
traordinary there." He pressed the "PAGE" key.
Smith watched the display roll up as new data
printed:

TAGGET, JOHN 0-4566231 FURTHER INFOR-
MATION REQUIRES A 012 CLASS CLEAR-
ANCE, FOLLOWED BY REQUESTOR'S ID #.
AUTHENTICATE.

Reynolds punched in the 012 clearance and his own
ID number. Turning to Smith, he said, "I'm supposed
to put your number in, too, but I know you've got
the 012 clearance."

TAGGET, JOHN 0-4566231 TDY'D OSS/MI-6 7
APRIL 1944. REASSIGNED SPECIAL OPS LON-
DON. INSERTED INTO FRANCE 15 APRIL
1944. ONE MAN OP. FOUND IN GERMAN
PRISON BY BRITISH COMMANDOS. NO MEM-
ORY OF OSS OPERATION. DISCHARGED 23
AUG 1947, WILLIAM BEAUMONT ARMY
HOSPITAL.

Reynolds shook his head. Then Hicks's name came
on the screen.

MI-6 1939 TO PRESENT . . . SERV. AIDE TO
LORD ENRIGHT 1939-1945 . . . AFTER WAR
DEALER IN RARE BOOKS . . . CONTINU.
ASSOC. WITH MI-6 . . . REG AGENT STATUS
1958-1964. DRINKING PROBLEM . . . PRES-

ENTLY BEING WATCHED BY OWN PEOPLE
FOR POSS. REMOVAL INACTIVE LIST.

"That's a bit of info the police lieutenant might
want to know," Smith smiled.

Lord Enright's name appeared, followed by:

MI-6, REMOVED FROM ACT STATUS. FILE
DELETED. NO OTHER INFO AVAILABLE.
FILE NAME DOES NOT EXIST.

Reynolds asked for the names of the individuals
who ran the Ops Center at 29 Russell Square:

INFO NOT AVAILABLE. FILE NAME DOES
NOT EXIST.

"Bullshit!" Reynolds tried to get the computer to
give him the names of the men who ran the missions
from 29 Russell Square by cross-referencing the street
name and number to Tagget and to Enright. Each
request drew the same response from the computer:

INFO NOT AVAILABLE.

Reynolds switched off the computer terminal and
faced Smith. "What's your reaction to this?"

"There's nothing that should have given Tagget a
code red with the Bureau . . . Lots of guys have
two stories, and as for the rest of it," Smith said, "it
seems that MI-6 has gone to a lot of trouble to protect
somebody. Maybe the Company is also trying to screen
the same people."

Reynolds nodded and said, "Enright's fatal stroke
last fall was probably induced, and there's little doubt
they put Hicks on ice . . . Whatever happened sure
as hell seems to be connected to Twenty-nine Russell
Square. Tagget too, from what you were told, has
some connection to the place. Only my guess is that
he doesn't remember what it is"—he looked at the

vacant screen of his computer terminal—"any better
than that thing does."

Smith was about to speak when the scrambler phone
on Reynolds's desk rang. He answered it, listened for
a moment and with his free hand wrote, *It's Langley
. . . Dep. Dir. Howell.*

Smith raised his eyebrows.

"I'll come straight to the point," Howell told Reynolds in his gravelly voice. "You asked for certain
information . . . We'd like to know why."

Reynolds explained the red signal from the Bureau.

"What else?"

"I wish I knew," Reynolds said. "But something is
playing I don't understand."

"Never mind what you do or don't understand . . .
Assign a man to watch Tagget . . . We want to know
who he meets and where he goes, at least for the next
few days."

"How long will that be?" Reynolds asked. He didn't
care for Howell on two counts: Howell came from the
outside, a former State Department man, and he was
bucking hard to form his own power base inside the
Company.

"Four days."

"How do you want the reports?"

"Make them every eight hours," Howell said. "You
can call me here or at my private number."

"Is there anything of a specific nature—?"

"Let's hope not," Howell answered, and hung up.

"That son of a bitch," Reynolds growled. "Thinks
the Company is run for his benefit."

Smith shrugged. He wasn't yet high enough in the
hierarchy of the Company to think in terms of whose
power base he wanted to be part of.

"You cover Tagget," Reynolds said. "Pick two other
men to spell you."

Smith nodded and then asked, "What about Alcantara, the police lieutenant? Do I make the call or not?"

Reynolds thought for a moment. "Cover him too.
If I know Howell, he's going to quash the investiga-

tion, and that might make the lieutenant do something
on his own."

"Like what?"

Reynolds shrugged. "Whatever a man with a con-
science might do." He said it with a straight face.

For the past fifteen years Albert Hentz, the senior
partner of the firm of Hentz, Defiore and Schiller, had
been Tagget's lawyer and friend. Tagget had phoned
him from Claudia's apartment and had arranged to
meet with him at three in the afternoon. Both men
were punctual, as usual.

Hentz sat behind the large table which he preferred
to a desk. The walls of his office were painted a light
blue, decorated with two large detailed landscape paintings and some arty photographs of circus clowns and
Bowery bums. They were a direct statement about
Hentz for anyone who knew him—he had done the
paintings, and the photographs had been taken by his
former wife, a woman he had divorced about five
years before.

Hentz was a smallish man, with gray hair and light
brown eyes that twinkled impishly despite his sixty
years. He was a dapper dresser, and unlike his other
partners, who preferred dark business suits, white
shirts and sensible ties, he often wore a sports jacket
and a loud shirt and tie.

"This is a bit outside the usual run of our business
dealings," Tagget began. "In fact, it's something you
probably won't be able to help me with, or may not
even want to become involved in."

"Tell me what it's all about, John, *then* I'll tell you
whether or not I'm interested," Hentz said.

"You remember I was going to buy a book from
Hicks, the London antiquarian?"

"Yes, as a matter of fact I thought you'd be calling
me today about drawing up the necessary papers."

"Hicks was killed Saturday afternoon, ostensibly
while being mugged."

Hentz shifted in his chair but showed no emotion. "Are you involved in any way with the killing?"

"Not in any way that you might think."

"Suppose you tell me how you are involved."

Tagget leaned slightly forward and asked, "Have I ever spoken to you about the war?"

"The war?"

"World War II."

"Not that I recall . . . I frankly didn't think—"

"You didn't think I was in it, isn't that right?"

"Your handicap—"

"I was a captain in the Fifth Ranger Battalion," Tagget said. "I saw action in North Africa, Sicily and Italy. That's where I got the handicap."

"Then you were wounded?"

"No," Tagget said. "Never wounded. Undernourished and delirious, but hardly scratched, as the saying goes."

Hentz arched his eyebrows.

"Until recently," Tagget told him, "I had managed to cut myself loose from any interest in the war, other than knowing my participation in it resulted in my disability and that because of it, I receive a seventy-five percent disability check every month."

Hentz hadn't known about the check. Someone else did Tagget's taxes. "Then your disability was service-connected."

"Yes, apparently . . . but where and how, that's the real question."

"Your records—"

"Let's back up a moment . . . As I said, I had given up on the war. The other night I was reading the autobiography of Sir William Enright. He's a well-established antiquarian who was with MI-6 during the war and wrote about his experiences in a brief chapter. In that chapter there's a paragraph in which he mentions the covert operations that were organized and run from Twenty-nine Russell Square, an address in London. He tells of one particular operation that successfully drew German armor away from Normandy, toward Brest, just before D-Day." Tagget paused to wipe his forehead with a handkerchief. Then he explained his peculiar reaction on first reading what Sir William Enright had written.

"But the army would have records of that," Hentz said.

Tagget shook his head. "The army records show that I went in *on* D-Day, and three days later I was listed as missing in action. Almost a full year later I was freed from a German prison by British commandos."

Hentz leaned forward and picked up a ball-point pen. "Do you mind if I make some notes as we talk?" he asked.

"No, not at all," Tagget told him, and then went on to describe what happened when he met Hicks. "You see, I didn't have the slightest inkling that Hicks was in any way connected with MI-6."

"What I don't see," Hentz told him, "is how all this connects you to Hicks's death."

"Even though I met him only once, I can tell you he was not the type of man to go walking in the park during a snow storm. He was the drinking type and a natty dresser, a bookish fellow, older than I am. He was with someone, and that someone killed him and made it look like a mugging."

"You think he was killed because of you?"

"Something like that."

"But the police—"

"They think it was a mugging." He told Hentz about the visit to his apartment by detectives Alcantara and Singer. "They also questioned Claudia Harris. I think we're their prime suspects, even though they won't say so."

"Did they advise you of your rights at any point?"

"No."

Hentz looked down at the notes he had made. "Why would Hicks be killed?" he asked.

"I don't know."

"Let me put another question to you . . . do you

think Hicks might have been killed for a reason other than his association with you?"

Tagget stood up and walked to one of Hentz's paintings, a rustic old world farm scene. "Last night," he said, staring at the painting, "for the first time I remembered the name of a man who in some way was also connected to Twenty-nine Russell Square . . . Cordez—"

"French by the sound of it," Hentz commented.

"Yes," Tagget answered, returning to the chair. "He was French." Then less sure, he said, "I think he was. . . . hell, I don't know, Albert. I only remember the name, not the man."

Hentz gently tapped his lower lip with the top of the pen. "I think I can settle one thing right now," he said, reaching for the phone. "I have a connection with the NYPD." He smiled. Within a matter of minutes, he was speaking to the chief of detectives, with whom he was on a first name basis.

"Tagget is the name," Hentz said, doodling on his pad. "John Tagget . . . the name of the victim was Donald Hicks . . . Yes, an Englishman . . . That's the one . . . So Tagget is not a suspect? . . . I see, you have photographs of the killing and the killer . . . Thank you very much. If I can return the favor in any way . . . Fine, I hope you will." He put the phone down. "So *that* absolves you of a crime you didn't commit."

"Good, but that wasn't the only reason I came here."

"You tell me what you want me to do."

"Find out about the information missing from my discharge papers . . . and anything you can about Hicks."

"The first half should be easy," Hentz said. "As for the second, my connections don't go that way . . . but I know Bill Schiller does have friends in the right places."

"Whatever the cost—"

Hentz held up his hand. "Bill's a partner and he has

the right connections for obtaining that kind of information. It's all in the family."

Tagget stood up and went to the window. There was snow on the narrow outside ledge, but the sky was clear and the city looked old in the light of a late afternoon sun. "Just suppose," he said with his back to Hentz, "that MI-6 was trying to hide something about the operations out of Twenty-nine Russell Square."

"Fine," Hentz answered. "But how would they know you and Hicks had met . . . And what's the connection between the information on your discharge and the hiatus in your memory?"

Tagget suddenly turned from the window. "Hicks must have contacted someone," he said. He walked back to the table but did not sit down. "He did it because he had met me."

"Why?"

"My interest in Twenty-nine Russell Square . . . See if you can follow this . . . Hicks sensed I had some connection with it . . . He probably was still feeding MI-6 information . . . He called someone in MI-6, told them about me—"

"And because he was doing his job," Hentz said in a gently mocking tone, "he was killed . . . It doesn't hold much water, John."

Tagget dropped down into the chair.

"You're asking me to accept the idea that something that happened in 1944, with which you may or may not have been involved, resulted in the murder of a man two days ago here in Central Park. Perhaps you could tell me what you know that could be important enough to be guarded by murder so many years later? And for that matter, if it's so important, why weren't *you* killed?" Hentz was sounding more like his psychiatrist than his lawyer.

Yet Tagget had asked himself the same thing as he had stepped into the office an hour ago. Now it was before him again. He was sweating again and shivered a little.

Hentz watched him, kept silent.

After a few moments Tagget regained his composure. "Call me as soon as you have something," he said, and stood up to leave.

"I most assuredly will. I hope I'll have something by the end of next week. Is that all right?"

Tagget nodded and offered his good hand across the table.

"What are you going to do in the meantime?" Hentz asked, showing him to the door.

"Find out what I can."

France, April 16, 1944

Tagget was prodded along a path that led into another copse. Two more men fell in behind him and his captor. He was ordered to halt and then blindfolded, and his hands were tied behind him with parachute cord.

No one had spoken since he'd been stopped. Whenever they wanted him to change direction he got a rough shove to the right or left. He had counted on his French to get him by, but ever since the first man had seen the Schmeisser he hadn't been allowed to speak.

He stumbled several times and once fell headlong. None of the men helped him regain his footing. Tagget had no way of judging where he was; he heard nothing more than the footfalls of the men behind him and the pounding of his own heart. They marched him interminably, three hours, maybe more, before they stopped and took the blindfold off. Directly in front of him was an old wooden barn, its lower half made of fieldstone and partially dug into the side of a hill.

He was pushed toward a small door to the right of the larger one. It was ajar, and inside he saw the yellowish light from a single lantern, hung from a low rafter, illuminating a group of five men and three women. The smell of hay and manure filled the air, though there were no animals in sight.

The man behind Tagget nudged him with the muzzle of his rifle and ordered him toward the group. They were armed with a variety of weapons ranging from a British Sten gun to a German Mauser. Several had ancient-looking bolt action French rifles he had never seen before.

One of the group stepped forward. He was about forty, dressed like the others in old clothes and peaked cap.

"We watched you," the man said. "You killed many Bosch." He spoke haltingly in German.

Tagget answered in French, telling him he was an American.

The man walked completely around him and stopped, facing him.

"Your name?"

"John Tagget."

"Well Monsieur Tagget," the man said with a sweep of his hands, "you drop out of the skies, but the plane that brought you blows up." Tagget recalled the detonation he'd heard while he was burying his chute. He opened his mouth to speak, but the man cut him off. "You kill many Bosch, but you have a Schmeisser."

"Some of your men have Mausers."

The man nodded. "Yes, but we have taken them from dead Bosch," he said matter of factly, "and that gives us the right to them, isn't that so?"

"The Schmeisser was issued to me by request," Tagget answered, "but I've used it before. On Bosch, as you say."

"Where?"

"Sicily and Italy."

The man did not even raise his eyebrows. "Before you tell me why you are here," he said, "remember I have but two choices. I can believe you or not. If I do not believe you, however, I have only one choice— to have my men kill you. Now let me hear what you have to say."

Tagget looked beyond his interrogator, who was

standing so close in front of him that he could smell the garlic on his breath. The other members of the group had not moved, though one of the women had a cigarette between her lips. The war was years old for them; they were used to killing and seeing members of their group being killed. If any of them was ordered to execute him, they would do it without hesitation.

"I was sent to find a man named Cordez. Like yourself he leads a Maquis group," Tagget said, shifting his eyes back to the man in front of him.

"Why?"

"I'm sorry, monsieur," Tagget said, "but I can't tell you."

"I know no one using the name Cordez." Looking toward the other members of the group, he asked if any of them had ever heard of a Maquis leader by the name of Cordez.

The answer was a chorus of no's.

"Cordez is the man I was sent to find," Tagget said. "I am not a German . . . I have a friend in this vicinity and before the war I spent time with him here. His name is Claude Suret. His family owns a farm just west of la Roche-sur-Yon."

"We are in your friend's barn," the man told him.

"Then for God's sake bring him here! He can identify me."

"A dead man can identify nothing," the leader said. "He was killed with all his family during the winter, when the Germans discovered he had helped a wounded man from another Maquis group."

Tagget said nothing.

"Where did you meet Claude?" the man asked.

"At the Sorbonne," Tagget answered in a low voice. "We had a seminar in philology together. The fall the war broke out, he was going to come back to the United States with me."

The man rubbed his chin and took a step backward. "I will wait," he said. "I do not want the blood of an innocent man on my hands."

"Have you a radio?" Tagget asked, annoyed with himself for not having thought of it sooner.

"Yes," the man said.

"Will it reach London?"

The man nodded.

"I have prearranged signals with my control in London," Tagget said. "If I prove to you who I am, will you help me find Cordez?"

He glanced toward the other members of the group. "We will help you," he replied. Unsheathing a knife, he walked behind Tagget and cut his bonds. "But let me warn you that if you try to leave us, you will be shot."

"I understand that," Tagget answered, rubbing the circulation back into his hands.

The leader of the group stopped in front of Tagget and offered his hand. "My name is Henri Dumas."

Tagget shook his hand and asked if he might have a cigarette.

"A Bosch cigarette," Dumas said, "but at the moment here in Bretagne it is the best one can get."

"It will do fine," Tagget answered, taking a deep drag on it.

Dumas offered him food, and Tagget sat down with the group, telling them as much as he felt he could to ease their suspicions. He leaned heavily on his recollections of what Claude Suret had told him about his home village. The Frenchmen seemed to be warming to him a little. After he had eaten bread and cold roast chicken and had drunk two cups of wine, he turned to Dumas, who was sitting next to him on the floor of the barn. "What I don't understand is how there could have been so many Krauts so close to the drop zone. It was almost as if they were waiting for me."

"In this part of France, the Germans are always waiting for Americans to parachute out of the sky," Dumas said in a weary voice. He looked at Tagget. "And, my friend, so are we."

VII

WILLIAM SCHILLER was tall, handsome and surprisingly muscular for his fifty-five years. His light brown hair was styled to give it the flowing look of a lion's mane, and his green eyes intrigued women easily. Though he was a bachelor, he had had several long relationships with various women. He had recently begun one with a twenty-five-year-old sloe-eyed beauty named Irene Regal, who acted as his hostess.

He was the wealthiest of the three partners in the firm of Hentz, Defiore and Schiller, and the one who spent almost none of his time on strictly legal matters. He held a law degree from Columbia and had passed the New York State Bar Examination some thirty years ago, but his role was to be the man who knew people on the city, state and federal levels—people who held important positions.

In his own mind he often pictured his role as that of a link—a link between one individual and another. His fees for the assignments he undertook were frequently in the tens of thousands, so he lived well.

For almost twenty years he had managed to stay close to the White House, regardless of who happened to occupy it. He had very strong connections with the State Department and the Internal Revenue Service, all well-known and often mentioned in the press. Schiller enjoyed seeing his name in print, especially when he was referred to as a "power broker." People who wanted to get things done, either for themselves or others, went to him because he knew the men and women who were in positions to do almost anything.

But Schiller's invisible ties were more significant than those that made the New York *Times* and the Washington *Post*. During World War II he had served with the OSS, and because of his fluency in German and Russian he had been one of the architects of a large CIA network established inside East Germany shortly after the war. Ten years ago he had decided he might be more valuable to the CIA if he could contrive to serve the Russians as well as the United States. He had managed it so well indeed that he had become an important link for the Soviet spy network in the United States.

Schiller had a duplex on the fourteenth floor of the Olympic Towers, across from Saint Patrick's Cathedral in Manhattan, and a lovely fieldstone house in the Chevy Chase district of Maryland, a short drive from Washington. He divided his time between the two locations.

When Hentz phoned him, he was still in New York. Schiller said that he would have left the previous day if the weather had not been so miserable and that he was now thinking about taking a late Washington shuttle flight out of LaGuardia. He invited Hentz down to his Maryland home for the following weekend, explaining cheerfully that he wanted to introduce him to a very rare and lovely woman.

Hentz said he would think about it.

Schiller suggested Hentz might be able to convince the woman to pose in the nude and told him to bring his palette and beret.

"With that kind of temptation," Hentz answered with a laugh, "I will come . . . but I have something to discuss with you."

"Your calls are almost never social," Schiller grumbled. "Go ahead. Ask." He pressed a button, actuating a voice recorder.

Hentz related all of what Tagget had told him, then asked if Schiller would be able to find out if Tagget had any connections with 29 Russell Square and whether Hicks had been current with MI-6.

"I will do my best," Schiller said.

They talked for another few minutes and when Schiller took the initiative and said good-by, he pushed the rewind button on the recorder. The whirr of the tape was the only sound in the room. He pressed another button and leaned back in his swivel chair, listening to the tape . . .

The Russians would be interested in anything having to do with MI-6, or the OSS. That it had happened over thirty years ago made no difference to them. They compiled information on people and events and stashed it away like squirrels. Schiller often wondered where these voluminous files were kept.

Russian logic, as Schiller had come to understand it, was as circuitous as it could possibly be. Nothing ever went in a straight line from A to Z. Yet for all their peculiarities they ran an extremely well-organized and productive intelligence network . . .

The tape had reached the part where Hentz was talking about Donald Hicks, who interested Schiller more than Tagget for the moment.

Hicks's past and present activities were known to the Russians of late, as was his weakness for drink. Schiller's Russian control, Colonel Uri Chelenko of the Soviet mission in New York, had suggested the previous Monday that he contact Hicks either during his stay in New York or in London sometime within the next month, with the aim of persuading the man to provide information to the Russians, through him. He was told by Chelenko that Hicks might possibly lead them to the heart of a fairly important Anglo-American operation. At the time of the conversation, Schiller had no idea that Tagget knew Hicks.

Schiller rewound the tape a second time and played it again, this time paying particular attention to Tagget's role. He had met Tagget several times in Albert Hentz's office but hadn't formed any opinion about the man. Now, as he listened to the tape, he realized

Tagget might be someone of considerable importance to him. And as for 29 Russell Square, he remembered it had existed, but nothing else, at least for the moment.

He played the tape a third time to be sure that he had all the essential facts committed to memory in their correct sequence, then erased the entire conversation with Hentz and reset the recorder so it would be ready to tape the next conversation.

Schiller lit a cigarette while he considered how to handle the situation. Serving, in his fashion, two masters required he treat each with a different focus, especially when the same or similar information was involved. Two parallel approaches occurred to him. Since he and Colonel Chelenko had already spoken about Hicks, he belonged to the Russians. Tagget would go to the Company, on two counts: the Russians had not as yet become aware of his connection with Hicks, whatever it was; and because the information Hentz had asked for would have to come from CIA files.

He stubbed out the cigarette, lifted the phone, dialed an 800 number followed by his own phone number in reverse.

After two rings a voice answered. "At the sound of the tone give your name and SS number."

A beep sounded and Schiller said, "Peter Grant, 101-22-8993."

Approximately thirty seconds passed before the voice on the other end said, "You will be contacted within five minutes. Thank you."

Schiller put the phone back in its cradle. Placing the tips of his fingers together, he closed his eyes and waited for the call back. He took several deep breaths, relaxed and began to feel his mind reaching back for some additional memory of 29 Russell Square, something that might help him understand why it formed a nexus between Hicks, Tagget and Lord Enright. That the three of them were antiquarians might be nothing more than a coincidence. Tagget, he knew from Hentz, had only started to collect rare books within the last five years; only Hicks and Enright had made it their lifelong work.

Suddenly he remembered that there had been two men at 29 Russell Square. "Two men," he said aloud, lowering his hands and opening his eyes. He had met them shortly after D-Day. One was an American, the other an Englishman. The American had bum legs, and the Englishman had a long horsey face with gap teeth. Their names . . . what the hell were their names?

The phone rang. This time Schiller turned on the voice scrambler before answering.

"This is Howell," a gravelly, synthetically reconstituted voice on the other end announced. "Go ahead."

"Copy the name John Tagget . . . I need to know whether the information on his army record is hard or a cover. And did he ever have a connection to Twenty-nine Russell Square, London, from April 1944 to May 1945?"

"Copied," Howell said. "Is there anything else?"

Schiller was about to say no when he realized how Howell's tone had changed. It was substantially harder, more clipped. He sounded nervous about something . . .

To protect himself, he said, "Nothing firm as yet, but Tagget might have wasted one of MI-6's men. Someone by the name of Hicks."

"Source of information?"

"Tagget's lawyer."

"Your business partner?"

"The senior partner . . . he has been Tagget's attorney for years."

"Will you be coming to Washington?"

"Yes, I'll be on the last flight out of LaGuardia tonight."

"Good," Howell said. "I should have the information by tomorrow afternoon."

"Thanks."

Schiller put the phone down and disconnected the secure-voice coder. He was certain from Howell's tone that Howell already knew something more than he did. They had a personal relationship from the time when Howell was with him in the State Department. In the present power alignment within the Company he had placed himself within Howell's group.

He went to the hall closet for his coat. He still had to reach Chelenko. The elevator stopped several times on the way down to the street level, and outside the streets were crowded with Christmas shoppers. His breath steamed in the cold air. Traffic inched along. He walked across Fifth Avenue and made for Forty-ninth Street, looking among parked cars.

Halfway there he found what he was looking for, a telephone company repair truck. It was always somewhere within a couple of blocks of his office. He smiled and wondered how the chairman of the board and his directors would react if they knew the KGB had dummied up one of Ma Bell's trucks as part of its communication system. He had visions of the utility coming up with a better cover story than the Russians could . . .

Schiller walked over to the truck and motioned to the driver that he wanted to speak to him.

The man cranked the window down. Schiller hadn't seen this one before.

"Excuse me," Schiller said, reciting the week's identification words, "but I'm somewhat confused. Which way is the Empire State Building?"

"Down Fifth Avenue to Thirty-fourth Street," the driver answered.

"Thank you . . . and would you know where the Aeroflot offices are?"

"The fourth phone from the end in the hallway just off that entrance," the driver said, gesturing toward the doorway directly in front of them. "It's tagged."

Schiller nodded and hurried inside the lobby. The phones were to his right, five booths. The first and second were occupied. The fourth had the OUT OF

ORDER sticker over the coin slots. He sat down, peeled the sticker off and waited. As soon as the phone rang he closed the door and picked it up. "I have a message for Chelenko," he told the woman on the other end.

"Go ahead," she said.

"I am sorry but it must be delivered directly."

"Would you be available—"

"No, I'll talk to him now," Schiller insisted. "Tell him it's a yellow situation."

For several moments there was no other sound on the line. Then a man asked, "What situation is yellow?"

Schiller recognized Chelenko's voice. "Hicks is dead," he said.

"How?"

"Supposedly a mugging in Central Park."

"Supposedly?"

"That's what the police think."

"But you don't?"

"There seem to be complications . . . something that happened during World War II . . . Connected with the Twenty-nine Russell Square ops . . . I can give you more information when I have it." He had thrown out enough bait.

"I take it you never made the approach to Hicks?"

"No, I didn't have time. He was killed shortly after he got into New York."

"Where are you now?"

"In one of our secure phone booths, off Forty-ninth Street."

"Can you meet me in a half hour?"

"We could get together for dinner—"

"No . . . I have previous arrangements. It will have to be for drinks."

"Where?" Chelenko was silent, so Schiller suggested, "There's a place on Twenty-eighth Street, off Park Avenue . . . It's called the Happy Cooker. I know the owner."

Chelenko agreed. "I'll leave in a minute, I'll meet you there in half an hour."

Schiller hung up and walked back to Fifth Avenue. He couldn't get a cab so he decided to walk over to Lexington Avenue and take the subway down to Twenty-ninth Street. It was still the evening rush hour, though why it was called that when it lasted a good three hours Schiller didn't know. The train was packed and it was all he could do to get a grip on one of the poles near the doors.

The brief ride to Twenty-eighth Street gave him enough time to place his two phone conversations in perspective. By the time he got off the train, Schiller had decided he would reverse his original plan and give Tagget to Chelenko—Howell already seemed to be on to Tagget—if Chelenko would in turn tell him why the KGB had been interested in Hicks as anything more than a low-level source of corroborative, historical information. He felt a familiar, intense sense of anticipation as he climbed the stairs up to street level. Chelenko would not have risked meeting with him unless he had come up with something important.

When Schiller saw Chelenko's chauffeured black limousine parked in the middle of the block, he guessed that Chelenko had brought one of his heavies with him. He was right; when he went inside the Happy Cooker, he spotted a beefy bodyguard at the front of the bar a few seats from Chelenko.

Schiller called over to Johnny, the owner, and remarked that the noise level hadn't dropped since the last time he had been there. They both laughed, and Schiller moved over to where Chelenko sat.

Chelenko was a chunky man of forty or forty-five. Schiller could never be sure. He wore an expensive turtleneck sweater, a herringbone sports jacket and gray wool slacks. He was proud of his Mongol heritage, but in America he could easily pass himself off as Chinese or Japanese. He spoke both languages fluently, as well as passable French and German. They exchanged greetings.

"Vito," Schiller called to the barkeep, "Stolichnaya on the rocks for me and for my friend."

"How did you find this place?" Chelenko asked. "Dust on the floor, disco music and—"

"Johnny is a friend of mine. And he's a damn good cook . . . You should take your comrades here for lunch."

When their drinks were set down on the bar they moved to a small table away from the wall.

"Tell me what you know about Hicks," Chelenko said. "Have you any information on who might have killed him?"

"I thought you could tell me that."

"We just wanted him turned, not killed. We had nothing to do with his death."

"I just meant you might know who did . . ."

"I'm telling you, he was a routine informational target, that's all. The situation, and what you told me over the phone, points to MI-6 or the CIA."

But not to a motive, Schiller thought.

"Hicks might have been an important source of information to us," Chelenko said, looking away.

"About what?"

Chelenko looked back at Schiller, apparently deciding whether to cut him in. Schiller's heart skipped a beat and began to race as Chelenko spoke.

"On the phone you mentioned Hicks's possible involvement with the Russell Square operations during the war. Well, the same sort of operation is being run now," Chelenko said, "only instead of sending men into occupied France or Denmark, counterrevolutionaries are being sent into Angola and other places in Africa."

"What was Hicks's connection to it?" Schiller asked. He had been given the missing motive. Hicks must have been killed because he knew too much about the operation. The alcoholic boasting that had attracted the KGB would hardly have escaped MI-6 if he had really known anything worthwhile, and they would have had one of their own people preemptively take him out. It would have been their responsibility, since

Hicks belonged to them. But Chelenko's answer surprised him.

"We're not even sure that there was any connection," Chelenko answered. "That's what we wanted to know. We think there was."

"But that was during the war . . . What has that got to do with men being recruited and sent to Africa now? Nothing unique about that. You do it . . . We do it . . . You know we do it and we know you do it."

Chelenko heaved a weary sigh. "Yes, but *the same two* are doing it for your British friends," he said. "The two who ran operations out of Twenty-nine Russell Square during the war. Now they have a different address, but it's the same game."

"And you want to put them out of business."

"Yes. We know who they are but not what they look like. Now tell me about the complications," Chelenko said.

Schiller suppressed a smile. "I have it on good authority that someone else is interested in that same operation."

"How good authority?"

"The Company," Schiller answered.

"And who is the someone?"

Schiller made a snap decision to hold onto Tagget as long as he could. "A man who worked for them," he said. "That's all I know."

"When?"

"During the war."

"Can you find out who wants them?"

"Yes, I think so," Schiller answered. "But I need to know their names."

"Ross and Fleming," Chelenko said, and finished off his vodka.

Alcantara was seething. He sat across the table from his wife and hardly ate the roast veal she had made for dinner. He had been in a rage ever since his chief had called him into the office and had told him to kill the composite and the photograph of the man who had murdered Hicks. . . .

"As of now," the chief inspector had said, "the investigation is over. It will be filed with the rest of the unsolved murders."

"But we have a good shot at—"

The chief shook his head. "This has come down from the top," he said. "I know how you feel."

Alcantara didn't answer. There was no way for the chief or anyone else to know how he felt.

Worse, on the way home he had discovered that he was being tailed. The spooks had started in with him again. He was really beginning to regret that he hadn't wasted a few of them in Nam. He had seen the dark blue Chevy turn off the highway with him, and he sensed it now, somewhere on the street outside with its lights out and some jerk dozing behind the wheel, keeping watch on his house. . . .

He looked across the small white kitchen table where he and Gene usually ate when he got home early enough to have dinner with her. The children were in the playroom watching TV. He shouted to them to lower the sound.

"I don't know why they have to have it up so damn high," he said.

"My, you're in a fine mood," she said. "You're not home for dinner that often to waste time yelling at the boys."

"It just was a lousy day," he said.

Gene waited for him to talk.

"We were pulled off the Hicks case."

"Is that so bad? . . . I'm sure there'll be another murder to keep you and Ralph busy."

"Yeah." He stood up.

"Where are you going? I baked an apple pie."

"I'll be back late . . . don't wait up for me . . . I have to see someone."

"Goddamn it, Peter, I don't know why you bother coming home at all . . . you should just drop by every

time you need to get laid . . . that's about all I'm
good for lately. . . ."

Alcantara heard her but didn't stop to answer; he'd
settle it another time, somehow. Slipping behind the
wheel of his car, he turned on the ignition. Without
giving the engine a chance to warm up he backed out
of the driveway and headed for the city. His tail followed. But as soon as Alcantara got onto the streets
of his own precinct in Manhattan he was able to lose
him.

He knew it was the Company who had him pulled
off the case . . . "Smith" and his people. He just wasn't
about to let those bastards walk all over him and get
away with it. He was going to go to Tagget and tell
him about Smith's visit. He was determined to move
this thing forward. What he couldn't do, he hoped
that Tagget would.

Claudia was with Tagget when the doorman sent
Alcantara up. The detective apologized for the late
unannounced visit and offered to come back in the
morning, hoping Tagget wouldn't take him up on it.
"I'm here on my own," he said.

"In that case," Tagget said, "come on in. I guess
you can call me John."

"My name's Peter. Thanks."

"Let me have your coat. We're just sitting down to
some Chinese food I brought up. Join us?"

Alcantara was clearly embarrassed to have intruded, and Claudia came to his rescue. "John always
buys too much and it will only go to waste. Since
you're not here officially then you can eat, drink and
be merry."

Tagget took his coat and the three of them sat
down to eat. "White or red wine—or some good
whiskey?" Tagget asked.

"Bourbon, if you have it."

"White wine for me," Claudia told him.

Alcantara didn't eat much. He was bothered by
what Gene had said, and by the truth there was in it.

He had his world, and she . . . well, had the house and the children. Only now and then did they share something other than their bodies. . . .

"Well," Tagget said when they finished, "let's go into the living room and talk."

"As I told you before," Alcantara said, sitting down in a high-backed chair, "this is not an official visit. In fact, the reason I'm here is that the department has decided to close the case and declare it unsolved."

"Wasn't that a rather hasty decision?"

"Seemed so to me."

Tagget, who had been sitting next to Claudia, stood up and went to the bar cart. "Another drink, Peter?"

"No thank you . . . I still have to drive home."

Tagget poured himself two fingers of scotch and returned to the couch.

"Earlier today," Alcantara said, "I had a visit from a Mr. Smith—that's the name on his ID card anyway. He's from the CIA."

Tagget frowned and bolted the whiskey down.

"He came to see me because I made a routine check with the FBI on you."

"I don't exactly understand that," Tagget said.

"The check was routine," Alcantara said. "Your fingerprints are on file and I imagine other information . . . we do it all the time . . . But I never got the information. Instead, this Smith came to see me, which brings me to why I'm here."

"Go ahead."

"Smith said you were 'coded red,' " Alcantara said, looking at Tagget. "That meant the Bureau had to notify the CIA if any request for information came in."

"Coded red," Tagget repeated.

"Yes, with some number attached to it that puts you under CIA protection and purview, according to Smith."

Tagget was on his feet. "Did Smith explain any more than that?"

"Nothing."

"And what did you tell him?"

"Everything we knew about the case and your involvement with Hicks," Alcantara said, looking down at his shoes.

Neither Tagget or Claudia said a word. The room was very quiet.

"I came here," Alcantara told them, "because"—he hesitated a moment—"because I can't do any more than follow my damn orders. But you can, and you're already involved. I don't know how, or in what, but you are."

"Thank you for coming here and telling me."

Alcantara stood up. "I thought you should know about the CIA's interest in you."

"Thanks again," Tagget said.

Alcantara asked for his coat, shook hands with Tagget and Claudia and took the elevator down. He had done all he could. Whatever else had to be done would be up to Tagget. Now he wanted to get home and square things with Gene. As he crossed the street to his car, he tried to think of an all-night florist where he could stop and buy some flowers for her. It had done the trick before. . . .

Alcantara saw the dark blue Chevy when he was halfway across York Avenue. Its lights were out, and it was coming down at him. Very fast.

He ran for the curb and just made it. Freeing his gun, he brought it up. Holding it steady with two hands, he squeezed off three shots. The bullets pinged off the side of the building across the street.

The car was alongside him.

A sudden explosion was in his chest, throwing him backward. He found himself looking up at the night sky and the windows of the buildings on either side of the street. His vision blurred, blood filled his mouth.

"Flowers for Gene," he mumbled, and died.

The car continued up York Avenue until it reached Seventy-second Street, where it turned east.

Smith reached forward and switched on the head-

lights. The man next to him picked up the mike and
turned on the transmitter.

"Homer," he said, "this is Flying Eagle . . . Do you
read me?"

"Ten-ten," a man answered.

"Tell Reynolds the talker is down."

Tagget went to his desk, filled a pipe and lit it. He
tried to act casual. He didn't want to upset Claudia
any more than she already was. He could tell from
the tightness at the corners of her lips that she was
having a bad reaction to what Alcantara had said.

He walked over to the TV and switched on the late
news.

"I'll tidy up the kitchen," Claudia told him.

"Thanks," he said, and settled down in a large
leather chair in front of the TV. The news was singu-
larly dull compared to his own situation. He was
deeply troubled by the things he had learned about
himself, that he had been assigned a special code with
the FBI, that the CIA was keeping tabs on him . . .
inconceivable, and yet it must be true—or was it?

There was the possibility that Alcantara wasn't telling him everything, that the lieutenant was part of
the cover up, part of the plan to keep him from the
truth about his past.

"But what the hell is the truth?" he said aloud.

"Did you say something?" Claudia asked over the
noise of the sink.

He turned toward her.

She was standing in the doorway of the kitchen.
"What did you say?" she asked, walking over to him.

"Do you think Peter was telling the truth?" he said.

"I was just about to ask you the same thing."

"If he was, he came here at considerable risk to
his career, and if he wasn't, he was sent here to keep
me from the truth," Tagget said, standing up. "The
hell of this whole thing is that I haven't the slightest
idea *what* it is that they're trying to keep from me
. . . Why would the CIA want to have my file color

coded? What the hell did I do? Or didn't do? It could just as well have been something I didn't do and should have."

Claudia moved close to him and put her arms around his neck.

"Albert Hentz said he'd have some information for me in a few days," he told her. "Maybe then I'll be able to make some sense out of all of this."

"You still think it's connected to that house in London?"

"Yes," he said, and after a pause added, "I feel as if I'm in a sack. I keep trying to fight my way out. But I can't."

She touched the side of his face. "I wish there was some real way I could help."

The TV newscaster was saying, "This just in . . . A man has been gunned down on York Avenue and Sixty-eighth Street in Manhattan this evening. One witness said that there was an exchange of shots . . ."

"Good God!" Claudia cried. "That's right outside."

"He said 'exchange of shots' . . . maybe it was Peter."

They released each other and faced the TV screen.

"There are no other details at this time . . . Members of the Channel Seven News Team are on the scene. We will bring you an on-the-scene report before the end of this program . . ."

Tagget switched off the TV. "I'm going downstairs."

She shook her head. "Please, don't . . . It won't do any good."

"It was Alcantara, and he was telling the truth," Tagget said, taking his coat from the closet. "He risked his life to cue me in on what happened."

"Well, don't leave me here alone. I'm going to go with you."

They had to wait a long time for the elevator. Claudia held on to his good hand. "And I thought you lived such a quiet life. That was one of the things that I liked so much about you."

"This isn't what I want," he answered. "Not what I want at all."

The elevator finally arrived.

On the way down, Tagget said, "I wonder if he knew they were following him. Following him, or maybe they knew he was coming here and they waited for him to come out."

"No more," she told him, shaking her head. "I already have goose bumps down my back."

"They could have been watching me too," he said unhelpfully as they stepped out of the elevator. Through the glass door of the lobby they saw the flashing red and yellow lights of a half-dozen police and detective cars.

"Terrible," the doorman said, as they approached him. "I saw the whole thing . . . a black car came at him, it was gonna hit him. He got to the curb and got some shots off . . . but they kept coming and blew him away with a sawed-off shotgun. He was one of the detectives who visited you the other day, wasn't he?"

Tagget was about to break away from the doorman when he saw Ralph Singer come toward the lobby.

Singer didn't wait until the doorman opened the door for him. He came in on his own. He was grim-faced. "I was on my way up to see you," he said to Tagget.

"We heard about it a few minutes ago on the Channel Seven news," Claudia began.

"Let's go back up to your place," Singer said with a glance toward the sidewalk.

Tagget nodded.

Singer didn't waste any time. As soon as they were in the apartment, he said, "Two things I want you to know about me. One is that Pete was my best friend. Two, I'm going to get the bastard that did this. Yes, there's one more thing: I'm a lot harder than Pete was, especially now, and I don't give a damn who I step on."

"I think we understand each other," Tagget answered. He sat down on the couch next to Claudia and took hold of her hand.

"Okay, was Pete up here?"

"Yes."

"Why?"

"That's as much as I can tell you," Tagget said.

Singer glared at him. "Don't play games with me. Two days ago you're with a guy and he gets killed . . . Tonight my partner visits you and he gets killed. I'm not going to settle for an answer like that."

"I don't see that you have much choice. I'm not suspected of anything am I? If so, I have the right to have counsel present."

Singer's face darkened. He balled his fist. "Listen, Pete left a wife and two kids—"

"Tell him," Claudia said softly. Tagget looked at her. "You owe it to him, John."

"All right, sit down," Tagget said in a commanding voice. "I'll tell you what you want to know, but if you try to use the information in any way against me I'll deny I told you anything and it will be your word against mine . . . And I assure you, I have enough money and influence to make mine the last word. You understand that?"

"You don't scare easy," Singer said, deciding to go along for the sake of information, and took the high-backed chair facing Tagget.

Tagget ignored that and said, "Peter came here to tell me what happened when he put in a routine request to the FBI for information about me . . ." Tagget went on to explain about his file, the color code and the numerical classification, the visit from Smith. "Then it seems word came from police headquarters to put Hicks's case in the dead file, even though you apparently had managed to get a good composite from that not-too-clear photograph of the man who killed Hicks."

Singer shook his head. "Pete hated anything or anyone connected to the CIA," he said. "But what's your part in all this?"

"That's what I really *don't* know."

"He was probably followed," Singer said.

"That was my guess too."

"If it's the CIA," Singer said, "then the chief will quash the investigation of Pete's killing just the way Hicks's was."

"Is there anything you can do to keep it open?"

"I can follow it on my own time without telling the chief anything. But it won't do any good if the CIA is involved. I've been through this before."

"There's no *if* about their involvement, according to Pete. They are involved . . . Now tell me what happened to the man who a few minutes ago told me he was going to get the bastards who killed his friend?"

Singer flushed.

"Could you at least do one thing for that friend?" Tagget asked.

Singer waited.

"Find out where I can find Smith."

"Look, I'm sorry," Singer told him, "if I start asking questions about a Mr. Smith, they'll get the word that I'm on to something. They won't think twice about coming after me. I think I can do more good by lying low. For a while, anyway. I don't want to end up the way Pete did—dead *and* empty-handed." He stood up and went to the door. "There are certain things you learn about in my game not to tangle with head on," Singer said before he opened the door and let himself out of the apartment. "You should think about that too, Mr. Tagget. It might help you stay alive." The door closed and he was gone.

Tagget stood up. "Guys like that make me want to puke."

"At least he was honest with you. He was afraid and said so."

Tagget went to his desk and filled his pipe.

"Aren't *you* afraid, John?"

"Yes, but I'm even more afraid to stop now . . . now that I'm finally maybe getting closer to what they're trying to hide from me. For all these years . . ."

Le Boulay, France, April 18, 1944

In the misty rain the village of Le Boulay looked like an impressionistic painting. There were at most a dozen buildings clustered around a small Romanesque church.

"Are you sure this Cordez is in Le Boulay?" Dumas asked.

"This is where I was told he'd be," Tagget answered.

The two of them stood up and moved back to a thinly wooded area, where the rest of the group was waiting.

Tagget looked at his watch. "Cordez will be in the third house from the end of the street."

Dumas made a face and spat.

"You came this far with me," Tagget said. "You might as well meet him."

"Why this place?" Dumas asked. "Look at it. Flat, with damn few trees and—"

"My orders were to meet Cordez here."

"Orders, shit!"

Tagget was not about to allow himself to become involved in an argument with Dumas. In the few days he had been with the Maquis group he had come to understand that Dumas lived only to kill Germans. For all practical purposes his life—according to what he himself had said—had not begun until he killed his first one.

Tagget moved away from Dumas and settled down with his back against a low stone wall. He lit a cigarette and let the smoke curl slowly out of his nose.

A young woman named Elaine sat down next to him. Without a word she took the cigarette from his mouth to light her own. She was tall and blond, slender, too, he guessed, though he couldn't tell much because she wore men's clothing. The heavy sweater and jacket made her body shapeless.

"Dumas is worried," she said after a while.

"I can understand that."

"Good," she said. "I thought you would." She smiled at him.

"I'm worried too," he told her.

The smile left her face. Looking away, she said, "I will be waiting for you." Then she stood up and walked to where two of the other women were sitting.

Tagget closed his eyes and in a matter of moments he slipped into a light sleep . . . Suddenly someone was shaking him. He awoke with a start.

"It is time," Dumas said.

Tagget rubbed his eyes and stood up. "We will go into the village separately, from east and west," he said. "If there's any trouble, you and your men pull back . . . Come back here . . . Wait fifteen minutes and then move out."

The group divided when they came close to the village. Half circled around to the east and the other half remained with Tagget. He waited until he judged that Dumas was in position, then moved forward, signaling to the men with him to do the same.

The village street was filled with mud. There was no sign of any of the villagers.

Tagget looked toward the church. The door was open. Because of the rain and the gloom inside the church he couldn't see too clearly, but he thought he saw figures a few paces back from the door.

He ran to where Dumas was standing. "Ever see anything like this before?"

"The Bosch sometimes take whole villages away," he said tightly.

A few more of the Maquis moved out into the center of the main street.

Tagget went toward the house where he was scheduled to meet Cordez. He had just about reached the door when one of the men shouted, "In the church tower!"

An instant later the street was raked by machine gun fire.

Tagget threw himself against the wall of the house as slugs chewed up the soft ground where he had been standing. The whole village seemed to explode around him. The Maquis were throwing grenades into every window and doorway.

Explosion followed explosion. Huge pieces of the walls fell out into the street.

German troops poured out of the church and were cut down by Dumas's men. Tagget kicked open the door to the house and fired a burst from his Schmeisser that brought screams from inside. He squeezed the trigger again, backed out, paused long enough to throw a grenade into the room and then, shouting to the Maquis to fall back, ran for the safety of the stone wall.

The firing was still fierce, and several of the Maquis were hit as they tried to break off the fight. Winded, dripping with sweat, Tagget dropped behind the wall, turned and watched for the other members of the group. Two more came running out of the mist.

"Set up covering fire," Tagget said.

They leaned their weapons on the wall and waited.
Several more members of the group came toward them. Elaine was among them. She dropped down next to Tagget. "Dumas is dead . . . the back of his head was blown away . . ."

Tagget clenched his fists. The firing stopped as suddenly as it had begun. Tagget took a fast count. Half the group had been killed. In the distance he heard the Germans shouting. "In another two hours it will be dark. Until then we have to keep moving."

"Which way?" one of the men asked.

"We'll keep circling the village," Tagget said. "Maybe we can get them nervous enough to start firing at their own men."

The men and women of the group followed Tagget as he left the shelter of the stone wall and at a run began to move back toward the village. Several times they were within a few yards of the Germans but the misty rain kept them hidden.

Twilight came early, and it was soon dark enough for them to risk leaving the area and move north.

They traveled most of the night and by morning were huddled in a burned-out barn some ten miles from Le Boulay.

"Now what do we do?" a man named Dandee asked.

"We rest," Tagget said. "Then we will find some food and decide what to do."

He found a dry corner and stretched out.

Elaine settled alongside him. "I keep my word," she said.

"I never doubted that," he said, putting his arm around her. He closed his eyes and was on the verge of sleep when she said, "There is no Cordez . . . Dumas didn't believe there was a Cordez, and now you too must know he doesn't exist."

Tagget was wide awake now. He propped himself on his elbow and asked, "Then why was I sent to meet him?"

Elaine shrugged.

Tagget eased himself down again. "It just wouldn't make sense," he said aloud.

"Not to you, not to me . . . but you're here now and so far there is no Cordez."

"What are you trying to tell me?"

"It must make sense to someone . . . to the people who sent you," she said.

He closed his eyes. He couldn't use the radio until the next night. He tried hard to think, but was too tired to do anything but sleep. Which was more of a blessing than he knew . . .

VIII

CLAUDIA LEFT Tagget's apartment at ten the next morning. He had offered to escort her back to her own place but she had told him, "Try to get some sleep." He had spent most of the night at his desk, or standing by the window.

The lobby was full of sunlight. Outside the weather was clear and cold. She paused for a few moments and looked across the street to where Alcantara had been shot down. There was a police car there and another pale green unmarked vehicle. Two uniformed officers sat in the patrol car, and two plainclothesmen were looking at the yellow chalk outline of Alcantara's body. The area was cordoned off with wooden horses. There was another parked car near the corner of Sixy-eighth Street with a man sitting at the wheel.

Claudia shuddered involuntarily and was about to continue on her way when one of the plainclothesmen looked in her direction. It was Detective Singer.

He said something to the other man, then started toward her. "How are you this morning?" he asked, coming up to her.

She looked past him. "Still horrified by what happened."

"And Mr. Tagget?"

"He didn't sleep much."

Singer nodded and admitted that he hadn't slept too well either. He offered to buy her a cup of coffee.

She was about to refuse but changed her mind. "Just looking at where it happened has chilled me," she said, going with him.

They walked quickly down the street. Neither of them spoke. When they reached a luncheonette, Singer steered Claudia to a booth. It was very warm; she opened her coat and Singer looked straight at her breasts. "Can I at least convince you to have something with your coffee? The pound cake's very good."

"Sounds okay," she said, blushing under his stare.

Singer gave the order to the waitress. He shook a cigarette from a pack and offered one to Claudia.

"I don't smoke," she told him. "But don't let that stop you."

He lit up. "Your friend Tagget doesn't think very much of me. Pete went in over his head. I don't have the hang-up he had about the CIA. He should have known better than to go against them."

"He didn't go against them, as you put it. He came to John to tell him what—"

"Say it any way you like, Mrs. Harris," he said. "It comes up the same thing . . . Your friend is in some sort of a jam with the Company—and he'll either square it with them or they'll blow him away too."

The waitress came with the coffee and pound cake. Claudia wrapped her hands around the hot cup. Without looking at Singer, she asked, "Do *you* work for them?"

"No, but you can bet that guy sitting in the car down the street from where Pete got taken out does . . . Don't you know what the hell you're getting into, or rather doesn't Tagget know?" Claudia raised her eyes. "He was right, you know. He's being watched. I wouldn't doubt his phone is tapped . . . What the hell is he into that they're so interested in him?"

"He told you."

"And you believe him?" Singer asked. "Okay, that was a dumb question, you do. Maybe Pete did. But I don't. I'm sorry. Something more has to be involved. Tagget isn't telling you the whole truth."

"Thank you for the coffee and cake," Claudia said,

gathering her coat around her shoulders. "I really have to go."

He reached across the table and took hold of her arm. "Did you know that Tagget spent two years in an army hospital after the war . . . Two years under intensive psychiatric care, hypnotherapy, a heavy drug regimen?"

Claudia pulled her hands away from his. "Yes, I know that," she lied.

"Isn't it just possible that he might need help again?"

"What, now he's imagined everything, Sergeant Singer? I thought you said that he's into something the Company—as you call it—doesn't think he should be. You can't seem to decide whether he's some sort of master spy or just a hair's breadth from going completely around the bend . . ."

"Maybe a mixture of both," Singer answered. "But I can't buy the story he's managed to sell you."

"As I said a moment ago, I must be going." And she eased her way out of the booth.

"You're angry—"

"Disgusted would be a better description," she answered, and hurried out. She turned up Sixty-seventh and walked swiftly. Her breath steamed in the cold air and her eyes watered.

Singer, of course, had given voice to her own fears. Several times during the last few days she had fought down the temptation to suggest to John that he seek the help of a good therapist. But then Alcantara had come and had told them about the CIA's involvement and she had begun to have other thoughts about it. She had found herself wondering if John had accidentally stumbled into something . . .

Claudia slowed her pace. As she saw it, she had two choices. She could tell him that if he didn't stop hunting down his past she would stop seeing him; or she could go along with him as she had been doing up to now, knowing that day by day, perhaps even hour by hour, the danger for him increased. The first way she knew she would lose him; he would not stop because she threatened to end their relationship. But the other way he might wind up dead.

She shook her head and fought back the tears. She had lived through the loss of her husband, being told that he had been killed in a freak crash but discovering some months later, while going through his papers, that there had been a hidden side to his life. Many of the business trips he had taken had been for reasons different from the ones that he had given her. He had two other women he had lived with. She had had her lawyer make some inquiries and after a brief period she'd been told by him to leave the matter alone. He had hinted that her husband had had connections with the Mafia, and that it was not in her interest for him to document them by investigation. She had let the matter drop.

And now when she had someone she could again love, she found herself having to face the realization that no matter what she did, he might be killed . . .

When she reached the corner of Second Avenue she saw a telephone booth. She went in, deposited a coin and dialed Tagget's number. It rang three times before he answered.

"John," she said, "I just wanted to tell you that I love you."

"And I love you."

"I'm glad."

They chatted for a few minutes and then she said goodby . . . When she stepped out of the phone booth she felt better. Much, much better. If there was ever to be a future for the two of them she at least had to go along with him now, never mind the consequences. She really had no choice. . . .

Howell had left Langley by helicopter before dawn and was in Reynolds's office by 8:30 A.M. He was a tall, blond, gray-eyed man with thin lips and a strong jaw. Though he was very angry, he maintained a calm appearance. He sat very still, listening to Reynolds's explanation of what had happened.

Howell cut in. "You told me all this last night. I don't like getting my information on the late TV news. I want to know *why* it happened."

"Alcantara came out of the house, saw one of our cars and just started shooting," Reynolds explained uneasily. Howell looked like a rattlesnake. And was, he knew, just as dangerous.

"How did he know it was one of our cars?" the deputy director asked.

"He must have figured it out . . . Smith had paid him a visit that morning . . . He must have known Tagget was under surveillance, and he certainly knew we were tailing him. According to Smith, he definitely had a thing against the Company."

Howell stood up. Reynolds was giving him a cover story.

Howell walked to the far side of the room and looked out of the window. Below him many of the roofs were covered with snow. In the distance he could see the upper bay, the Statue of Liberty and Staten Island.

He turned . . . Reynolds would be more useful to him if he could be manipulated from antagonist to friend. Howell knew which men in the Company were still opposed to his appointment and which were willing to accept it. Reynolds was an old Company man with a record going all the way back to the closing days of the OSS and the beginning of the Company as it now was organized.

"Anything in the files on Alcantara?" Howell asked as he approached the desk.

Reynolds smiled. "I would have checked that myself, but your visit—"

"Have one of your people develop something," Howell told him, "then run it through in the usual way so the FBI has it for the press."

"Do you want to see it before we put it through to the Bureau?"

Howell waved the suggestion aside. "I know you'll do the right thing."

Reynolds nodded appreciatively.

"Were there any witnesses?"

"The doorman, where Tagget lives."

"Have two of your men pay him a visit . . . Shake him up a little, but not enough to put him in the hospital."

"Right."

"Now we come to Tagget," Howell said. He leaned back in the chair. "How much do you know about him?"

"Only the information that came through on the computer readout just before you called the other day."

"What I am about to tell you," Howell said, "must not go beyond this room."

"You can be sure it won't."

"The two men, Ross and Fleming, who ran Tagget out of Twenty-nine Russell Square, are putting men into African countries . . . They're still very much part of MI-6, and the Agency is now cooperating. Fully."

Reynolds nodded. "So that's why Tagget came up red in the Bureau's files?"

"Only partially . . . Tagget was sent into France just prior to Overlord . . . to be captured and broken by the Germans. Never mind the details . . ."

"And you think he knows that?"

"I don't think he knows *yet*," Howell said with a shake of his head. "And we don't want him to know it, or anything that followed . . . After the Germans had him, he spent the next two years in an army hospital."

"The William Beaumont in El Paso?"

"That's when we—I mean the OSS—got hold of him again . . . Some very fancy work for that time was done on him. It's still an ongoing project. Everything about his mission in France was wiped clean from his brain, in a manner of speaking, and the damage done by the Germans was reinforced, so that the limp and inability to move his left arm were given a kind of permanence."

"I'm not sure I follow you," Reynolds said.

"The initial damage came from the beatings he had taken . . . I don't know the details, but what remained was more psychological than physical . . . When the OSS got hold of him, he was used for additional experiments in what they now call mind-control."

"I didn't realize things were that far along thirty-five years ago—"

"That and much more . . . He was given various drugs and the pattern was set . . . And through the VA we were able to monitor him every year. So far so good. Tagget proved to be a very successful experiment, he was teaching us a lot . . . until something happened to disrupt the pattern that had been set for him . . . The doctors who had worked on him foresaw that possibility. They knew if he ever came in contact with something that somehow revived the memory of what had really happened, there would be a strong possibility that a kind of psychological domino effect would set in . . . Eventually all or most of it would start to come back, and it would take a lot of treatment to offset it."

"And you think it's happening?"

"Maybe yes, maybe no. But the signs are pretty strong that it might be. Now just suppose you are Tagget and you find out what was done to you—I mean during the war—what would you do?"

"Go after the people who set me up."

Howell nodded.

"But first he would have to find Ross and Fleming," Reynolds said.

"Right. And that's what we can't allow to happen."

"Take him out?"

"Only if necessary," Howell said. "We'd *very* much like the experiment to run its course. It's valuable as hell. There have been setbacks before, like a few years ago when Tagget began having nightmares, and that was overcome with drugs and hypnotherapy during his annual VA visits. Three years ago his wife died of cancer; that shook him up again and threw things back a couple of turns. We have to be very careful about what we're doing with this guy. He has the potential to be a very dangerous man, physically and politically. He has some very important connections. One of the President's aides—Nathan Pierce—is a very good friend of his. We have to watch it."

"I understand."

Howell stood up again and went back to the window. "We know just about everything there is to know about Tagget," he said. "We know things about him he doesn't know. We know he has been having an affair with Claudia Harris, a woman whose husband worked for us until we discovered he was working two sides of the street and not paying attention to our side. She started to investigate the circumstances of her husband's death but we had someone talk mob to her lawyer and he got her to drop it." He faced Reynolds. "If we didn't have the Mafia to blame for certain things, I think we'd have to organize it and run it ourselves." He sat down again. "I would have preferred it if Mrs. Harris and Tagget had never met, but there are things we can't control. . . ."

"Do you want to keep a tail on Tagget?"

"For another few days, until he goes back to normal," Howell said. "If we luck out, this whole flap will die down. There's nowhere for him to go. Everything is a dead end. We'll just wait and see . . . But there is one thing—"

"Yes."

"I might need a couple of your men to take someone else out . . . This person is very close to the Washington scene and I would prefer not to have anyone in headquarters connected with it."

"Give me a few hours' notice and I'll have them wherever you need them."

"Good," Howell said. "I think we've had a productive meeting this morning."

"So do I."

"I'm a firm believer in working with my field people. From now on, I'd like to think that you and I have the kind of working relationship that will put us on the same side."

"Absolutely," Reynolds said.

Howell reached across the desk and shook Reynolds's hand, then said, "I could use some coffee. I'm just about dead on my feet . . . After your phone call I went back to headquarters and pulled out Tagget's file . . . It was six inches thick but I read the whole damn thing before I left for the airport."

"I didn't get too much sleep either," Reynolds told him. "I kept wondering how you were going to—"

"I'm a reasonable man," Howell said with a smile. "We're in a difficult line of work. People like Alcantara, with certain political leanings, can't understand how important our work is."

Reynolds nodded, picked up his phone and asked his secretary to bring in two cups of black coffee.

Singer was in the inspector's office. He'd tried, but he couldn't stay out of it. Neither he nor the inspector was seated, though each stood on opposite sides of the inspector's desk.

The inspector was a thin, bespectacled man with a balding head and a tracery of red veins on a bulbous nose. He eyed Singer for a long time before he said, "Ralph, you're not going to have another man with you on Alcantara's case . . . We're short-handed and can't spare anyone . . . In fact, I don't want you to spend too much time on it."

"Why not just file it away," Singer said, unable to keep the sarcasm out of his voice. "It's as good as dead anyway, the same as Pete was as good as dead when you pulled the rug out from under him on the Hicks case."

The inspector's face got redder. He had never gotten along with Singer, but he was even more standoffish than usual. "Listen," he said, "I know how you feel. He was your partner and I respect your feelings . . .

But sometimes, even in a close relationship, men don't really know each other. It's something like a marriage in which you think you know the other person, then one day you discover that you didn't at all, that she was cheating or playing around . . . know what I mean?"

"I can't believe I'm hearing this," Singer said. "Pete was straight . . . He was a damn good man." He walked out of the inspector's office, and by the time he reached his desk he was so angry that he went to the men's room and splashed cold water on his face. When he got back to his desk he pretended to be busy with paperwork but he was thinking about Alcantara's wife. Sometime that evening he was planning to drive out to the house and see if Gene needed anything. He had already been out there once, after he had spoken to Tagget. Gene had told him that she and Pete had argued before he had left the house the night he was shot. "I loved him," she had said. "And I was afraid of losing him to another woman." And then she had started to cry. . . .

The phone on Singer's desk rang. He let it ring. He didn't feel like talking to anyone.

"Aren't you going to answer it?" one of the other detectives asked.

"Yeah," Singer said, and picked up the phone. It was one of the women he was sleeping with. "I'm busy," he told her, and hung up. "This I don't need," he said, looking at the phone. He left his desk and signed out at three-thirty. He hurried down the steps of the precinct house and onto the street.

The sky had clouded up and strong wind whipped through the street, kicking papers along in front of it. Singer stopped at the corner newsstand, slapped twenty-five cents down on the marble and picked up the afternoon edition of the *Post*. He looked at the headlines.

DETECTIVE SHOT TO DEATH—SUSPECT UNDERWORLD TIES

For an instant Singer couldn't believe what he was

reading. "Those fuckers couldn't leave it alone . . . They just couldn't leave it alone."

"Whatdyasay?" the newsy asked.

Singer glared at him and turned away, heading for his car. The inspector had known about this story, he had known and, what was worse, he expected him to believe it because someone in headquarters was saying that connections between Alcantara and the mob had suddenly come to light. Yet he was talking about limiting the investigation . . .

"Bullshit," Singer said, walking across the precinct parking area. "Just bullshit." He got into his car and pulled out of the lot with his tires screaming.

When he was stopped at a red light he finally picked up the newspaper and read the lead paragraph.

"Detective Lieutenant Peter Alcantara was shot to death in a gun battle last night. A spokesperson for the police department has indicated that Lieutenant Alcantara had been under departmental investigation for his alleged connections to underworld figures. This same source said that this investigation will continue, even though the lieutenant is dead. According to police sources, the shooting took place at about 10:30 P.M.—"

Someone behind Singer gave him the horn. He glanced up at the green light and drove across the intersection.

It wasn't enough for them to kill Pete, Singer thought angrily, they also have to destroy his reputation. The effect of the newspaper story on Gene and the children would be devastating. And to cap it all, because of this noninvestigation Gene might well have difficulty collecting Pete's pension.

He spotted a telephone booth and double parked next to it. In a few moments he was listening to Tagget's phone ring. As soon as Tagget came on the line he said, "Have you seen the afternoon *Post*?"

"No."

"The story on the front page says that Pete Alcantara was connected to the mob."

"It's as good a cover story as any, isn't it?"

Singer was breathing hard. "Listen," he said. "I changed my mind. Don't ask me why now. Can you meet me about seven?"

"Tell me where."

"The Weathervane . . . it's on Twenty-ninth Street."

"Okay, but come alone."

"Yeah, I'll see you there."

Singer hung up and leaned against the side of the telephone booth. He wasn't completely sure what he was up against. He was scared. He wasn't, especially in his own estimation of himself, the hero type. So far he had been able to live with the compromises he had to make. But to take a dead man's reputation from him . . . no way was he about to let that happen to Gene and the boys. Somehow he would make them retract the story, make a decent investigation . . .

Singer left the telephone booth and slid behind the wheel of his car. With the paper still on the seat beside him he drove slowly east toward Fifth Avenue.

"This is just in from London," the code room clerk said as he entered Bright's office with a sealed envelope and a receipt.

Bright signed for the message and waited until the clerk left before he broke the seal and took out the decoded message. He read:

HICKS SITUATION WELL-HANDLED. TAKE SAME ACTION FOR TAGGET.

SIGNED GEN. FINNEY, CHIEF OF OVERSEAS OPERATIONS

Bright leaned back in his chair. He knew there was no mistake. The message was too short for someone to have made an error. He stood up and walked to the other side of the room, where he fed the message and the envelope into a shredder. Then he returned to his desk and dialed Sands's number. As soon as Sands answered, Bright said, "Would you come into my office please."

"Now?"

"Yes," Bright answered. "It's rather important."

Within a matter of minutes Sands was seated along-side Bright's desk, curious to know what was so urgent that it would not keep until morning.

"A message from London," Bright said. "To take care of Tagget."

"I was wondering when that would come," Sands said, adjusting his tie.

"You were?"

"More or less sensed it . . . it comes with the turf, as the Americans say."

Bright had only a vague notion of what Sands meant. In all his years of service, he had had occasion to kill only twice, once during the civil war in Greece, to save his own life, and a second time when he had killed a double agent on orders from London. Since those two incidents he had always been in a position to order someone else to do the necessary work for him.

"When do they want it done?"

"No specific time was indicated, but I assume the sooner the better."

"I'll see it's done within the next twenty-four hours."

"Can't be a mugging this time," Bright told him.

"I'll think of something . . . By the way, did you happen to catch the late news last night on the telly?"

Bright shook his head. "I was in bed before eleven," he said, beginning to stand up. "I haven't had time to look at the papers."

"That Detective Alcantara, the one who was on the Hicks case, was shot down on York Avenue between Sixty-eighth and Sixty-seventh streets."

Bright sat down. The color drained from his face. "That's where Tagget lives," he said.

"Think the Russians—"

"I don't think so, I would guess it was the CIA."

"But why?"

"I'll let you know when I find out," Bright said. "In the meantime be very careful . . . Tagget and dead people tend to go together . . . I'll do some checking tomorrow morning. For now I think it would be a good idea for you to trail Tagget . . . Get to know something about his habits. Make sure you're not the only one following him." Bright jotted down Tagget's address on a piece of paper and slid it across the desk. "You can pick up a picture of him in our files."

Sands pocketed the slip of paper and stood up. "Thanks. I'll go down with you."

Tagget left his apartment at six. When he walked through the lobby the doorman was busy explaining to a well-dressed young man that there weren't any apartments available. The young man asked if he might speak with the manager of the building. His accent was distinctly British.

Tagget opened the door himself and left the building. Halfway to First Avenue he realized he was being followed. He hailed the first empty cab he saw and told the driver to take him to 30 East Twenty-ninth Street.

Almost immediately the traffic slowed the cab to a crawl. Tagget looked out of the rear window, but there was no way for him to know if his tail was in one of the dozen cabs he saw behind him.

"You in a hurry, mister?" the cabby asked, glancing back at him.

"No . . . are you?"

"I've gotta bring the cab back to the garage in the Bronx . . . The night driver is goin' ta throw a shit fit if I'm late."

"When are you supposed to be there?"

"Six-fifteen."

"You're late already," Tagget said, looking at his watch. "It's already twenty after six."

"This friggin' traffic, it's been like this all day."

"Mr. Henshaw," Tagget said, reading the man's

name off his ID card on the dashboard, "drop me on the Lexington Avenue side of Bloomingdale's and you can go back to your garage. But before we get there I want you to do some fancy cutting in and out."

"I thought you wanted Twenty-ninth Street."

"I'll add ten dollars to whatever shows on the meter."

"You got it!"

They changed lanes, moving to the left and then swerving over to the far right between a bus and a delivery truck.

"Very good," Tagget said, "very good."

When they reached Bloomingdale's, Tagget jumped out and hurried into the store. He worked his way through the crowds of Christmas shoppers and went down into the subway. He rode the train to the Twenty-eighth Street Station and walked back up to Twenty-ninth Street, where the Weathervane was.

Singer was already there and made room for him at the long bar.

"Busy place," Tagget said, looking around the room.

"Mainly from the garment trades and some publishing people," Singer explained. "A few hookers over in the corner near the door."

Tagget ordered a Chivas neat and took a few pretzels from a nearby bowl.

"Did you pick up the paper?" Singer asked.

"No, I haven't seen it," Tagget answered, chewing on a pretzel.

Singer didn't say anything. He finished his drink and gestured to the barkeep for another. When it came, he drank most of it in one swallow.

"I'm going out to see Pete's family later on."

Tagget nodded. He could see that Singer had already had a few. The pupils of his eyes were contracted. He looked very unhappy.

"Let's sit down over at one of those tables against the wall," Singer suggested.

They took their drinks from the bar and set them down on a round table top.

"After I phoned you I went back to the precinct," Singer said. "These were supposed to go to the newspapers, but orders came down to sit on them." He handed Tagget a white business envelope. "They're photographs and a composite of the man who killed Hicks, the ones that Pete told you about. Look at them when you're back in your apartment. If what you told me is true, then the guy in the pictures is either from the Company or MI-6. He might even be Smith, the CIA agent who leaned on Pete."

"Why the change?" Tagget asked, putting the envelope in his jacket pocket.

"All Pete's wife and kids have left of him is his reputation, and when the Company gets through with it, they're not even going to have that . . . I won't buy the crap about Pete's underworld connections. He was straight."

"How much information can you get for me?"

"I'll feed you whatever comes my way," Singer said. "But as far as the Bureau is concerned, you won't get anything more than you already have. From what Pete told you, the Company has a lid on it. You're going to have to watch yourself. They're going to get a tap on your phone if they haven't done it already, and you know they're following you and probably your lady friend as well."

"Have you got any idea why all of this is happening?"

"A couple of good guesses but nothing more."

"I don't even have that," Tagget said.

"The Company and MI-6 are protecting something. Whether that something happened in the war, or whether it's something in the present, I don't know. But you're connected to it either way."

A waiter set two plates of hors d'oeuvres on their table, and Singer ordered another round of drinks. "Listen," he said when they were alone, "I know you're good with your hand . . . But I think you should have a gun."

"Can you get me one?"

"Yeah," Singer answered. "I'll wrap it up in Christmas paper or something and leave it with the doorman."

"How will you get the information to me?"

"We could work out a drop . . . I guess this place will do as well as any. I can tell the owner you're working undercover."

"Can he be trusted?"

"Yeah, I scratch his back, he scratches mine . . . I'll have an ID card and a shield for you the next time we meet."

"I didn't know you could buy those things."

"Why not? You can buy just about everything else."

They finished their drinks and Singer asked for the check. When they were outside he offered to drive Tagget back to where he lived. "I can take the Fifty-ninth Street Bridge and drive out on either Northern or Queens Boulevard."

"Thanks, but I think I'd like to walk a bit."

"Well, my car is up toward Madison Avenue," Singer said. "I'll get that piece to you."

They shook hands. Singer went off uptown. Tagget walked slowly. The night was cold and there were ragged clouds overhead. He went as far as Lexington Avenue before turning uptown. He hoped that Albert Hentz's partner would come up with something that would explain what really had happened to him from April of 1944.

At Fifty-second Street Tagget stopped at the Stage Delicatessen for a corned beef sandwich and bottle of beer. While he was eating he fished Singer's envelope out of his breast pocket and scanned the two photographs. One showed the killer striking at Hicks's head; the other was of the killer's face, badly blurred.

The third item was a Xerox copy of the sketch of the killer's face drawn by an artist in the police labs. It looked familiar, but no more than that. He replaced the pictures in the envelope and put it back into his pocket. He finished his sandwich, trying very hard to remember where he had seen the killer, or a man who had a similar face. . . .

Colonel Uri Chelenko sat in a large easy chair watching *Red River* on the nine o'clock movie. He enjoyed American television as much as he enjoyed American food or the marvelous atmosphere in New York during the pre-Christmas season. He had seen this movie once before; the great open spaces of the American West reminded him of the vast openness of his own country, and for a moment or two he remembered how he had learned to ride a horse almost before he could walk . . .

The secure phone rang and he went to the table and picked it up without speaking.

A man on the other end said, "Good morning."

He answered, "The day has long been over."

And the man said, "Alcantara was one of the detectives assigned to the Hicks murder."

"Anything else?"

"Everything is sealed."

Chelenko put down the phone.

From the bedroom his wife Sonia asked if the phone had rung.

"Yes," Chelenko answered, "it was mine." He turned the television volume off and sat down.

Since his meeting with Schiller his mind had been filled with thoughts about the dead detective and reasons why the CIA would have killed him. He knew exactly what had happened because one of his men had shadowed Alcantara, seen the shooting and then joined the crowd of bystanders that had gathered around the body. The information that had just been phoned to him came from his source inside the police department.

That the dead detective had been assigned to the Hicks murder made his death even more interesting. Now he could compare what he had learned to whatever information Schiller brought him.

The connection between the dead former MI-6 agent

and dead detective was the kind of coincidence that aroused his suspicion, or what his subordinates jokingly referred to as his twisted oriental mind. It was true enough that he took nothing at face value. He gave his trust to very few and kept his own counsel.

It was obvious to Chelenko that Alcantara had been either coming from or going to a meeting that the Company had objections to. Now the question was, who was Alcantara seeing? And what was this person's connection, if any, to Hicks. Alcantara could have met with more than one individual . . . but Chelenko knew there was a remote possibility that he might be on the wrong track altogether, that it was possible that the Company was watching someone else and Alcantara had blundered into something. . . .

Chelenko decided to have two of his men check around the neighborhood to see if they could find out what Alcantara had been doing that night. He would have comrade Krilov, the man who had witnessed the shooting, do most of the leg work and assign a junior man to help him, perhaps Kerenski. Both men spoke English fluently without trace of an accent. He made a mental note to follow this up in the morning and was about to turn the sound on the television back up when the secure phone rang again.

This time it was a different man, who said after an exchange of passwords, "Deputy Director Howell left the New York office shortly before noon."

"Interesting."

"The rumor is that when he first arrived he was angry about what happened last night, but was in much better humor when he left."

"Any other details available?"

"None."

Chelenko put the phone down and returned to the big chair to watch *Red River*. When the film was over, he would have one or two vodkas and think about why Howell would pay Reynolds a visit and what connection it might have to Alcantara and Hicks. But for the next hour or so Chelenko could afford to enjoy

John Wayne and Montgomery Clift as they portrayed another portion of the American myth that so fascinated him.

Schiller walked into the library of his Chevy Chase house and switched on the desk lamp. The two couples Irene had invited for dinner had left a while ago and she had gone upstairs to get ready for bed.

Ordinarily he would have gone up with her. But he had much to think about from a day that had been very productive. He had learned some interesting things about John Tagget and his connection to 29 Russell Square, and about the two men who had operated from there during the war.

Schiller had obtained the information from a bright young man who worked in the records section of the Company's headquarters in Langley and whose expenses were greater than his income. Schiller was always on the lookout for men or women in sensitive government positions who needed additional funds and didn't mind doing something extra for a colleague. He paid two thousand in cash for the information. At five times that he would have considered it a bargain. He was making an investment in his future both with the KGB and the law firm of Hentz, DeFiore and Schiller.

Schiller unlocked his top desk drawer and withdrew a flat manila envelope, opened it and removed a set of black and white photostats marked TOP SECRET— RESTRICTED TO SECURITY RATING 12.

The first three pages explained in detail the particular mission that Tagget had been sent on and the following two pages detailed the type of mind-conditioning that Tagget had undergone at the William Beaumont hospital.

The next page was devoted to the current activities of Ross and Fleming. As Chelenko had told him, they were recruiting mercenaries to fight against rebel forces in Angola, Rhodesia and half a dozen other African nations. They were in London, using the magazine

New Wars and Weapons as a cover. Ross was publisher and Fleming was editor-in-chief.

The last page dealt with Hicks and revealed that
MI-6 had become very concerned about his loose
tongue and had ordered their area chiefs to eliminate
him if he should in their judgment endanger any of
the listed operations or areas of interest. The recruitment of mercenaries was first on the list of areas of
interest.

Schiller went to the French doors overlooking a
barren rose garden. A light snow was falling. With
the information he had, he could satisfy Chelenko *and*
Hentz. Chelenko would be pleased to get Tagget's
name, and Tagget would be grateful to Hentz for the
information about Ross and Fleming. From that point
it would be up to Chelenko to use Tagget, if he could,
or if Tagget was not interested in a face-to-face meeting with Ross and Fleming, then Chelenko would
have to use the wide services of his own organization
to go after the two men.

Schiller decided to phone Hentz first, in the morning, and to have Tagget come down late in the day or
the following morning. That way he could take the
measure of the man and report to Chelenko what he
thought Tagget might do.

Schiller went back to the desk and replaced the
pages in the envelope. After locking the envelope in
the desk drawer, he switched off the light and made
his way upstairs to the bedroom where Irene was
waiting for him.

As soon as Tagget turned onto York Avenue from
Sixty-seventh Street he saw the blue car diagonally
across from the entrance of the building where he
lived. There were two men in the front seat. He over-
came his inclination to go up to the car, knock on
the window and inform them he would not be going
out again for the rest of the night.

Tagget was surprised to see a new doorman on duty
and asked where the regular man was.

"Don't know, sir," the new man answered. "I'm just a temporary . . . I got a call from my boss tellin' me to come over here, so I come . . . That's all I know."

Tagget didn't say anything more and headed for the elevator.

The conversation with Singer ran through his mind. Tagget was suspicious of the man's rapid turnabout, though it was obvious that he was genuinely upset over the story in the *Post*. He just hadn't figured Singer to be so sensitive to the effect of the story on Alcantara's family.

The elevator doors opened and Tagget stepped into the car. He was emotionally exhausted. The last few days had totally unsettled his life. The past was rushing at him, but it was a gossamer thing, totally insubstantial in spite of his feeling that it was all around him.

Tagget reached his floor and walked into the hallway with his thoughts still on the past. All he had so far was his intuition—and the name Cordez.

He stopped. The doorway to his apartment was directly ahead of him, no more than thirty feet away. His heart began to pound. He took several deep breaths and a few steps forward, then stopped again.

He glanced over his shoulder. The doors to the elevator were closed. Above them green numbers flashed on the indication panel as the car passed each floor on its way down to the lobby. Unconsciously Tagget began counting backward with the descending numbers. His eyes moved to the other doors in the hallway. There were three, all of them closed. Someone must have been watching TV because he could hear the sound of gunfire.

Tagget realized he was having an experience very similar to the one he had during dinner with Hicks. He had the intense feeling that he was crouching outside a building in a European village. The hallway in front of him was a street being torn up by slugs fired from a machine gun. The air was filled with the staccato crack of small arms fire and grenade explosions.

"Dumas, I'll work my way around to the right and try to knock out the machine gun."

"We will cover you from here."

It was over as quickly as it had begun and Tagget was still looking at the door to his apartment. He walked toward it but his stomach twisted into a hard knot. Dumas was another name out of the past and like the name Cordez, he couldn't connect it with a face. But the voices he had heard were speaking in French. . . .

Tagget unlocked the door and swung it open. The light from the hallway made a rectangle on the floor of the foyer. He brushed his hands along the wall toward the light switch.

"I would rather you left the lights *off*," a man with a decided English accent said. "I have a .357 magnum pointed at you, Mr. Tagget. Please step inside and close the door. Your eyes will become accustomed to darkness very quickly."

Tagget did as he was told. He couldn't see a thing.

"Now move away from the door," the man said. "Very good."

As soon as Tagget's eyes adjusted to the darkness, he saw the man he'd seen talking to the doorman earlier. He could also be the man in the composite, the one who had killed Hicks. The pistol had an oversize silencer on its barrel.

"I see you recognize me," the man said.

Tagget remained silent, wondering whether the man belonged to the Company or MI-6.

"I think you know why I am here."

"Suppose you tell me," Tagget answered, forcing himself to remain calm.

"I was rather hoping you might tell me something about it," the man said. "Understand, Mr. Tagget, I have nothing against you."

"Of course not, you don't even know me. This is your assignment."

"Exactly," the man said. "But it would be helpful if I knew—"

"I'm afraid I won't be able to help you," Tagget said.

"I was quite certain you'd say that . . . Too bad, I had hoped you would be helpful."

Tagget remained silent, expecting to feel the crushing blow of a .357 slug. If the Englishman was a good shot, he would take him out with one round in the heart or in the head.

"Mr. Tagget, will you please walk slowly into your library, go to your desk, switch on the light and then sit down."

Tagget hesitated. With that silencer the man could shoot him with no more noise than someone sneezing.

"Please do not give me any trouble . . . It will be much easier for the two of us if you cooperate."

Tagget forced himself to move, disgusted with the phony melodrama of the man's British understatement. Switching on the desk lamp, he sat down.

"Now please pick up a pen and write the following. 'I, John Tagget, have become too deeply involved with agents of the Russian government and have no other way out. I am guilty of treason and had I been tried, I would have been found guilty. I regret all the pain I have caused.' . . . Good. Now will you please sign it."

"Do you really think anyone who knows me will believe this?"

"Oh, I will not know for sure until it's tried," the man answered. "Now please stand up, turn around and walk toward the terrace."

Tagget followed his instructions, thinking furiously.

"Remove your coat and hat, then open the door."

Tagget put his hand on the brass handle but did not open the door. His only chance was to get his would-be assassin to move closer and surprise him somehow . . .

"I know it is difficult," the man said. "But it will soon be over."

Tagget kept quiet.

"So far you have done everything right," the man told him, and moved closer. "I would hate to have to knock you out, drag you onto the terrace and then drop you over . . . I would much prefer to have you leave with—"

Tagget suddenly wrenched the door open and the icy wind roared into the room, scattering papers from the desk and blowing the drapes wildly around the two men.

Tagget turned. The man with the gun looked like a drowning swimmer.

"Don't move," the man shouted, trying to protect his eyes from the wind's blast, but Tagget already had the man's gun hand in his own good one. The man grunted and struggled to keep the gun, using his free hand to grab hold of Tagget's throat, and the two of them fell to the floor.

Tagget couldn't breathe. His lungs ached and a thumb was jabbing into his throat. He had to break the hold or he'd be out within seconds.

Tagget *willed* his left arm to move. And, by God, it *did* move . . . He balled his fist and crashed it awkwardly against the side of the man's face, breaking the hold on his throat.

The man tried to roll free but Tagget slammed his head against the parquet floor until he dropped the gun. Tagget went for it. The gun slid onto the terrace.

The man was on his feet and through the door. He got hold of the gun by the silencer, but Tagget rushed him, driving his head into the man's stomach and at the same time lifting him over the railing into a cold updraft full of traffic noises.

The man dropped the gun, terror in his face as he struggled to hold onto the iron railing, and couldn't. Tagget butted him farther over with his shoulder, breaking his grip. He screamed and fell to the street, twenty-two floors below.

Tagget stepped back, sagged against the glass door, sweating and breathing very hard. The wind beat against him. He was cold and shaking. He took several deep breaths. Every part of his body hurt, especially his neck. He could barely think, but he resisted the impulse to go to the railing and look down.

"Move," he told himself. "You've got to move."

The high-pitched wail of sirens drifted up from the street. Within a few minutes, Tagget realized, the police would be all over the street. He looked for the man's gun and saw it lying near the railing. He couldn't leave it there. Forcing himself to move, he retrieved the gun and stepped back into the livingroom, closing the glass door behind him. All six chambers of the cylinder were still loaded, so the gun had not gone off and he needn't search the room for bullet holes. He set the gun down on an end-table and switched on a lamp. He looked around at the papers scattered across the room. Nothing else had been upset during the struggle.

He put the room in order, then went to the bar cart, and poured himself a double Chivas. He downed the drink in one long swallow, poured another and drank until the glass was empty.

He became aware of a tingling sensation in his left arm and leg. He looked at his arm and felt it with his right hand. He tried to raise it but found he couldn't, though he had been able to move it during the fight. He began to walk and tried to move his leg in a normal manner, but he couldn't do that either.

"Why then and not now?" he asked aloud, rubbing the arm with his right hand. He stopped in front of the end-table where the gun was. He picked it up, unscrewed the silencer, put the safety on and placed the revolver in his belt.

Again he tried to move his left arm. The tingling sensation gave way to a burning one, and the arm moved slightly. He held it up without support, lowered it and raised it again, only this time he couldn't get it to go as high as it had been before. He tried his leg again but he was unable to move it normally,

though it was filled with the same burning sensation
as his arm.

"All right for now," Tagget told himself. He walked
into the den, tore the note he had written into small
pieces, then went into the bathroom and flushed the
scraps down the toilet.

He returned to the living room. He had to keep
thinking. Sooner or later the police would determine
the general area—if not pinpoint the exact terrace—
the body had fallen from. The gun was probably un-
traceable, and the police might not believe—or choose
to believe—that he had killed the man in self-defense.

He checked his wallet. He had one hundred fifty
dollars and his credit cards. Enough for a while, but
not enough if he'd have to remain away for any length
of time. He went back into the den for the key to his
bank vault where he always kept at least twenty thousand in cash.

Tagget slipped on his coat and put on his hat. He
paused in the hallway. Using the elevator would be
out of the question. He decided on the service stairs.
He'd go down to the garage in the basement and then
out the side entrance, which would put him on Sixty-
eighth Street.

He closed his door behind him, locked it and started
toward the service stairway when the doors to the
elevator opened and the middle-aged couple who
lived across the hall stepped out. They were very
agitated, and the woman said, "The police are downstairs . . . someone jumped from one of the terraces
. . . I don't know what's happening. The other night
there was a shooting and earlier two thugs beat up
the doorman . . ."

Tagget put on his most astonished expression, and
before he could say anything the husband said, "I
heard one of the cops say that they'd have to pick up
the guy with a blotter . . . The only way they knew
it was a man was because of the way he was dressed."

"Terrible," Tagget said, "terrible," and walked into
the elevator. When he reached the lobby, the door

opened. There were several plainclothesmen. A harassed Detective Oliver Blanchard from homicide was ordering his men to disperse the large crowd so he could begin his interrogation of the tenants in the building. Tagget, taking advantage of the diversion, backed away and managed to fade into the crowd and limp unnoticed—he hoped—out of the building. There was a very large crowd in the street, a half dozen blue-and-whites and as many unmarked cars. He turned up Sixty-eighth Street, went as far as Second Avenue, hailed a cab and told the driver to take him to the Summit Hotel on Lexington Avenue and Fifty-first Street, then sat back, grateful that he had somehow managed to get away.

A few minutes later he was at the hotel registration desk, explaining to the night clerk why he didn't have any luggage.

"Listen," he said, "I just walked out on my wife. I called it quits after fifteen years . . . What did you expect me to do, stop and pack?" He spoke loud enough to attract the attention of other people in the lobby. "I'll pay in advance," he said, taking out his wallet. "Cash."

"If you had offered to do that in the beginning," the clerk told him, "we could have avoided any difficulty."

"I thought I had. I'm sorry, but I *am* upset."

He paid for the room and was escorted up to it by a bell-hop. As soon as he was alone, he switched off the light, kicked off his shoes and dropped down onto the bed. He was too keyed up to sleep, too tired to think. He lay staring at the ceiling, wondering whether if he ever did manage to put his life together again there would be anything worthwhile left over . . . .

London, April 20, 1944

Ross and Fleming were seated at a round, highly polished table in a small room. Rain pelted against the single window, which looked out on a courtyard.

With them were two other men: Hugh Williams, a representative of General Sir Stewart Menzies, chief of MI-6, and Robert Patch, aide to General William J. Donovan, director of the American counterpart of MI-6, the Office of Strategic Services.

Williams was a young blond man whose father owned a small weekly newspaper in Northumberland. Patch, a former college professor from Columbia University, was older, with cool gray eyes.

"According to our last communiqué from our friend Gunner," Williams said, "Tagget has not only eluded capture but has linked up with a Maquis group."

"We are trying to find out more about the Maquis group without compromising our special operation," Ross explained.

Patch made a low clicking sound with his tongue before he said, "The director wants to know how you now intend to put Tagget in the hands of the Germans."

"We will tell him that the mission is cancelled and have him go to a particular place on the coast to be removed by a submarine . . . Gunner will be there to take him."

"General Menzies has had some further communiqués from Admiral Canaris," Williams said. "Tagget must be in the hands of the Abwehr within the next fortnight or Canaris will not be in a position to bring the information to Hitler in time to be of any use to us . . . Canaris needs time to prepare his case."

Fleming leaned forward. "Suppose he runs into a regular German patrol and gets killed. Then what?"

Ross frowned. Though the question was legitimate, he did not appreciate it coming from his own quarter.

"That is a possibility," Patch replied, "which now must be given serious consideration." He directed his gaze to Ross. "You must also consider the possibility that if he is *not* captured, he may eventually figure out that he was set up, especially if he stays alive after Operation Overlord takes place. He could become a problem. He might cause trouble in several different ways. The press for one . . . Could you imagine what they would do with his story?"

"To prevent that from happening," Williams said, "it is General Menzies's opinion that Tagget must be neutralized if he is not captured within the fortnight specified by Admiral Canaris."

"I don't think the director would have any objections to that," Patch said, "though we didn't specifically discuss that possibility. I have no objections."

"Nor I," Williams told them. "The general suggests that you make every effort to identify the Maquis group and if they can't be manipulated into executing him, have one of our own men go into France, seek them out and eliminate Tagget."

"Well, gentlemen," Patch said, "we won't keep you any longer." Then, "Even if your plan doesn't succeed, it was a damn good try."

"Absolutely marvelous," Williams added.

IX

As soon as he was awake, Tagget listened to the early morning news on the radio and then sampled the television news on several channels. No mention was made of a man having fallen to his death from an Upper East Side apartment.

Tagget wasn't surprised. Sometime during the night he had reached the conclusion that CIA or MI-6—perhaps both acting jointly—would have blacked out any news coverage. He also decided that the police would have been told, once again, to back off and leave the matter to them.

He had slept fitfully, often waking to the brazen sounds of fire engines or the wailing sirens of police cars, and once startled awake by the violence of his own dreams.

He had not been able to decide, with any degree of clarity, what he wanted to do. For the first time in his life he saw a terrifying meaning in the pronoun *they*. He switched off the radio and left his room. He went down to the coffee shop in the lobby for breakfast and sat in a booth. Out of habit, he used only his right hand, though he felt he could use the left one too. For the same reason, when he walked, he continued to limp, but during the night he had proved to himself several times that he was regaining the use of both limbs.

He did not believe in God, or in miracles. He thought he had lost his belief in both somewhere in Italy, before he lost that part of himself he was trying to find. But regaining the use of his arm and leg after so many years was close enough to a miracle for him. Only the danger he was in kept him from shouting, "Look I can walk like other men . . . I can use my arm like other men . . . I'm a whole man after thirty years of being less . . ." He realized that he had already taken too big a risk by coming down to the coffee shop instead of calling room service. His situation did not even permit him to phone Claudia, for the time being at least.

He finished his coffee, paid the cashier, crossed the street and bought a *Times* and a *Daily News* at the corner stand; from there he went into the Bancroft store and bought three wash-and-wear shirts, some socks and some underwear to get him through the rest of the week. He stopped at the drug store in the hotel lobby and bought a razor, shaving cream, after-shave lotion and body cologne. He went upstairs, shaved, showered and changed. By eleven he had gone to his vault in the Seaman's bank and withdrawn ten thousand in cash. Then he went straight to Hentz's law offices.

His arrival at the offices of Hentz, Defiore and Schiller without an appointment brought out the best in the receptionist. She recognized him from previous visits but was surprised to see him now and ostentatiously checked her appointment book.

"You won't find me there," Tagget told her. "Just ring Mr. Hentz, tell him I'm here and that it is urgent I see him now."

"He has someone in his office—"

"Just tell him I'm here."

While she spoke to Hentz on the phone she kept her eyes on Tagget, making him feel she sensed something different, even threatening? "Mr. Hentz will be with you," she said.

Tagget nodded and was about to sit down when Hentz came out of his office. "We can go into the conference room." He was clearly annoyed.

Tagget offered no apology, and as soon as the door

to the conference room was closed said, "I need your advice and help."

"How long is this going to take?" Hentz asked. "I'm sorry, John, but I have a client waiting."

Tagget didn't answer. He walked to the other side of the desk without limping, then he lifted his left hand.

Hentz stared at him.

"Last night," Tagget said, "I killed a man. I want you to get rid of these." He put the magnum and its silencer on the desk. "I can explain the whole thing—"

"Sit down," Hentz told him. "I'll be back in a few minutes." He left the office, closing the door quietly behind him.

Tagget went to the telephone and called Singer at the precinct house. When Singer came on Tagget said, "I'll be at the same bar at the same time."

"Okay," Singer answered, and hung up.

Hentz came back into the room, locked the door and sat down. "I called you about ten-thirty," he said. "Schiller had phoned me earlier and asked that you go down to Washington today if possible, or early tomorrow morning. He says he's uncovered something that would interest you . . ."

"I'll go tomorrow morning." The two of them were now seated across from each other. Tagget had removed his coat and was filling a pipe.

"For God's sake, John, what happened?"

Tagget gave a complete explanation of how he had spent the evening, without mentioning the photographs of the man in his apartment who had killed Hicks and had tried to kill him. He described the strange feeling he had experienced before entering the apartment.

"It was as if I were actually living the experience," he said. "And someone named Dumas was with me. But as with Cordez, I was unable to match Dumas with a face."

He went on to tell Hentz how he had wrestled the assassin over the balcony. "After it was over," he said,

"I managed to fade into the crowd in the lobby and make my way to the Summit Hotel."

"And what do you intend to do?" Hentz asked.

"Stay alive and hope I find out who is trying to kill me, and why."

"I want to know two things," Hentz said. "First, about your previous physical disabilities. As I remember, you said you have been required to report to the VA three times a year. And once a year you spent a few days in the hospital?"

"That's right," Tagget replied, smoking again. "You know I have a seventy-five percent disability and shortly after I was discharged from the army I was asked if I would be part of an experiment having to do with nerve degeneration. I hoped it might help find a cure for my problem and I agreed. Why do you ask?"

"Because," Hentz said, "nerves that truly degenerate never regenerate . . . I suspect that you never suffered any organic nerve degeneration, which was why you were able to use your left hand last night to break this man's hold on your throat. But let's go to the other thing. You said that in this vision or whatever you and someone named Dumas were fighting in a French village?"

"Yes, that was the distinct impression I had. The machine gun fire was coming from the church tower."

"Are you sure it was France?"

"I spoke in French to Dumas."

"But according to what you told me before, you don't remember going into France during the war."

"That's right."

"What kind of clothing were you wearing? Try hard to remember."

"Clothing . . . Pants, jacket . . . I'm sorry, Albert, I don't know what you want."

"Were you wearing a uniform?" Hentz waited, then repeated the question. "Were you wearing your army uniform?"

Tagget shook his head. "I might have been, but

Dumas wasn't . . . He was wearing the clothes of a
. . . of a French peasant."

"Are you sure?"

"Not as sure as I know you'd like me to be."

Hentz frowned and stood up. He walked to the
window and said quietly, "It looks as if we might
have more snow." Then he returned to the table, sat
down and said, "Now, I'm thinking back to your
dinner in the hotel with Hicks, the time you passed
out. Didn't you tell me before that you had the feeling
that you were jumping out of a plane?"

"Yes, that's right. I remember falling, hearing
planes around me . . ."

"Is it possible that you jumped into France, became
separated from your unit and wound up fighting with
the French?"

"That's not what the army said."

"So? The army said you had suffered nerve damage
too, and it's now obvious that you didn't. How else
would you have acquired such distinct and vivid mem-
ories of combat experiences in France?"

"You tell me."

"I have some idea," Hentz answered, "but for right
now, what do you want me to do?"

Tagget asked him to contact Claudia and assure
her that he was all right. "Have her come to your
office, tell her I'm staying at the Summit and tell her
to join me there. I'll leave word at the desk. Warn
her that she's being followed."

"How do you know that?"

"I know it. Then I want you to—never mind. I can
get those things from someone else."

"What things?"

"A whole new set of identification papers. Social
Security, driver's license, credit cards and a passport."

"You understand," Hentz told him, "what you intend to do is against the law?" He followed Tagget's
eyes to the handgun and the illegal silencer on the
desk between them. "Sorry, just professional reflex."

Tagget smiled. "To borrow an expression from my

son's generation, I'm going underground. I'll give you power of attorney and you'll send me money as I need it. I don't think you'll be in any jeopardy, but if you should feel that you are, contact my son David. Have him come east, explain the situation to him and let him take it from there. But I don't want him involved unless he has to be. I'm sorry to have involved you too, Albert. Let's not put anything in writing."

"I understand. If you wait a moment I'll give you Schiller's home address." He locked the pistol and silencer in his safe.

"Would you risk lunch with a hunted man?" Tagget asked.

"We can't go to my club."

"I know, too many people recognize me there. I'd like some more anonymous place."

"Put on your coat and we'll go." Hentz opened the door. "I'll join you in a few minutes."

Tagget walked out into the reception room. The receptionist smiled at him and busied herself with the document she was typing.

Hentz came out of his office carrying his coat and hat and handed Tagget a piece of paper. "I spoke to Schiller. Breakfast at nine at his home. You take the first shuttle flight out of LaGuardia, that gets you to the Washington airport at eight. You can take a cab to Chevy Chase from there."

Tagget pocketed the piece of paper. "Any idea what he's got for me?"

"None."

Because there were other people in the elevator, neither of them spoke on the way down. When they were out on the street Tagget wanted to know something more about Schiller.

"A charming, clever and ruthless man," Hentz said.

Tagget was surprised by the answer and said as much.

"Notwithstanding my own feelings," Hentz explained, "he has been a valuable asset to the firm."

"But what about the man himself?"

"That's just it. The man would be difficult, if not impossible to really know. He's something of a woman-izer and right now has a beautiful woman living with him who is probably half his age. You'll probably meet her when you're down there. He likes to show off his women. They're another one of his possessions, like his antiques, works of art and, oh yes, rare books. He's something of a collector, just like you."

"Then he can't be all bad."

"Never said he was. He's just not the sort I would choose as a friend."

"Then why have him as a partner, especially in such a small firm?"

"Because I know how to keep my business dealings and my friendships mutually exclusive. My relation-ship with you is one of the few exceptions."

"Thanks. I do value our relationship—both halves of it."

"So do I," Hentz answered, putting a hand to his friend's shoulder.

It was three o'clock in the afternoon. Howell was in a foul mood. Nothing had gone right since the time he woke up and tried to make love to his wife. His lack of potency had become a frequent embarrassment in recent months, as was his inability to sleep through the night without waking up and thinking about the assignments under his control, the options he saw for "his team," as he referred to the men who supported him within the agency . . .

At first his wife had been understanding and sup-portive, then she'd urged him to seek medical help, but he hadn't responded to the idea and she had ceased to be sympathetic. Now she was just angry. This morning she had shouted, "If you don't do some-thing about it, I will." They never discussed their problem—but he knew she would eventually find someone who could satisfy her needs.

Howell had left the house angry and hurt, but by the time he got to work he was beginning to put it behind him. At the daily morning briefing he was informed by an aide that MI-6 had ordered the elimination of John Tagget. Rationale: The operations being conducted by Ross and Fleming were too valuable to be disrupted or compromised.

Since MI-6 had elected to take action, Howell had anticipated the corresponding order from the director, which arrived that afternoon by special messenger. Howell phoned Reynolds on the scrambler. "Take Tagget out," he said.

"We're scrapping the Beaumont mind-control experiment?"

"We're scrapping Tagget."

"Right. But we've got a problem." Reynolds sounded nervous. "Tagget killed an MI-6 agent last night."

Howell said nothing, though the tension in his jaw increased.

"He managed to get past my men," Reynolds said finally.

"Find the son of a bitch and take him *out*." Howell slammed the phone down hard enough to send it over the edge of the desk, taking a box of paperclips with it.

To add to his problems, he was informed by an aide from security that a clerk in archives named Philip Redding had removed Tagget's file and had photocopied a dozen documents. Redding had just confessed to passing them to Schiller for two thousand dollars.

Howell shook his head. Ever since he had been with the State Department he'd had suspicions about Schiller. Nothing he could really tie onto, though. When he joined the Company his suspicions deepened and he made some preliminary investigations, which again came to nothing. But as soon as Schiller had mentioned Tagget's name, Howell guessed he would want more information about the man and the only place it could come from was the Company files.

Howell had been aware of Schiller's relationship to Redding for several months, and he had been certain

Schiller would tap him one last time to obtain the information on Tagget. And Schiller had. Now Howell had to re-bait the trap . . .

By four o'clock in the afternoon Chelenko was in possession of several pieces of information he considered extremely important, especially since the operation against Ross and Fleming had been given an upgraded priority by his superiors at 2 Dzerzhinsky Square. The new code designation number was, appropriately, 29.

Each piece of information had come to Chelenko from a different source. The first had been phoned in by Schiller: the name and address of John Tagget, the man who was interested in discovering the whereabouts of Ross and Fleming. Chelenko felt certain that Schiller knew why Tagget was looking for the two men and that for some reason he was sitting on the information. But Schiller had said that Tagget was involved with Claudia Harris, the widow of one of Chelenko's former agents.

Chelenko had noted that Tagget lived on the street where the detective assigned to the Hicks murder had been shot. Chelenko had been trying to establish the connection between Tagget, Hicks, and the death of the detective when he had received a message from his counterpart in London:

RECENT INTERCEPT FROM GEN. FINNEY CHIEF OS/ OP. MI-6 ORDER "BRIGHT" N.Y. TO KILL JOHN TAGGET. IDENT "BRIGHT" AND PURPOSE MI-6 ORDER.

SIGNED,
PETER OISTERAKH

The message from London had at first appeared to confirm Chelenko's speculations. The British had ordered Tagget killed because he had killed Hicks, who obviously had been more important to them than KGB headquarters in Moscow had realized. It also had seemed possible that Tagget could have been responsible for the murder of detective Alcantara, although if that were true, why had nothing been done by the police to arrest him?

That question had stood between Chelenko and the full understanding of the order from MI-6. He had mulled it over for most of the day and then the third piece of information had come in from Serge Krilov, one of the men he had assigned to investigate the shooting of the detective.

Krilov, under his cover as a newspaper reporter, had discovered what had not been in the New York papers: the doorman in Tagget's apartment building had said that Alcantara had been shot from a moving vehicle, and a man had jumped or been pushed from the same building—on the side where John Tagget lived.

Chelenko sent Krilov back to the area where Tagget lived with instructions to find out whatever he could about John Tagget. Then he went to a pay phone several blocks away from the mission and called the police headquarters telling the desk sergeant that he was the brother of the man who had jumped from the building on York Avenue.

The sergeant asked him to hold the line and said he had no knowledge of anyone jumping from a building in that vicinity. When he tried to engage him in a conversation, Chelenko knew that an attempt was being made to hold him at the phone in order to trace the call. He hung up and hurried away, walking downtown to Fifty-seventh Street and then west to Rockefeller Center. He stopped to watch the ice skaters in the rink below the plaza. He was a man who admired beautiful form, especially in pretty dancers and figure skaters. Several of the people around him took flash photographs of the skaters and he obliged a group of tourists by taking a picture of them. He was enjoying himself.

It started to snow. Chelenko pulled up his collar and walked across the street to Saint Patrick's Cathe-

dral. He found a seat in the rear of the church and
began to reexamine what he had.

He assumed that the man who had fallen from the
building where Tagget lived had probably come to kill
Tagget and been overpowered. That would explain the
lack of information on the dead man from the media
and the police. He had been the MI-6 agent assigned
to kill Tagget.

Chelenko decided to have the central files of the
KGB in Moscow run a check on Tagget. They might
come up with some information that would help him
understand why Tagget wanted Ross and Fleming
enough to make the British feel the operation was
endangered.

Chelenko was almost startled by the realization
that he was staring at a woman who was kneeling in
silent prayer in front of a small altar nearby. Her
long black hair flowed out from under the white silk
kerchief she wore. He had seen such a beatific expression only in certain religious paintings, and to see
it on the face of a beautiful woman was an experience
he was not prepared for. The incongruity of the sight
of her praying and his own thoughts was enough to
make him stand up and start for the door. But he
allowed himself a lingering look as she stood up, lit a
candle and dropped a few coins into the box.

Chelenko imagined that she was offering thanks,
or perhaps praying for someone who was ill, remembering someone who had died.

The young woman buttoned the collar of her coat
and passed close to where Chelenko was standing. For
a fraction of a second he felt like reaching out to stop
her and tell her that her prayers would be answered.
He pulled up his own fur-trimmed collar and walked
out of the cathedral behind her, but she was quickly
lost in the crowds and he began to walk back toward
the mission.

By the time he returned to his office he found himself wondering if there might be a possibility of having
Tagget work for him. Both of them were interested

in finding the same two men. Tagget could be used to endanger the London operation further, while at the same time keeping the KGB one step removed and creating a picture of disarray and rebellion within the Anglo-American espionage establishment. Yes, he thought, rebellion *from within,* against their own clandestine program of combatting legitimate African revolutionary movements. The idea appealed to him, but he wanted to wait and see what kind of information the central files would give him on the man.

On his desk were two messages. One was from his wife, asking him to phone her. The other had been called in to his secretary by Krilov. It read: *J.T. is missing.*

Tagget spent the rest of the afternoon at the Metropolitan Museum of Art. He thought it would be the least likely place for anyone to look for him. For a while he sat on a bench in the Rembrandt gallery admiring the master's painting, *Aristotle Contemplating the Bust of Homer.* As he wandered from gallery to gallery, Dumas's name moved in and out of his thoughts.

At four o'clock Tagget left the gallery and a few minutes later was on a bus heading down Fifth Avenue. Because of the snow, traffic was slow and it took more than forty minutes to reach his stop at Twenty-ninth Street.

He walked rapidly, without limping. The street was full of people on their way home and Tagget found himself envying them. They were not running from anyone; they were not fearful they would be killed. He sighed deeply, making his breath steam in the cold air.

He entered the Weathervane, handed his coat and hat to the hatcheck girl and looked down the length of the crowded bar. Singer hadn't arrived yet.

Tagget found a place at the bar and asked for Chivas, neat. He helped himself to a cocktail frankfurter and listened to the men on either side of him discussing their businesses. Draperies and importers; he tuned them out.

He was at a bar drinking less than twenty-four hours after he had killed a man. He wondered how the men on either side would react if he interrupted their conversation to mention that the night before he had killed a man.

He started on his second drink and watched his reflection in the mirror on the other side of the bar. There wasn't anything different about him—or was there? His face seemed more drawn, his eyes appeared different. He hoped it was only the dim lighting . . .

Suddenly he knew what Dumas looked like. He remembered the bristly beard, the scar on the forehead over the left eye; he remembered the low rough sound of the man's voice. *"We will cover you from here. . . ."*

Tagget picked up his drink and finished it. He churned with excitement. Dumas seemed real and if he was, then the context in which he had remembered him was also real. Somewhere in France he had fought alongside Dumas . . . He was sure of it, but he just as surely had no other memory of having been in France during the war.

Tagget became aware of a man to his left, staring at him. His heart began to race. Had he been followed . . . ?

"You clutch it that hard," the man warned, "you're going to break the glass."

Tagget's eyes moved down to his right hand. He relaxed his hold on the shot glass and said, "I just remembered something I should have done."

The man shrugged and turned away.

Tagget reached for another frankfurter. Though it was cold and rubbery tasting, he had to do something with his hand. He was becoming impatient and concerned that something might have happened to Singer when he saw him come through the door.

"Sorry I'm late," Singer said, dropping a small package on the bar. "That's for you. I got you two different holsters, a clip for your belt and an ankle rig for your leg."

"Thanks. I just got rid of one of these things today."

"Is that right?" Singer helped himself to a handful of bar nuts and said, "I heard about the guy who fell. The lab boys figured out it came from your terrace . . . How'd it happen?"

Tagget told him, explaining how he managed to use his left hand. "Look," he said, raising his left arm. "It still feels a little strange. But I can use it."

"What about the leg?"

"The same . . . I can walk without limping."

"That's going to be a big help to you," Singer said, "in a way you wouldn't have guessed. They're going to be looking for someone with a bum wing and a gimpy leg. Now all you have to do is grow some hair on your face and dye the hair on your head black."

"I'll have to do something," Tagget agreed.

The barkeep brought Singer his vodka.

"It's all been hushed up," Singer said, before he picked up his drink. "No one says why, but the general feeling is that the pressure came from Washington."

"Any reasons given?"

"Mob ties . . . Working for the commies . . . Nothing definite."

"Who was he?"

"That's the crazy part of it, the best I can make out is that he was another MI-6 agent."

Tagget nodded and said, "He pretty well matched the composite you gave me. I think he killed Hicks."

Singer gave a low whistle. "You'd never prove it by us. The guy landed face down. I guess nobody has made the connection yet." He looked at the older man. "You know, you don't stand much chance against them."

"I don't see that I can do anything about that now . . . I'm going to do everything I can to stay alive, no holds barred. I didn't go looking for them, they came looking for me."

"Because you went looking for yourself." Singer picked up his drink again. "Are you really certain that you never worked for them? Not even in the days of the old OSS?"

"There's only one part of my life that's a blank," Tagget said. "I remember everything else. Just before you came in I managed to connect a name with a face. It was someone named Dumas . . . We were together fighting in a French village . . . The only trouble is, I don't remember even having *been* to France during the war."

"Maybe it was in Italy?" Singer suggested. "You could have gotten the place mixed up, confused the experiences you had at that college in Paris before the war. You told me yourself you were in bad shape when you were found."

"I remembered two names, Cordez and Dumas, both French."

Singer didn't answer. Then touching the small package on the bar, he said, "The piece is German-made but it looks like our Smith and Wesson."

"How much do I owe you?"

"A friend of mine gave it to me."

"Thanks. Maybe someday I'll be in a position to return the favor. You need any rare books?"

Singer laughed, asked the barkeep for another round.

"How is Pete Alcantara's family doing?"

"The rough part will be the funeral and what happens afterwards," Singer answered, his smile fading.

"If I ever get clear of my own thing I'll be able to do something for them . . . In fact I'll speak to my lawyer about making the necessary arrangements just in case I don't make it."

"That's generous—"

Tagget stopped him. "Pete tried to help me," he said. "I can do as much for his family."

Each of them sipped at his drink in silence. Then

Tagget said he was going to Washington in the morning.

"They might be watching the various terminals," Singer told him. "The police do, anytime they think one of their suspects is going to skip. My advice is to drive down to Philly, or even to Newark early in the morning and take a train from there. Come back the same way; drive into the city."

"Okay."

"And stop smoking a pipe . . . Try to change as many of your habits and characteristics as possible. That's why I said that regaining the use of your arm and leg would be so important to you. As much as you can, give yourself another self. If you can change your tone of voice, your way of speaking, it will help too."

"I understand."

Singer straightened up, looked around and commented that most of the commuters had gone home. "What's left are bachelors like me," he commented, "and guys who don't want to go home and be with their wives."

"By now I expect Claudia should be at the hotel."

"I'm glad you mentioned her," Singer said. "How well do you know her?"

"What do you mean?" Tagget asked, unsure of himself for a moment.

"Her past."

"She was married. Her husband was killed in a plane crash. She has money of her own. What else is there? . . ."

"On a hunch I had a friend of mine in the Bureau run a check on her."

Tagget stared at him.

"She came up clean—"

"I could have saved you the trouble," Tagget cut in.

"—but her husband Frank Harris didn't," Singer said. "Look, before you get angry, listen to what I have to say."

"I'm listening."

"Frank Harris was killed by the Company . . . His plane was rigged with a time bomb. He was a Company man who decided to sell to the other side. He maintained a mistress or two in Washington and was heavy into gambling."

Tagget picked up his drink and downed it.

"Now Claudia is with you . . . right?"

Tagget nodded and said, "And the Company might think—" He was staring at his reflection in the mirror again.

"The coincidence of the way you two met works in their favor. She didn't know what her husband was doing. He ran an import-export business as far as she was concerned."

"The Company knows that?" Tagget asked, his voice still unsteady.

"Sure. They used a lawyer to tell her that her husband had been killed by the mob," Singer explained, then added, "don't think they would hesitate to use her to get to you."

Tagget shook his head. He had never pried into Claudia's past; it protected him from revealing his own. What little she had told him seemed to give her pain and he had no need to know any more than she had been willing to tell him. She had not said a word about her husband's supposed underworld connections, or that there had been anything suspect about the plane crash that had kiled him.

"I'm sorry," Singer said, "but I thought you should know."

"Yes," Tagget answered, "it's best that I do know . . . At least I can do something to protect her. What was your hunch? What made you run the check on her?"

"She was being tailed . . . I figured maybe there was more of a reason than just her connection to you that made them interested in her. I guess I was wrong. Every time a check was run on her in the last three years, she's come up clean."

"They've been checking on Claudia?"

"Always do, especially in a situation where espionage was involved."

Tagget fished a twenty-dollar bill out of his pocket but Singer said, "It's on me, I have a house account." Tagget looked at the bill, then put it back in his pocket as Singer said, "Good luck, John. Remember, you can leave word for me here."

"Thanks . . . I owe you."

They shook hands and Tagget took the package from the bar with him to the front, where the hatcheck girl helped him into his coat. He tipped her and went out into the street. It was still snowing and now that the rush hour was over snow was sticking to the sidewalks. He pulled up his collar and walked to Park Avenue, where he turned uptown. The cold air felt good and he decided to walk back to the Summit.

Claudia was in the hotel room when he returned. As soon as he opened the door she rushed across the room to him.

"I've been so worried," she told him. "I thought something happened to you."

Tagget held her close to him, using both arms fully for the first time. He wondered how long it would take her to notice.

"John," she said, "Albert Hentz didn't tell me very much at all."

"I told him not to, for your own good. Are you sure you weren't followed?"

"I don't think so . . . After I left Hentz I went into several different department stores." Suddenly she drew back from him and looked at the arms he had around her waist. He was holding her more tightly with his left arm than his right. She reached up and ran her hand down his arm until she came to the bend in the elbow. "How?" she whispered. "For the love of God, tell me how this happened." She brought his left hand to her lips, kissing his fingers.

"Watch," he said. "Watch closely." He put the

package Singer had given him on the top of the dresser and walked across the room without limping. Claudia ran to him. "When did it happen? Tell me how it happened." She was in his arms again. "I can't believe it . . . I never told you this but I was going to suggest that you go to a specialist and see if anything could be done to give you better use of your arm and leg . . . But now you have *full* use of them . . ."

Tagget took off his coat and hat. "Did you bring any clothes?"

"A nightgown and a pants suit for tomorrow. It's all I had time to get."

He nodded and said, "Sit down, we have to talk."

She shook her head. "Not now." She had her arms around him again, massaging his back. "I don't want to hear anything except that you love me, and I especially don't want to *do* anything except get in that bed." She closed her eyes and whispered into his ear, "I want to screw . . . I want you to . . . fuck me until we're both unconscious. I know you never expected to hear me talk this way, but I never expected to wait in a hotel room for you after going to your lawyer's office to be told that I'm being followed. I've been here at the window for almost three hours and I told myself that when you come through that door, we're not going to do anything until—until you've made love to me . . . I want you inside of me." Her eyes were alive, almost wild, and her breasts rose and fell as she breathed.

Tagget ran his fingers up into her hair and kissed her. She had always been uninhibited in bed but had never turned him on with talk this way.

"Get undressed," he told her.

She turned around and looked back at him over her shoulder. "Unzip me."

It's remarkably easy with two hands, he thought as he drew the zipper down to her waist. He turned her around to ease the dress down over her shoulders and as she stepped out of it he reached around and undid her bra, taking her breasts in his hands. He had not caressed a woman's breast with his left hand since the war. He bent down and kissed one nipple and then the other.

"You'd better do the rest," he told her. "Four hands are better than even two." In his haste to get his clothes off he followed his familiar habit of doing everything with his right hand, but as soon as they were naked in bed he moved both hands all over her body and moved his left leg against her thighs. "I love you," he told her.

She took his left hand and put it against her sex. "I meant what I said," she whispered. "I was afraid that I'd never have you to touch me again."

She eased herself onto her back, reached up and guided him into her.

"A new position," he said, "at least for us."

"God, yes," she answered dreamily, moving slowly under him in rhythm to his movements. She arched her back and he took the tip of one breast into his mouth.

They quickened their pace and he could feel her begin to tense under him. Deep in her throat she made small sounds of pleasure and rolled her head from side to side. "John," she gasped, "oh John, there are so many things I can give you . . . do for you . . ."

He kissed her, told her again that he loved her as she wrapped her thighs more tightly against his back and drew herself against him, wordlessly crying out her delight.

At that instant Tagget's passion exploded into her. They held each other for a long time before Claudia said, with her eyes still shut, "In another minute I think I'll be ready to listen to what you have to say."

Tagget pushed himself up, propped the pillow against the headboard and leaned back into it.

Claudia snuggled close to him and waited for him to start.

"Singer says I should give up smoking my pipe and take up cigarettes, if I must smoke . . . It will help confuse them, they'll be looking for a lame man, someone with a bad left arm who smokes a pipe—"

"That's not what you wanted to tell me."

"No," he admitted after a long pause, "it's not." He reached down and stroked her shoulder. "Last night a man tried to kill me."

Claudia gasped.

"He was sent by MI-6. I know he was the same man who killed Hicks. We fought . . ."

"But how could you fight with—"

"That's when I first had the use of my arm and leg. If I hadn't, he would have put a bullet into me and . . . anyway, he didn't. I killed him, God help me."

Claudia looked stricken.

"Singer figures that the Company will also try," he told her in a low voice.

"God."

"Now," he said, putting his arms fully around her and holding her tightly, "comes the hard part."

"Don't say it." She put her hand over his mouth. "Don't say it, John. I don't want to hear." Tears were sliding down her cheeks and he brushed them away. "Where will it end?"

Tagget looked away. He didn't know. The odds, if there were any, were surely against him.

For a moment neither of them spoke, then Claudia asked in a suddenly calm voice, "Why?"

"They're hiding something that has to do with my connection to Twenty-nine Russell Square," Tagget answered. "Whatever it is they think it's worth killing for, even if it happened over thirty years ago."

"Suppose it's not that," Claudia suggested. "Suppose it's something that's going on now?"

"How do you mean?"

"Suppose that by looking for something that happened to you during the war, you're . . . endangering something they're doing now?"

Tagget shook his head. It was a left-field suggestion.

"You didn't answer my question," she said. "John . . ." Her eyes were wet.

"I'll keep in touch with you," he told her, forcing the words out, "through Hentz . . . If anyone questions you about me, tell them the truth, I guess, but don't say anything about Hentz, or anything I might write to you."

"All right, John . . . What can I say to all this?"

Tagget drew her face to his with both hands and kissed her gently. It was the only answer he had.

TAGGET LEFT enough money with Claudia to cover
the hotel bill. Looking, he hoped, like any other businessman heading to work, he carried a small valise
and a leather portfolio. Following Singer's advice, he
rode a cab to the PATH station on West Ninth Street
in the Village and then took a train to Newark, where
he boarded a Metroliner train for Washington, D.C.

He sat next to a window. He had said nothing to
Claudia about her late husband's activities. It would
serve no purpose to make her life any more difficult
than it already was. Leaving her had been difficult
enough.

The industrial landscape that flashed past the window was depressing. Even the newly fallen snow did
little to relieve the panorama of junked cars, tank
farms and asphalt lots littered with scrap and garbage
from factories along the way.

As soon as the dining car opened, he went in for
breakfast. He had ham and eggs, toast and a cup of
coffee which he took back to his seat after he finished
his meal. The train was moving through southern
New Jersey, where the land was given over to farms.
Now and then he caught sight of the Turnpike running parallel to the path of his train but visible only
at intervals.

Tagget closed his eyes and listened to the ticking
rhythm of the wheels on the tracks. He was being
carried along, carried back to a place and time that
he could visualize clearly but of which he had no

previous recollection. . . . The countryside was
rolling farmland, close to the sea. He was near some
railroad tracks and a dozen men and women—he
had become their leader. It was late May. The air was
soft and carried the scent of flowers and of the nearby
sea. . . .

Next to him was Elaine. The previous night they
had slept in a bed for the first time in the four weeks
that they had been lovers.

"The train will come out of that curve and slow
down," she said, pointing up the right-of-way, "when
the engineer sees the barrier and the sections of track
we tore up."

Tagget nodded. "I want our heaviest fire to come
from that small rise there," he said. "Get as many
soldiers as you can with the first burst. Aim just below the windows."

"We will try our best."

"I'll take four men and hit them from the other
side," Tagget said. "We'll use grenades. I'll knock out
the engine and then go for the last car, where they'll
have the weapons and ammo. . . ."

Tagget's heart began to pound as the memory
swept over him. He could hear the clicking of the
streamliner's wheels beating a tatoo on the joints of
the rails. . . .

Elaine reached up and touched his bearded face.
"It was good last night," she told him. Then with a
smile she said, "But the bed made a lot of noise."

He moved his hand through her blond hair. She
had almost made him forget the war and he loved
her for it.

'We won't have a bed again for a long time," he
said. "After this they will look for us night and day."

She kissed his hand. "Soon it will be summer," she
told him. "We will be able to live out of doors."

Suddenly, in the distance, they heard a single short
bleat of a train whistle. Elaine ran across to the hill
where the other partisans were already taking their
positions, while Tagget and his four men moved

quickly down the far side of the railroad bed to a large drainage ditch.

Among them they had fewer than two dozen grenades—stolen German potato masher types, some American pineapples and the rest French. Earlier that morning Tagget and his band had torn up about forty feet of rail and stacked some ties across the tracks in preparation for the attack on the train. . . .

Tagget slowly opened his eyes. The Metroliner had slowed down to cross a small bridge. The memory of the attack on the German train stayed with him. . . .

They could hear the chugging of the locomotive as the train, just out of sight, came closer. Tagget looked up at the sun. It was almost midday. Here and there a crow swooped low over the nearby fields. In the distance he could see a barn, and two cows standing in the meadow across the tracks seemed for a moment to be looking straight at him. He shrank lower into the ditch, feeling foolish. A large fly buzzed close to his face and he brushed it away with a nervous movement of his hand as he watched the bend in the tracks to the east. In a few seconds he saw the front of the engine.

One of the men said, "They should be slowing down . . . now."

Tagget nodded. His stomach was hard with the familiar knot of fear. His hands were wet and his breath seemed to be stuck somewhere in his throat.

A long shrill whistle came from the train and it began to slow down, moving toward the depression where the men were waiting. He picked up one of the grenades, pulled the pin and held the plunger in place. He looked down the line at the other men with him. All of them were ready.

"Only five cars," Tagget whispered, "besides the engine."

The decelerating train rolled slowly past them, blocking their view of the hillock from which the rest of the partisans would open fire at the sound of the first explosion.

With a hiss of leaking steam the train jolted to a halt.

"Now," Tagget shouted and pitched the grenade through an open window into the car in front of him. Explosion followed explosion.

The Germans were shouting; some were screaming in agony. The huge drive wheels of the locomotive began to turn slowly backward as the engineer attempted to back the train up the track. Tagget ran toward the engine and tossed a grenade into the cab. The train crew might be French but it couldn't be helped; the explosion blew the head off one of the men and sent his body rolling down into the drainage ditch.

A steady stream of small arms fire was coming from the hill on the far side of the train, and several of the officers were trying to get their men into some sort of defensive stance.

"The last car," Tagget shouted, leading his small group down the length of the train. As they reached the middle car the doors at both ends opened and soldiers began to jump from them. Tagget opened up with a burst from his Schmeisser, but someone inside the car returned the fire with an automatic rifle and two of the men with him were hit. He ducked back almost under the car, out of the field of fire, and got close enough to toss a concussion grenade into the open door. The explosion blew half the wooden slats loose from the walls of the car and collapsed the roof at the end nearest him. Tagget motioned to the two remaining men and they raced for the last car.

A sandbagged machine gun mounted on top of the car was firing at the hill, and a group of Germans had managed to set up a small mortar. Tagget started up a rusty ladder on the side of the last car as one of his other men went up the rear. The mortar crew was dropping rounds on the far side of the hill, where the explosions sent plumes of dirt fifty feet into the air.

The machine gunners were too intent on their work

to be aware of the other man until it was too late.
Tagget was on them with a knife, killing one with a
quick slash across the neck from behind and the
other with a thrust to the stomach that drove the
knife to the hilt. Then he turned the light machine
gun on the surprised mortar crew and was about to
send them over the edge of the roof when he realized
that the firing around him had stopped. The three
German soldiers in front threw down their arms **and**
raised their hands over their heads, saying *"nicht
schiessen,"* and Tagget released his grip on the machine
gun to signal the men and women on the hill to rejoin
them. They came trooping slowly down toward the
burning train. Two of them carried Elaine. She had
taken a machine gun slug in her chest.

The sight of her made him turn on the Germans
and fire his Schmeisser until the magazine was empty,
then grab another weapon from the partisan beside
him and empty it into the corpses that lay sprawled
over the sandbags. By the time he had been wrestled
down by his men, rivulets of blood and sand trickled
from dozens of bullet holes. When he came down
from the car a few minutes later, he knelt down beside Elaine's body, his rage momentarily expended,
his pity for her . . . for himself in his loss only beginning. . . .

Tagget's eyes were wide open, tears in them. His
hands were gripping the armrest of his seat, and he
fought down the desire to call out, "I was there, I
was in France . . . I killed Germans there, I loved a
woman there. . . ."

Schiller was in the study when the door chimes
sounded. He glanced at the grandfather clock in the
far corner of the room; it was ten minutes to nine.
He was expecting Tagget, but not quite so early. He
went to the door of the study and opened it, ready
to welcome his breakfast guest.

The butler was at the front door. He turned to

Schiller and said, "This gentleman asks if he might speak with you, sir."

"I'm expecting him." Schiller stepped out of the study. He was so absorbed in thinking how best to play Tagget that he scarcely heard what the butler said and was halfway to the door before he stopped.

The man—one of Reynolds's enforcers—was already in the foyer.

Schiller said, "You came sooner than I expected." He turned and walked slowly back into the study, feeling sick.

The agent followed him.

Schiller thought about going for the gun he kept in the top drawer of the desk. But the man behind him was trained; he wouldn't have a chance against him and the others outside—he knew they would be there —would kill him. And there was Irene to think about. He didn't want to endanger her.

As soon as they were in the library the man said, "It's cold out. Bring your hat and coat."

Schiller nodded.

"And if you give me the documents on Tagget now," the man said, "it will be less difficult for you."

Schiller nodded, went to the desk and handed over the brown envelope.

"Your coat and hat," the man said again.

"They're in the closet, near the door," Schiller said with a sigh.

The man gestured for him to leave the library first.

"Don't worry," Schiller told him. "I'm not about to do anything foolish."

A minute later Schiller was seated next to him in the back of a black Mercedes. There were no inside handles on the doors. The two men in the front didn't turn around, and no one spoke. Schiller glanced through the rear window at the house, and for a moment he thought about Irene. She was still upstairs, asleep. Over the past few months he really had developed a great feeling of fondness for her—more,

anyway, than he had felt for the other women he had
known over the years.

He faced forward as the car pulled away from the
house. He had not expected to be taken this way.
The truth was that he hadn't expected to be taken.
He had managed to work both sides for so many
years that he often had the feeling that he operated
with the consent of each.

"You'll have to be blindfolded now," the man next
to him said.

Schiller removed his hat and turned his head
toward the window as a band of cloth was placed
over his eyes and secured at the back of his head.
The car continued straight for a few minutes, made
three left turns, then a quick right jog and for a while
seemed to be on a highway before it once more turned
onto a smaller road. Schiller guessed that they rode
for over an hour, although he knew that his percep-
tion of time was thrown off by the blindfold. He also
tried to stay calm, but was undeniably afraid.

The car slowed, made a right turn and rolled to a
stop. Then it moved forward slowly and stopped again.
Schiller heard some sort of overhead garage door
closing. He was helped out of the car and led through
another doorway, up a steep flight of steps, across to
another door and into a dimly lit room where the
blindfold was removed. He was still flanked by the
three who had picked him up, and directly in front
of him was a man seated at a desk, someone he had
never seen before.

"Well, Mr. Schiller," the man at the desk said, "we
have a great deal to talk about. Will you sit down."

Schiller took the chair to the left of the desk. As he
sat down he studied the man he took to be the interrogator. He was tall, thin and well-tanned. Schiller
guessed he had probably been flown in for this.

"Let me begin by telling you," the man said, "that
we already have Redding's signed statement of his
extracurricular activities on your behalf."

"I see."

"I won't waste time by reading you the statement," the man said. "Here's the point. There are certain questions I want you to answer. You can choose to answer them directly and save a great deal of unpleasantness. But you will answer them."

Schiller nodded.

"I'm glad you see things in a realistic light," the man said. "First I will begin at the end, so to speak . . . What is your interest in John Tagget?"

"None, actually," Schiller answered.

A sudden explosion of pain struck the left side of Schiller's head. He could not focus his eyes and there was a roaring in his left ear.

"What was your interest in Tagget?" the man asked again.

"I was asked to find out why the army had falsified certain information about his activities during the war."

"Who made the request?"

"Albert Hentz, the senior partner of my law firm . . . Tagget is one of Hentz's clients."

"What is your relationship to the KGB?"

"Naturally, in the course of my work for the Company, I'm aware—"

Another blow sent Schiller sprawling on the floor. A sharp kick in the stomach forced him into a fetal position, groaning. After he regained his breath he was helped back into the chair.

"Your contact, who is it?" the man asked.

"Chelenko, Colonel Uri Chelenko, in New York," Schiller said haltingly. He was still doubled up with pain. He was not accustomed to physical violence and despite the care he took of his body it was not tough enough to take this kind of abuse.

"Tell me about Tagget."

"You know as much as I do."

"And how much of what you know did you tell him?"

"Nothing."

The blow to the back of Schiller's neck threw him

forward and brought a sudden paralysis over his body. He was on his knees beside the desk, unable to move.

Once again he was lifted up and put back in the chair.

"I never talked to him, Hentz did," he gasped. "Tagget was coming to my house this morning. I was to—" The room began to spin and he felt a wave of nausea. The sharp scent of smelling salts pulled him out of the spin, but he still wanted to gag.

"How long have you been working for the KGB?" the man asked.

"Ten years," Schiller answered, coughing up blood.

"Tell me your method of contacting Colonel Chelenko," the man asked.

Schiller explained about the phone company truck and the booths located in the lobbies of buildings around Rockefeller Center.

"And how did you make the contact from Washington, or any other part of the country?" the man asked.

"Initially from any pay phone," Schiller explained. "The receptionist in New York would know my ID number and password for the particular day . . ."

"What is your partner's role in your connections to the KGB?" the man asked.

"None. Hentz has nothing to do with it."

The man leaned back and said, "Tagget killed an MI-6 agent the night before last."

"I don't know anything about that."

The man accepted his response, lit a cigarette and offered one to Schiller, who sat hunched in his chair, afraid to move.

"Now tell me," he said, "why the KGB is interested in Tagget."

Schiller thought about denying that the Russians had any such interest but he doubted that he could withstand another blow. He was already in more pain than he ever believed possible. Still, he tried to lead the questioning away from the subject of the KGB.

"They're not," he said.

"Then why did you give his name to Colonel Chelenko?" the man asked.

For a moment Schiller was too stunned to reply, and the man said, "We have our people on their side as they have someone like you on ours. And if you're wondering whether I knew about your relationship with Colonel Chelenko before you told me, the answer is yes, I did . . . Now you have verified things. So tell me, why would they be interested in Tagget? We really do want to know the answer to this, Mr. Schiller."

Schiller took a deep breath. His stomach felt torn. "They want to get at the two men—Ross and Fleming—who are running the recruiting operation for African mercenaries . . . Tagget—"

"Tagget doesn't know a thing about Ross and Fleming."

Schiller lowered his eyes to the floor.

"But you were going to tell Tagget about them, weren't you?" The interrogator's voice was again hard with anger.

"No," Schiller shouted back. "I wasn't going to—"

He was tumbled backward and before he could move a foot smashed into his chest. He screamed and tried to crawl away, but another blow caught him in the face, starting a flow of blood from his nose. He clawed at the air with his right hand and someone lifted him to his feet. He thought they were going to have him sit down again but he was pulled away from the chair.

"What *were* you going to do, Schiller?"

"Please let me sit," Schiller gasped. He was pushed down into the chair. The blood was still flowing from his nose and his lips had begun to swell.

"I'm waiting to hear what you were going to tell Tagget," the man said.

"No names," Schiller said. "Just that they were operating out of London."

"Just that?"

"Yes."

"And what did you think Tagget would do?"

"Try to find them," Schiller answered.

"And what were you going to tell Tagget about the time he spent in the hospital and his visits to the VA and—"

"Nothing," Schiller said. "So help me God, nothing . . ."

The man stubbed out his cigarette. "All right, you give Tagget's name to Chelenko and you tell Tagget where to find all the answers to his questions."

"Yes . . . yes . . . That's all . . . It was like a game," Schiller said, aware of the childish desperation in his voice. "A game."

"Chelenko would then try to make contact with Tagget and use him to find Ross and Fleming, is that right?"

Schiller couldn't follow the man's words.

"I asked a question."

"Probably."

"Probably *what?*"

"Probably it would happen the way you described . . ."

The man at the desk took a deep breath, then said, "If I were you, Schiller, I'd blow my brains out before I let the KGB question me . . . You'll be taken home later this afternoon, and I expect you to take my advice."

Schiller slumped down into the chair. "It would be better if one of you did it for me," he said in a low voice. "I won't be able to do it myself."

"Then you will most assuredly be questioned by the KGB," the man said.

Schiller knew full well that they had no intention of letting Chelenko wring him dry, but still, even with the thought of Krilov and Kerenski on him . . . it was small comfort that he was going to die first. He leaned forward and placed his hands on the man's arm. "Kill me," he said, hoping they had the drugs. "Kill me."

The man shook his head.

Tagget composed himself. He went into the men's room, washed his face with cold water and looked at himself for a moment in the small mirror above the washbasin. He now felt certain that sometime during the year he was trying to account for he had actually been with a Maquis group. Obviously he had been in combat with them *before* he had been captured by the Germans. But how he had gotten to France still eluded him . . . there was the possibility that he had gone in on D-Day, had been separated from his unit and had somehow linked up with a Maquis group. But he had no memory of going in on the day of the invasion. If he had been in the initial assault, he was sure he would have remembered something about it— hundreds of ships, tens of thousands of troops, tons of equipment coming ashore . . . It had been too massive an event for *some* part not to have lodged in his memory. He left the washroom and headed back to his seat.

The train slowed down when it reached the outskirts of the capital, then stopped entirely. The conductor walked through the train announcing that there was some difficulty with switches ahead and that they would be delayed at least a half hour.

Tagget went back to the dining car and ordered another cup of coffee. He hoped that Schiller wouldn't hold breakfast for him. He disliked being late for an appointment and hated to be kept waiting himself.

He rubbed the fog off the inside of the window and looked out. Snow was falling so heavily that he couldn't see more than a few feet away from the train. The snow would make it difficult for him to find a cab in Washington and he decided to try to rent a car for the drive to Schiller's home.

Tagget lingered over the coffee, thinking about Claudia. He wondered if they would ever have the chance to have a real life together. At the moment the prospects were dim, and he didn't see them improving in the immediate future. That Claudia's husband had been a Company man and also an agent for the KGB was the worst of all. He could hardly believe it. Obviously Frank Harris had managed to keep his wife thoroughly in the dark about his espionage work, and presumably both sides knew that— Singer had told him as much—but it was a terrible complication and a dismal omen for them now.

The train jerked forward, rolled for a few yards and jolted to a halt with a loud hiss of compressed air just below the window next to Tagget. The sudden burst of sound startled him and he overturned his cup, spilling the coffee over the top of the table.

Tagget tipped the waiter who came over to wipe up the spill, then returned to his seat. It was unlike him to be startled by loud noises and he knew he had to face up to the effect the events of the last few days had had on him. He was feeling what it was to be frightened, and hunted.

The train started to roll again and he settled back, trying to relax. He wasn't looking forward to driving in the snow. He thought of vacations he had spent in warmer climates, like last winter when he had flown down to the small, still fairly unspoiled town of Manzanillo on the west coast of Mexico. It would be nice to take Claudia there . . .

He looked out of the window again. The snow obscured everything. A long freight train passed by in the other direction, and for several seconds he had the sensation that he wasn't moving. By the time the caboose of the freight passed by his window, the Metroliner was in the yards just outside Washington, crawling into Union Station.

As soon as Tagget left the train, he went to the car rental booth in the station's rotunda and picked up a car for the day. Because of the unaccustomed heavy snow, Washington traffic was moving slowly.

He found his way out of the city and headed into Maryland on the Beltway toward Chevy Chase.

Schiller's house was easier to find than he had expected. He swung up the long curving driveway and parked off to the side of the front door, impressed by the size of the grounds and the house.

Tagget rang the front doorbell. Somewhere deep in the house he could hear the chimes sound. His watch read twelve-twenty. He had arrived for lunch, rather than a late breakfast, and would owe Schiller an apology. He pushed the bell again, impatient to be out of the wind-blown snow. He noticed that there was another car around the side of the house.

The door was opened and Tagget found himself facing the butler.

"I'm John Tagget," he said. "Mr. Schiller is expecting me."

The butler was a shaky, infirm-looking old gent whose lips now trembled when he replied, "I will tell him you're here, sir."

"Thank you." Tagget slipped off his coat and hat. The foyer was very large, with a beautiful curved staircase going up to the second floor.

The butler returned from the study to take Tagget's hat and coat. "Please go right into the study, sir. It's the room down the hall . . . the first door on the left."

He started across the foyer, sensing that the butler was watching him, resisting an impulse to turn around and catch him at it.

The study door was closed and Tagget knocked lightly.

"Come in," a voice called out.

Tagget opened the door and stepped into the library. The chair at the desk was empty.

"Close the door, Mr. Tagget."

A man was standing behind him, next to the book shelves, with an automatic pistol in his hand.

"Your friend Mr. Schiller had an unexpected meeting to attend," the man explained. "He's still tied up. He's very active in our community, you know." He

waved Tagget farther into the room. "I don't suppose
you'll tell me why *you* became so deeply involved in
this situation?"

The man moved away from the wall and went
around to the desk. He was heavy set, about forty-five,
with brown eyes and hair. He looked as if he had
once been an athlete. "This can be done here among
all these old books you and Schiller love so much,"
the man told him, "or somewhere else."

From the agent's cocky manner Tagget guessed that
the man was not yet aware that he could move normally.

"Actually, I guess I would rather do it here," the
man went on.

"Shot while burglarizing, is that it?" Tagget asked.

"Nope, then I'd have to do the butler and the lady
upstairs," the man answered. "*I'm* the burglar. But you
do get shot, don't worry." He laughed, "Maybe you
should help me pick out what I take when I leave.
You know, an assortment of books and paintings."

Tagget remained motionless.

"Schiller told us you were coming here. He told us
a great deal more. Just for the record, we'd like to
know what you intended to do with the information
he was going to give you."

"Since I don't have the information, how can you
expect me to answer that?"

"I know you had some ideas."

This time Tagget shook his head. He realized that
there must be at least one, possibly two other men
close by, covering the servants. It was all but hope-
less.

The man made a slight movement with his gun
hand. He looked like he was getting ready to squeeze
the trigger.

"I'm surprised you don't want to talk, Tagget. From
what I hear, you sure sang loud and clear about thirty-
five years ago, told everybody what they wanted to
hear. You're just lucky the home office doesn't care
about sweating you now . . . Walk over here, away

from the door." When he pointed impatiently with the gun to the open space between two chairs, Tagget dropped to the floor and pulled Singer's .38 from the belt holster. He snapped off a shot that caught the man in the shoulder, and sent him staggering backward.

The man fired. With a loud ping the bullet smashed into a brass vase, sending it crashing to the floor.

Tagget got off another round, hitting the man in the stomach. He slipped face down on the floor.

The door to the study was flung open.

Tagget whipped around and fired twice. The side of another man's face dissolved in a mask of blood.

Tagget was on his feet, running out of the library to the front door.

A shot came from the steps, Tagget saw another man. Behind him was a woman. She was screaming as Tagget fired wildly and missed.

Another slug embedded itself in the floor in front of Tagget, splintering the highly polished wood. He moved quickly around the corner of the foyer and made for the front door as the man on the steps came down after him.

Tagget flung open the front door and ran for his car, fumbling in his pants pocket for the key. He jumped in and turned over the engine without stopping to close his door. The third man was running up the driveway, shouting at him. Two rounds punched into the side of the car and a third starred the rear window. He was not going to make it; in a moment the agent would reach the car.

Using the car for cover, Tagget twisted around in his seat and got off two more shots. The first went wide but the second struck the man in the chest.

Tagget put the car in gear and pulled away from the house with his foot holding the accelerator to the floor.

Uri Chelenko was in his New York office, with his door locked. The report from the central files of the

KGB on John Tagget was not as detailed as he would have liked. It contained two extremely interesting pieces of information, but unfortunately there was no evidence of follow-up on either one.

The first stated that on April 1, 1944, Captain John Tagget was transferred out of the Fifth Ranger Battalion. The nature of the reassignment was unknown. Unidentified sources in Italy at the time had said he had been transferred to SHAFE Headquarters, London, but this had never been confirmed. The second piece of information indicated that a John Tagget, with the same army serial number, had been a patient in the William Beaumont Army Hospital for a period of almost two years. He was assumed to have undergone what the OSS then euphemistically termed "therapeutic reorientation." The report also stated the KGB had not been able to establish a connection between Tagget and the operations conducted out of 29 Russell Square during the war.

Chelenko was always a little amused by the informational lacunae in the central files. Tagget had been connected to 29 Russell Square—everything that had happened in the past few days was proof of it. Yet no one had followed this connection, even after the present mercenary operations in Tanzania and Angola had become a high-priority target. Well, he would not point out the missing inference to Moscow until he had more details about whatever function Tagget had served, or was serving now.

He was particularly interested in Tagget's stay at Beaumont. Therapeutic reorientation had been a program devoted to the development of drugs and psychological techniques to control various functions of an individual's mind. Shortly after Germany's surrender, the OSS had initiated the research using materials and specialists the Americans had captured in Germany.

The doctor in charge of the secret facility at the William Beaumont Army Hospital had been Ludvick Gottenberg, a man who had performed hundreds of experiments on inmates of various concentration camps. By the time Gottenberg had begun his work at the Texas hospital, he had developed a chemo-hypnosis technique that could apparently be sustained indefinitely if supportive treatment was administered a few times a year.

Chelenko was almost certain that Tagget had been and still was part of the therapeutic reorientation program. Moreover, from the time Tagget had been found in a German prison, the OSS and the MI-6 had tried to hide something from him. Now they were trying to kill him. . . .

Tagget, Chelenko thought, it is time we met—

The phone rang, a call from comrade Zhukov in the Soviet Embassy.

"Schiller has been taken in," Zhukov said.

Chelenko sighed deeply and asked, "Much damage?"

"Too early to know. There was a shootout at the Schiller house just after noon . . . One man was killed; two were critically wounded. Our sources in the CIA say it's the work of a man named John Tagget. Do you have anything on him?"

Chelenko explained that he had been monitoring Tagget's activities with a view to using him to put an end to the Ross and Fleming recruiting operation.

"Apparently he is not going to be easy to find," Zhukov commented.

"A man on the run never is."

Zhukov brought the conversation back to Schiller. "If he is alive, do you want him liquidated?"

Chelenko considered the question. Over the years he had come to enjoy Schiller's company. The man was charming, knowledgeable and an excellent source of information. "Not if there is a way to interrogate him first. I'd like to have him debriefed up here."

"I understand. Good-by."

Chelenko put the phone down. He didn't really think that Schiller would wait to be questioned by the KGB. He would probably summon up enough courage to take his own life. Chelenko hoped he would. He had no further value, and Chelenko did not think he would be the kind of a man to withstand the rigors of a KGB interrogation . . . But then very few men could. He wasn't even sure that he could if he were put to the test . . . He dismissed Schiller from his mind. Back to Tagget . . . That Tagget had shot his way past three men was incredible, especially since Tagget didn't have the full use of his left arm and leg . . . Something was wrong, very wrong with the story. . . .

Howell stood by the window in Schiller's study. It was still snowing, perhaps more heavily than it had been earlier. Howell was in a rage over Tagget's escape.

"I send three experienced men here to do a simple job," he said, speaking more to himself than the men behind him, "on *one* guy, and they can't take him out." He turned around and asked, "Will one of you tell me what the hell is going on?"

There were three of his aides in the room. None of them ventured an answer.

Howell walked away from the window. Had Tagget been taken out, his life, at least for the present, would have been much simpler. "All right," he said, "let's go over what happened again."

"According to the butler," one of the younger men said, "Tagget came into the library and almost immediately the shooting began."

"What was the woman's statement? Was she able to describe the man who shot his way out of the house?"

"No . . . She just keeps asking for Schiller. She wants to know what's happened to him. She's halfway around the bend."

"Has she got any idea who we are?"

"She still thinks we're Maryland police," the aide answered.

"What about the men who were here?"

"Art thieves, as far as she's concerned. We asked her a lot of questions about Schiller's collections."

Howell walked over to one of the walls and looked at the books and said, "I want this place gone over by our lab people . . . Every book, every paper." He faced them again. "What about the local and state police? I don't want them involved."

"I'll talk to some people at the Bureau . . . I don't think it will be any trouble."

"And the press?"

"I already took care of that," the third man said.

Howell didn't bother to ask for a clarification of his aide's statement. He was eager to return to Langley, where at four o'clock he was going to meet with Roy Perkins, the chief of the Agency's Psychological Experimental Program. He picked up his coat and hat. "I suspect Schiller will return here sometime late this afternoon, or early evening. He is going to be released near Baltimore and because of this snow it will take him a while to reach here . . . Two of you stay in one of the cars . . . Let me know if we have any of the Russian friends around."

The three aides quickly decided which of them would stay.

"If our Russian friends decide to finish him, don't stop them . . . All I want you to do is let me know."

"What about the woman?"

"We just string her along," Howell said. "She's not in any problem—she has nothing to do with this. Schiller will be the one they want."

A few minutes later Howell and his aides were seated in the rear of the limousine on their way back to Langley. Howell remained silent for the entire ride. The escalating difficulty with Tagget was getting to be a threat to his standing. He regretted not having suggested to the director that Tagget be taken out as soon as his involvement with Hicks had come to light, regardless of his value as a showpiece of the agency's mind-control handiwork. Now it might look to the director, and to anyone else who had a reason to

undermine his position, that he had not been on his
toes and that he had bungled the situation by allowing
Tagget to escape. Someone would be called to account
for what had happened, and he was on deck.

Howell reached his office at 3:15. On his desk was
a message to call his wife. He dialed his home phone
number. The line was busy. Annoyed, he dropped the
phone back into its cradle.

He took time out to have his secretary bring him
a cup of coffee and a doughnut before he called his
wife again. This time the phone rang five times before
his wife answered.

"I wanted to remind you that we're having Colonel
Fuller and his wife for dinner," she said.

Howell closed his eyes. Fuller was an aide to General Hartland, chief of Air Force Intelligence.

"You did remember?"

"Why yes, of course," Howell said, rubbing his
eyes with the back of his hand. He was beginning to
have one of his tension headaches. "But something
has come up . . . I'm afraid I'll be late."

The line went dead.

He looked at the phone.

"Goddamn bitch." He slammed the phone down.
On his feet, he glared at the phone, then began to
pace. His marriage was damn well heading for a
breakup and he felt there was nothing he could do
to save it, short of quitting the Company. And he
wasn't about to—not for his wife or, for that matter,
any woman. The Company at least gave him a feeling
of what real power was. He could have things done
for himself, or done to others, just by picking up the
phone and speaking to someone in the Company, or
someone with connections to the Company. And if he
managed his opportunities with any acumen at all,
there was an excellent chance he would one day be
the director of Central Intelligence. In that position
he would have, in some ways, more power than the
President. He would command a small army of agents
who were completely loyal to him. He would be in

an excellent position to be the power behind the presidency, no matter who the current President happened to be . . .

But for all this he needed a faultless record, and so far what was happening with Tagget was anything but a success. It was rapidly turning into a disaster, with one MI-6 agent dead, one of his own men dead, another not expected to live and a third who would need extensive plastic surgery to rebuild his face.

And *she,* Howell thought bitterly, just doesn't understand what this whole game is about. He returned to his desk, sat down and finished the tepid coffee.

At five minutes to four Howell told his secretary he would be in the small conference room down the hall and to hold all his calls. Then he collected Dr. Perkins and his paraphernalia in the waiting room.

Perkins was a chubby, bald man with bifocal glasses who came armed with several file folders. When the two of them sat down, he asked, "Just how serious is the situation?"

"Tagget has killed two men and possibly a third," Howell answered. "Suppose I bring you up to date, and then we'll take it from there."

Perkins nodded and Howell gave him a fifteen-minute recap of how Tagget had suddenly been brought to their attention, what had motivated the man, how MI-6 had eventually attempted to take him out and what had happened when three Company men had tried to do the same thing. "You can see," he concluded, "that we'll need to know more about this man if we're going to stop him."

Dr. Perkins nodded and said, "Tagget is, as you know, one of our more successful experiments . . . He has been kept going for thirty-five years." He began to refer to his folders. "Because of our work with him, we now have the capability to—"

"Yes, I know about that . . . what I really want to know is your assessment of the likelihood that he could go even further out of control, and some idea of how we can best track him down."

"Well, before we got him, he was in a German prison camp, where he had been tortured . . . From what we learned when we put Tagget under deep hypnosis, he had been hung from the ceiling by his left wrist for hours at a time, or sometimes he was forced to stand on his left leg, only to have it knocked out from under him . . . He had also been given massive dosages of drugs. Their names wouldn't mean anything to you, but they robbed him of all identity . . . When he came to us, it soon became apparent his only reason for living was to someday find and kill Ross and Fleming, the two men who had sent him into France . . . The conditions for motivational redirection were ideal, and quite challenging, so we immediately contacted the OSS and were given permission to use him for our experiments in psychological reorientation. The transient injuries to his left arm and leg were given a psychological permanence, linked with the memory control phase to act as a visible physical indicator of how solidly we were keeping his mind in check. We were asked to place special emphasis on removing any memory he might have of Ross and Fleming. We were able to control it, of course—that phase of the treatment worked well. But we knew that if he ever came across something that would act as a trigger, then his behavior might become unpredictable, which is obviously what has taken place now. Of course all of this occurred long before my time. I only came to know about him because of his visits every four months, when we are given the opportunity to measure the permanence of the induced motor dysfunction and to reinforce our original reorientation as necessary. This is done in a variety of ways, most recently through the administering of chemical supporters of the phenothiazine group. He is given several injections while under deep hypnosis. Naturally this is done so that he has no idea that he is under hypnosis."

"Then what happened?" Howell asked. "How did

he make the connection between himself and Twenty-nine Russell Square?"

"Nothing is perfect," Perkins answered. "Besides, thirty-five years is a very long time for him to have gone without making the connection. Books, TV, movies—there are a variety of ways in which he could have picked up some cue to his past, then simply struggled to remember more."

"Then it is reasonable to assume that he no longer has a lame left leg or left arm?" Howell asked.

"I think that would be a reasonable assumption," Dr. Perkins answered.

"Would it also be a reasonable assumption that he had remembered Ross and Fleming?"

"He might and then again he might not . . . It would depend on the circumstances. We tried to lock that away from him completely. But you can be sure that bits and pieces of what had been effectively screened from him all these years would come back."

"And how would that affect him?"

"It would be most unpleasant. We ensured that such recollections would be accompanied by symptoms of severe anxiety. It might frighten him, but then again it might also serve to further stimulate his need to know more."

"Can you tell me anything that might help us to get him?" Howell asked.

"Only that when he was in France, before his capture, he was apparently an effective killing machine, and from what you have told me I suspect he has become one again. He is a very dangerous man really —sensitive, but also quite ruthless and intelligent. His reflexes are very sharp for a man his age. He has compensated for the induced dysfunction on the left by developing great strength and speed on his right side. If he were to overcome the block . . . well, he would just be lethal."

"We have found that out," Howell said dourly.

"If he is bent on finding Ross and Fleming, even though he may not yet actually know they exist, he will not stop pursuing it until he is stopped by one of your men . . . My guess is that he senses some deeper connections to Twenty-nine Russell Square, something that already made him aware of bits of his past, and ravenous to know more."

Howell leaned back into the chair, squinting. His head felt as if it were taking hammer blows between the eyes.

"Can't you give me anything that might give us an edge? If he does hit the London operation somehow, you can imagine the propaganda the Russians would make—you know, 'American spy rebels against neo-colonial policies of CIA . . .' "

Dr. Perkins shook his head.

Howell stood up and extending his hand, he said, "Thanks for coming."

"I'm sorry I couldn't be of more help," Perkins responded. "But I told you what the situation is without any embellishments."

"That's the way I have to have it."

They moved to the door and Perkins said, "If by some chance you might capture Tagget, we would like to have another crack at him . . . It might be interesting if we could effect a second erasure . . . I think it can be done."

"If we find him, he's yours," Howell said.

"By the way," Perkins said, "if I were you, I'd do something to ease that tension . . . Tagget or no Tagget, you have to continue to function. Stop by the lab and I'll give you a few pills that will make things easier for you."

"Thanks, but no thanks," Howell said. "I'd rather work it out myself."

Perkins nodded and they parted. Howell returned to his office, sat down, opened the desk drawer and helped himself to two aspirin, which he swallowed without water. Then he remembered that he had not yet called Reynolds. He picked up the phone and explained to Reynolds what Tagget had managed to do.

"We've just got to get the bastard," Howell said, "before he gets to Ross and Fleming, or a lot of heads are going to roll. The director is bound to ask how Tagget managed to slip past your men in New York . . . No, I'm not asking . . . I know that Tagget is going to be difficult. Look, I'm on your side . . . Listen, Tagget has probably regained the use of his left leg and arm . . . Tell your men to shoot first and ask questions they might have afterwards. I want Tagget and I want him dead. The hell with the doctor. They've played with him long enough. . . . Yes, I think he'll be going back to New York . . . That's right . . . all we can do now is stick together on this one . . . Sooner or later we'll get him . . . Good luck to you too."

He put the phone down. Lacing his fingers, he wondered if he should take a few days off. He decided he would, once the business with Tagget was out of the way. Maybe he would go fishing, or just lie in the sun and do absolutely nothing for a while.

Howell put the palms of his hands over his eyes. His head pounded terribly.

The taxi slowed and then swung up the driveway leading to Schiller's house. The long December twilight had fallen and there were lights in the windows of the dining room, the upstairs bedroom and kitchen.

Schiller paid the cabbie and gave him a generous tip. He had been set free in downtown Baltimore after he had been given the opportunity to wash the blood from his face. In Baltimore he had stopped at a men's shop and had bought a shirt, explaining to the proprietor that he had been mugged a few minutes before. The man had been sympathetic and had even given him a drink of scotch, which had helped to steady him.

As he pushed the bell button, Schiller saw the black limousine at the far end of the driveway. He knew they were from the Company. If they had been from the KGB they would already have come down on him and he would have been off for another ride—his last.

The butler opened the door and was about to speak, but Schiller said, "I forgot my key. Look, I'm going to my study . . . I don't wish to be disturbed."

"But there's been—"

"No one." Schiller silenced the old man. "Absolutely no one." He crossed the foyer, entered the study and switched on the lights. The chalk outline where one of the men had fallen was clearly visible. There were other signs of a struggle. In several places the flooring was splintered, as was one of the corners of his desk. His Syrian brass vase was gone.

He went to the chair behind the desk and sat down. The game he had managed to play so successfully for some fifteen years was up. For the first time he saw clearly that no matter whether the game ended now or later, he had to be the loser. Still, he had never expected his involvement with the Company or the KGB to end over something or someone as trivial as John Tagget.

Schiller had recently considered the idea of dissolving his connections with both intelligence organizations. He had enough money to be considered wealthy and in Irene he thought he had found a woman who pleased him physically as well as intellectually. He had thought about asking her to marry him.

A soft knock at the door made him look toward it.

"It's Irene."

He knew it was she without her telling him.

"Please, can I come in?" she asked.

"We'll talk later," he said. "I'm working now."

"God, William," she called out, "terrible things happened here today . . . I'm so afraid."

"Later," he answered. "Now I must take care of something." He heard her pad away. Picking up a pen, he wrote a brief note to Hentz, instructing him to transfer his estate and assets to Irene after his debts were paid.

Schiller left the desk and went to the sideboard where he poured himself half a glass of bourbon. He drank it quickly and poured another. Holding the glass in his hand, he went to the window that overlooked the garden.

The light from the library fell across the snow in the shape of a parallelogram and several nearby trees threw their shadows outward toward the deeper darkness. Schiller loved the garden, regardless of the season. He took pleasure in watching the coming and going of the seasons in it. He looked around at the various shelves of books. He took pleasure in them too.

Schiller turned to the window again and raised the glass to his lips. Suddenly there were the sounds of many voices in the foyer. He didn't remember hearing the bell. Finishing the bourbon, he placed the glass on a Parsons table and went directly to his desk. From the top drawer he picked up his .32 caliber revolver. His eyes were on the door.

The voices grew louder; there were the unmistakable sounds of a scuffle.

Irene was yelling for him.

The door opened. Schiller pointed the gun at the first man who charged into the room and squeezed the trigger. The explosion was deafening. The man tumbled forward and a second man squeezed off two shots in rapid succession, striking Schiller in the head. He twitched for several moments before he died.

Chelenko was genuinely sad when a phone call from the Embassy in Washington informed him that Schiller had been killed in a shootout with two of his agents. Schiller had been a gentleman and Chelenko was old enough to appreciate that quality in a man. He had appreciated Schiller's motives for having become a double agent, that the danger of the situation had been the real appeal for a man who had no physical courage and knew it.

That was his private tribute to Schiller. Now Chelenko had to find a solution for his own problem, which was made more difficult by Schiller's death. He had hoped Schiller would have been able to generate more information on Tagget. But now he had to find Tagget himself and see how far the man would be willing to cooperate.

Chelenko had already decided that if the situation required it he would go to Claudia Harris and try to reach Tagget through her. He guessed that Tagget would attempt to get in touch with her sometime during the next few days, so at six o'clock in the evening he dispatched one of his men to a florist near her apartment building and sent her a bouquet of roses with a note reading: *From a friend. Meet me at 8 P.M. this evening in the cocktail lounge of the hotel Pierre. Be careful.* He was certain that Mrs. Harris would think the flowers were from Tagget.

Chelenko busied himself with paperwork until half past seven, then left the mission. He had looked at some file photographs of Mrs. Harris from the time her husband worked for him and would be able to recognize her.

The Pierre was only a few blocks from the Soviet mission and Chelenko walked. The air was cold and the sky clear. He kept up a brisk stride and within ten minutes he was checking his coat and hat in the lobby.

There were several couples at the small round tables in the long cocktail lounge. Then he saw Mrs. Harris at the bar and sat down at an empty stool to her left. He ordered vodka from the barkeep and, turning toward Mrs. Harris, said, "I hope you liked the roses."

She faced him.

He nodded and said, "I have come here to speak to you about John Tagget."

The look of surprise gave way to a softness. But almost as quickly as the softness came, it vanished and was replaced by an expression of wariness.

Chelenko's vodka came and he politely raised his

glass to her. "May you soon be reunited with your beloved."

"Who *are* you?"

"Would you care for something to drink . . . perhaps another of the same?"

"No thank you," she said. "But please, who are you?"

"Colonel Uri Chelenko."

"You're Russian?" she asked incredulously. "Oh God. Is John all right?"

"As far as I know, yes," Chelenko answered. "Now listen to me. Your husband worked for me . . . He also worked for the CIA. Now you know who I am. When the CIA found out that he worked for me as well as for them, *they* put a bomb aboard his plane. And that, very simply, is the reason I've come to you. I do not want to see the same thing happen to Tagget."

"John works for the KGB?" she asked, too astonished to control her voice.

"No, but my hope is that he will now agree to join with us."

"Why should he want to do that?"

"Because I know something about his connection to number Twenty-nine Russell Square that he would like to know. I know a great deal about his past, about the time he is trying to account for and something about what happened to him afterwards."

"And you are willing to tell him in return for his cooperation?"

"Absolutely. Our ends happen to be peculiarly identical." He paused to study her face. "At least if he decides to work for us, he will have our protection."

"That didn't do my husband much good, did it?" she shot back. "It's all too vague . . . give me something more concrete."

"There are two men who are responsible for what happened to John Tagget, and when he learns their names, he will want to find them."

"You want John to kill them? For you?"

"As well as for himself," Chelenko answered. "I just want you to tell him this. Will you?"

". . . Yes, I suppose I will . . . But the way you talk about the deaths of two men as if you were swatting a fly—it makes me sick."

"In my profession," he answered, holding the glass in his hands, "it is the way we come to look at things . . . Doctors have the same detachment . . . The two men I spoke about are obstacles that must be removed. There is seldom anything personal in our actions, though with Tagget it is completely personal."

"And how was it with my husband?"

"My purpose is to possibly help John Tagget . . . I no longer have any interest in your husband's activities . . . His file is closed."

"You don't give much, colonel," she said.

A brief smile crossed his lips. "That only shows that I have not lost touch with the ancient art of horse trading, which was something of a talent with my people."

A short time later Chelenko put her in a cab and handed her a ten-dollar bill for the fare. "Please think on the matter we discussed."

"I will," she answered.

"Call me at this number any time during the day or night," he told her. "Make the call from a pay booth."

"Don't you ever sleep?" she said, shutting the door.

Tagget drove north on Interstate 270 to Frederick, where he stopped for gas and a cup of coffee. Then he continued to Interstate 81 and turned north into Pennsylvania.

Late in the afternoon it began to snow again and he was forced to slow down to forty miles an hour. He had hoped to return to New York sometime during the night but the snow was going to make that impossible.

The shootout had left him with a strange feeling

of exhilaration. He had managed to stay alive though the odds were greatly against him. He also realized that he had probably killed three men and that the Company would redouble its efforts to kill him.

By five o'clock Tagget had seen enough snow and stopped for the night at a motel in Shippensburg, a small town about fifty miles from Harrisburg. The motel owner noticed the smashed rear window on his car.

"Some character with a rifle in Maryland," Tagget explained, taking the room key from the desk.

The man shook his head and said, "Happens up here sometimes too . . . Somebody goes out hunting and fires across the road. Now and then the driver or a passenger gets hit."

"It was just lucky," Tagget said, "that whoever it was wasn't shooting at me." He left the office, parked the car and went into his room. It was comfortable enough, furnished in Spanish motel decor complete with color TV in an ornate plastic cabinet.

He hung his hat and coat in the closet, took off his jacket, opened his collar and loosened his tie, slipped off his shoes and dropped onto the bed. He was too tired to reach over and turn off the lamp, so he just put his arm over his eyes to shield them from its glare. . . .

The following morning was cold but clear. Tagget drove to Harrisburg, where he abandoned the car and bought a one-way train ticket for Newark. By four o'clock that afternoon he had checked into the Hotel Seville in Manhattan.

He put through a call to his lawyer's office and was told that Mr. Hentz had left early. He hung up and called Hentz's home number. His friend answered the phone.

"I'm back in New York," Tagget said. "Can you meet me this evening?"

"Yes."

"The Weathervane in an hour . . . It's on East Twenty-ninth Street, south side of the street."

"I'll find it."

Tagget put the phone down. He had nothing to do
but wait—and think. . . .

The Weathervane was not as crowded as it had
been during his two meetings with Singer, the snow
was probably keeping many of its patrons away. Tagget sat down on a stool toward the end of the bar,
ordered scotch and helped himself to some meatballs
from a tray on the counter. He was very hungry and
realized he hadn't eaten more than a sandwich and
coffee since the morning.

The owner, Mario, recognized him and came over
to chat. Tagget asked him if Singer had been by.

"Not tonight," the man said. "But it's still early."

Tagget noticed that there were four other men at
the bar. Two were alone and seemed to concentrate
on their drinks just as he was doing. From somewhere
behind him came the light sound of a woman's laugh-
ter . . . Tagget was suddenly in the grip of an over-
whelming sense of loneliness, much the same as he had
felt just after Helen had died.

He downed the rest of his drink and signaled the
barkeep he wanted another round . . . He couldn't
help feeling he was on the outside of his own life
looking in. He was a fugitive, a man with very little
hope for tomorrow. It was as if he had been thrust
back to the time when he had been a Ranger, when
he had lived from day to day, sometimes from hour
to hour. Now, all over again, he couldn't count on
having a future. The present was really all that could
matter to him. . . .

As soon as Hentz came in, Tagget saw him and
signaled. Hentz took off his coat and sat down on the
stool to the right of Tagget. "Word has it that you
were one of the two gunmen who attacked Schiller,"
he said.

"Never saw him," Tagget said.

The bartender delivered Tagget's second scotch and
asked Hentz what he wanted. He pointed to Tagget's
drink and said, "I'll have the same."

Tagget waited until the barkeep was out of earshot before he asked, "How did you get word about me?"

"A man called. He said he was letting me know because Schiller had been my partner. He said he knew I was your legal counsel. He hung up before I could ask any questions."

"When did he call?"

"About ten-thirty this morning."

When Hentz's scotch came, Tagget suggested they get a table and have dinner at the Weathervane. Hentz agreed, and they moved to a booth.

"Do you still want to represent me?" Tagget asked.

"I'll answer that when you tell me what happened in Washington."

Tagget explained how he had arrived at the Schiller house late and how a man had asked him into the study. "I couldn't see him until I was inside, then I saw he was holding a gun. Whoever he was, he was a talker. I dropped to the floor . . . there was an exchange of shots . . . I hit him and as I ran out of the room another man came after me . . . I hit him too, and the third—"

"You mean you shot three men?"

"Yes. By the time I arrived, Schiller was already gone . . . My guess is that the Company had picked him up and he told them about my coming to the house."

"Do you really think they'd kill him just for trying to meet with you?"

"I think he had something he wasn't supposed to have."

"Information about you, about where you were?"

"Yes." Tagget was almost on the point of telling Hentz about what Schiller had been up to, and about the Russell Square connection, but he changed his mind. He did not want to give his friend any information that might needlessly endanger his life.

A waiter came to the table. They each ordered a steak and another scotch.

"John, the more I think about this situation," Hentz

said, "the less sense it makes—unless you're keeping something from me. Are you?"

"It doesn't make any sense to me either," Tagget told him. "Do you still want to represent me?"

"I'm probably a fool, but the answer is yes."

Tagget nodded.

"These are for you," Hentz told him, taking a business-size white envelope from his inside breast pocket. "Your new identity . . . driver's license, Social Security card, an American Express Card and a Master Charge Credit from Chemical Bank. There's a passport to which you have to affix your photograph . . . All of the papers are in the name of Henry Morrison."

"And what's my new profession?"

"You choose one," Hentz told him, "I did all the rest."

Tagget picked up the envelope and asked, "How much did all this cost?"

"When this is settled, I'll send you a bill."

"Well, if I don't make it, you have that power of attorney over a sufficient share of my funds to pay for these. I would like you to draw up the necessary papers to set up a trust fund for each of the Alcantara children, with the money to be used for college."

"Only for that?"

"Yes."

"How much?"

"Twenty thousand for each of the two children," Tagget said. "My will already leaves the bulk of my estate to my son . . . I would also like to leave a hundred thousand dollars to Claudia."

"I'll take care of it," Hentz said.

"You know it's going to become more and more difficult for me to be in touch with you, or with Claudia. I didn't even try to contact her last night."

"Do you want me to call her?" Hentz asked.

"Yes," Tagget answered. "Tell her I'm all right . . . tell her—" He pursed his lips and said, "The best thing you could tell her is to forget about me."

"You don't mean that."

"Yes, I do," Tagget said quietly. "The Company is not going to lay off until one of their agents puts me away. You know it's true, and so do I. She'd be a lot better off without me."

"You're probably right," Hentz answered, "but I don't think that's going to change her attitude one bit. Love is blind, as the old adage says, especially when it comes to looking at what's right and logical."

The waiter brought their food and drinks.

"As I started to say before," Hentz said, "the only way all of this would make sense would be if you were involved with them—a defecting agent, or a double agent, or something that would have put you in possession of information they want to protect."

"But I'm not," Tagget said, cutting into his steak.

Hentz raised his eyebrows. "I'm not sure this whole story sits so well with me."

Tagget set his knife and fork down. He ran his hand over his chin and said, "Albert, during the war I was sent into France by the OSS."

"Why didn't you say so before?" Hentz asked, sounding a bit peevish in spite of himself.

"I didn't even know before last night," Tagget said. "It's only come back to me in bits and pieces. I was sent in by the OSS from Twenty-nine Russell Square. I don't know where in France, or what my mission was. But I do know that I was with a Maquis group, and I remember a love affair with a woman named Elaine."

"And how did you suddenly find all this out?"

"I just remembered it," Tagget answered, shaking his head, "the same as I was suddenly able to use my left arm and leg . . . I don't know."

"Suppose you did go on some OSS mission. What could be that important about it now that would make the CIA take such drastic measures to protect it? Why wouldn't they have killed you years ago?"

"Answer that," Tagget replied, "and I'm sure you'll have the answer to everything else."

"Is it possible that the mission or whatever it was is ongoing?"

"For thirty-five years?"

'It was just an idea," Hentz said.

France, April 25, 1944

The radio signal from London ordered Tagget to proceed immediately to Port Manech, a small village on the coast of Brittany, south of Port-Aven, where on the night of April 25th at 2300 hours he was to be joined by Captain Horace Justine, a British commando, who would be put ashore from a submarine. London said that Captain Justine was being sent to assist in an extension of the original mission, now designated Pitfall.

Tagget moved his group of Maquis toward the coast. The location of Port Manech forced him to alter his previous line of march and come uncomfortably close to large units of German troops deployed along the coast to repel an expected invasion from England.

By the afternoon of the 25th, Tagget and his force were in sight of Port Manech. The village went straight down to the water's edge, with a stone quay leading to the square where there was a small café, a church and several stores, including a ship's chandler. From what he could see through his field glasses, the village was quiet in the warmth of the April sun. There were several men seated at the tables outside the café and a few more fishing off the quay.

"No Germans," Tagget said. "At least not any I can see." He handed the glasses to Jacques DuBois, a tall, red-headed man with startling blue eyes who had become his lieutenant after he had taken command of the unit. DuBois studied the village. He was Tagget's age and spoke English with a charming French accent. He had been born and raised within sight of Mont St.-Michel. His father had been a fisherman and had hoped his son someday would enter the church. But DuBois had responded to another calling. Before the war he had left home and lived in London and then in Paris where he had earned his living making sketches of people in cafés and clubs. His real love had been and still was painting. When he wasn't reading, he was sketching. He had a good eye for detail.

"I think one or two of us should go in and look it over," DuBois said, returning the glasses to Tagget. "I'll go. I speak Gaelic." He looked back to where the others of the group were resting. "Rambeau can come with me."

Tagget nodded.

DuBois called to Rambeau and told him what they were going to do. Both men slipped off their rifles and left them with other members of the band.

Tagget watched them disappear over the rise before he moved back to the rest of the group and sat down next to Elaine. He picked a blade of grass and chewed on it.

"You looked worried," Elaine commented, touching his arm.

"I don't know why London is sending another man now," he answered. "This time there'll be more to worry about with a sub sitting offshore. Suppose the Germans pick it up?"

"London knows what the dangers are," she told him. "If they're sending in a man by submarine, then they must think it is the best way."

"But *is* it? Do they really know what they're doing? I mean—"

"You're finally beginning to doubt that Cordez can be found, aren't you?"

Tagget's silence spoke for him. From the first night he had been in France he had tried to find Cordez, but there was no sign of him anywhere. Local people who should have known every leader of a Maquis force of such considerable size had never heard of him.

"There's the possibility," Tagget said, "that Captain Justine will bring new information about Cordez . . ."

He stood up. The wind off the sea had freshened, giving the air a wonderfully pungent scent. "If as you say there is no Cordez," he said without looking at her, "why was I sent to find him? There were photos of him, a complete plan for establishing contact, moving on Brest . . ."

"I can't answer that," she said. "But I know there isn't any Cordez." She stood up and took hold of his hand. "After tonight, you will know too."

In two hours DuBois and Rambeau returned. They reported that the village was free of Germans and that the nearest Wehrmacht garrison of any size was at Port-Aven.

When evening came it turned cold and a fog began to roll in from the north. Tagget and his men waited in the hills behind the village until 2200, then moved down to the beach south of the village where there was a small cove in which the rendezvous was to take place.

Tagget divided this group into four units of four men. Three of the units covered the cove from three sides, while the fourth remained inland, about 500 meters from the cove. He placed them along a narrow dirt road that twisted back through the dunes so that if for some reason they had to fall back, this group could cover their retreat to a wooded area about two kilometers from the cove.

Tagget and DuBois, the only two men left on the beach, huddled back against a sand dune. The fog was very thick.

"They're going to have to practically beach the submarine to land the captain in this fog," DuBois said.

They fell silent and peered intently into the fog.

Tagget checked his watch. It was 2245 hours . . . If the submarine was on time, it shouldn't be more than two or three kilometers offshore.

"Let's move down to the water—" Tagget began.

"I hear something," DuBois whispered. The two men stopped.

"A diesel engine, I think," DuBois said, pointing north into the mist.

The heavy throb became louder.

Tagget's heart began to pound. "That's loud enough to wake up every damn German along the coast."

As if in reply to his words the sound of the diesel died away.

DuBois started forward. Tagget grabbed hold of his arm. "Wait," he said in a whisper. "The sub must be all the way into the cove."

But suddenly a battery of floodlights came on, and the two men saw not a submarine but two landing craft moving at them. One had its ramp down and troops were already splashing up onto the beach.

Tagget dropped to the sand. DuBois followed suit. They bellied their way toward the road as the men in the dunes began to fire down at the Germans.

Tagget reached the road and began to shout to the three groups around the cove to fall back.

The Germans were pushing up from the beach. The crack of small arms fire was everywhere, but the fog prevented either the Maquis or the Germans from inflicting casualties.

Tagget and his men ran from the beach and the group melted into a nearby woods. The entire action had lasted no more than six minutes, but Tagget continued to move inland for the remainder of the night and well into the following day before he felt it was safe to stop and rest.

He hardly spoke to anyone, and when he finally settled down next to Elaine, she said, "So. You see now that there is no Cordez. What are you going to do?"

"Radio London and say that I've found him," he said in a fury, and started to clean his gun.

London, April 27, 1944

Ross looked up at Fleming and blinked. "Say again?"

"I have *two* messages," Fleming said. "One from Gunner and the other from Tagget."

Ross drummed on the desk with the fingers of his right hand. The previous day he had heard from Gunner that Tagget had managed to elude the Germans at Port Manech. There had been no explanation of how it had happened. "Gunner's message first," he said.

" 'Imperative Tagget be taken alive. Rundstedt convinced invasion will be on Brittany coast. Tagget's capture will supply proof he needs to swing panzer divisions south to Brittany. Repeat, imperative Tagget be taken alive.' "

"That should have happened twelve days ago," Ross said angrily. "Tagget is either the luckiest man in the army or just too damn good for the Krauts."

"Something of both, I think," Fleming said, moving back from the desk.

"And what does Tagget say?" Ross asked.

" 'I've found Cordez,' " Fleming said.

Ross started out of the chair, but the effort was so painful that it robbed him of his breath and forced him to sit down again.

Fleming came forward, poured some water from a pitcher into a glass and handed it to Ross.

"He's on to us," Ross said, as soon as he could speak. "He knows . . . he knows that we have been trying to have him killed. I don't think captured would enter his mind. He is telling us that if he survives, we're going to be his number one target. His Cordez."

Fleming frowned. "But he can't very well blame us for—"

"He blames us," Ross said, "but if he is captured or killed, then the problem is automatically solved. We must make him think that the mission, at least, is real. Send him the following message . . . Tell him the man he knows as Cordez is a German agent . . . Tell him Cordez was killed three days ago by a

German firing squad. Tell him to proceed to Monteneuf as per the original plan . . . That should at least confuse him . . . It's time we sent in one of our own people. If the Germans can't capture Tagget, we'll just have to deliver him to them . . ."

XI

TAGGET PLANNED to remain in the hotel until his beard grew in; then he was going to dye it and his hair gray. He figured that anyone looking for him would be thrown off the trail by the gray beard and gray hair, even if they might know he no longer was physically handicapped.

But it was impossible to remain in the room all of the time. He not only needed exercise but he also wanted to know there was a world beyond the confines of his own struggle for survival. He thought about calling his son, calling Claudia. Finally, at two o'clock in the afternoon, he left the hotel, walked to Third Avenue and started uptown. He paused now and then to look at displays in a shop window and used the window glass as a large mirror, to see if anyone was following him. He looked unshaven but his beard was still a good week away. To get out of the cold he went into an antique shop and priced a hand-made model of a gaff-rigged fishing schooner. The proprietor, a small owlish-looking man, said he was asking two thousand dollars for it.

Tagget thanked him, left the shop and continued uptown. Had the circumstances been different, he would have offered twelve hundred dollars for the model, which he thought was a fair price.

A few blocks later he went into a pet shop. It was very large, warm and full of not altogether unpleasant animal smells. At the front of the store there were tiers of tanks with all sorts of brilliantly colored tropical

fish, and behind them an array of cages holding para-
keets, parrots, mynah birds and some pert yellow
canaries. Cages with dogs and cats came next, then
more glass tanks with snakes, turtles and lizards. At
the back of the store there were some cages with
various kinds of small gibbons and monkeys. One of
them was hanging from a bar by one hand, while
trying with his foot to make contact with a small
wooden stool.

Tagget stopped and watched. He was suddenly very
cold and almost choked on the smell of the cages. He
wanted to scream but his tongue felt too swollen to
move, and there was a twisting pain in his left wrist
and in his left leg. He shut his eyes and took several
deep breaths, then turned and almost staggered out
into the street to lean against the side of a building. . . .

He remembered. With startling clarity he remembered having been given powerful injections by some
doctors and being hung by his left wrist and trying
desperately to set his left foot on a short stool . . .
The room was square, or nearly so, with gray rock
walls. There was a small, semicircular barred window
near the ceiling. A blue-eyed man in a black uniform
was seated behind a table.

"We could let you hang there for a few more
hours," the SS officer said. "Or days."

Tagget said nothing. His left foot had just found a
purchase on the wooden stool. He breathed a sigh of
relief, but the next instant someone kicked his leg
away and pulled the stool out from under him. His
body dropped and he winced from the flash of pain
that tore across the left side of his body. Sweat poured
from him and he struggled with his right hand to pull
himself up on the iron shackle that bound him to the
bar overhead.

"The war is over for you," the German said. "Why
not make it easy for yourself and tell us what we
want to know?"

"I have nothing more to tell you," Tagget answered,

forcing the words from his dry mouth. He was fighting
the effects of the drug, but the German's words were
beginning to sound reasonable.

"But we do not even believe what you *have* said.
Tell us something we can believe and I promise you
will be well-treated. . . ."

Tagget pulled himself together and started back to
his hotel with the memory of what had happened to
him still twisting in his mind. He remembered he was
not given any food, though every few hours a guard
put a dipper of water to his mouth. He remembered
the SS officer saying, "You force me to use more
persuasive methods than I want to, techniques we've
developed that we know you can't resist. . . ." And
then came more drugs and the beating with cane rods
that had been split at one end. Each stroke drew more
blood. When the pain became unendurable and his
screams no more than a hoarse croaking he agreed to
tell them what they wanted to know. He was taken
down and put on a chair; then he fainted . . .

Or had he? Tagget stopped walking. The memory
came to an abrupt end as he entered the lobby of
the hotel.

He realized that in the end he had told the Nazis
what they wanted to know. He had told them all
right, and they had turned him over to the doctors
and the prison camps, and now, thirty-five years later,
he could not remember what it was that he had betrayed, what had been worth enduring so much pain
to protect, worth spending thirty-five years with a
handicap that wasn't real.

When he was back in his room he dropped on the
bed, so exhausted he wanted to die.

The Manhattan conference room was soundproof,
windowless and illuminated by fluorescent lights re-
cessed in the ceiling. Reynolds was at the head of the
highly polished rectangular table. Smith and eight
other agents were seated in front of him, four on either
side and Smith at the opposite end.

He looked at his watch. It was six o'clock. He had already phoned his wife and told her not to hold dinner for him.

Reynolds cleared his throat. "At four-thirty yesterday afternoon," he told them, "Deputy Director Howell called to tell me Tagget had killed one agent and critically wounded two others in the shootout in Maryland. The two surviving men have both been unconscious since going into surgery and haven't been able to tell us anything."

The men at the table looked questioningly at each other.

"However, Tagget's movement from Washington to New York has now been traced. A car belonging to the Rent-All Agency was found in Harrisburg . . . the rear window had been shattered by a bullet and a motel owner on Interstate 81 gave a positive ID, with the exception that the man he described was not handicapped in any way."

"Can we be sure it was Tagget?" Smith asked.

"The motel owner had the license number in his registration book, and the fingerprints taken from the room where he spent the night identify him as John Tagget. And that includes prints taken from his left hand and matched with those on file at the Bureau and at the VA hospital. We're going after a man who knows how to use his hands as well as, or perhaps better than, any of you. But Langley wants him taken out and we're going to take him out. Howell has given this some real priority. He's sent a team of four men up here to augment our force."

"Even if we had ten times that number of men," one of the other agents commented, "we wouldn't be able to touch all the bases . . . We're covering the building where he lives and the one where his girlfriend lives. We have taps on her phone and on his. But it's no picnic to shadow her. She goes into a department store, or makes a quick subway connection and we're left behind."

"Has Tagget tried to call his son?" Smith asked.

"No," Reynolds said. "Our San Francisco office has been monitoring his phone too. Nothing."

"What we have to do," Reynolds said, "is brainstorm—come up with something that will enable us to find this man and stop him fast. Apparently there's heavy pressure from the British as well."

"It may not be easy to find him," one of the men spoke up. "He's not part of any intelligence network. If he were, we could just tap someone who'd be willing to sell him out . . ."

Reynolds pressed a button under the table. A section of wall on the far side of the room moved away. "Gentlemen," he said, "I'm going to show our findings on the screen so we'll be able to keep track of what we have said and what our final plan will be. Now, yes, it would be easier if Tagget were an active agent, but he's not."

"I suggest going over a profile of the man," Smith said. "Let's look at everything we know about him."

Reynolds agreed and since he and Smith were the two in the room who knew more about Tagget than anyone else, they presented the profile. He was described physically; the men were told about his penchant for collecting rare books, where his money had come from, and his relationship with Claudia Harris.

"What about his friends?" Smith asked. "Who is there beside the Harris woman?"

"None that are close with the exception of Hentz, his lawyer, whom we've been watching."

"Is his phone tapped?"

"It's being done now . . . What else do we have?"

"Damn little," the agent to his right sighed, tapping a cigarette from a hard pack.

"What about using his son to get to him?" Smith asked.

"Tagget is here in New York," Reynolds said. "He's hiding. Maybe if he contacts his son and plans to meet him, we'd make the intercept . . . But I don't think Tagget will call his son. I don't think his son has any idea about what his father is involved in."

A cigarette haze hung over the table.

"All right," Reynolds said, "let's begin at the beginning. As far as we know—and this information comes from MI-6 and the police files—Tagget first got a clue to his connection to Twenty-nine Russell Square from something he read in Lord Enright's autobiography, a chapter that mentions the place. Tagget apparently had a powerful psychological reaction to that paragraph. Then the following day he had a run-in with two muggers he managed to fight off using only his hands."

"Do you believe that?" a man to the left of Smith asked.

"They might have seen he was handicapped and figured him for an easy mark," Smith said.

"But was he?" the man persisted. "Do you think he managed to deck two muggers with only one hand?"

"You're suggesting that he used both hands but remembered using one?"

"Or that he lied."

"Interesting point," Reynolds said. "Let's go on. That afternoon he met Hicks for lunch. In conversation Hicks tells Tagget at some point that he knew Enright and served as his aide during World War II. Tagget asks Hicks about Twenty-nine Russell Square and has another violent reaction—he faints. Later in the afternoon Hicks is killed. Peter Alcantara, an NYPD detective, wires the Bureau for information on Tagget; the result is that we are alerted; this leads to the unfortunate death of Alcantara and the case is closed."

"Wait a minute," Smith said. "What's the name of the other detective who was on the Hicks case?"

"Singer," Reynolds answered.

"Wasn't he pissed about the cover story given out on his partner, Alcantara?"

"That's what I got from his captain," one of the men said.

"Was he pissed enough to pick up where Alcantara left off? I don't mean officially. I mean there's a good chance he and Tagget might be in touch and might get together in the next few days."

"Okay, that's the first real break we have," Reynolds said. "Smith, go over to police headquarters after the meeting and get everything you can find on Singer . . . Maybe tomorrow I'll have a talk with him. Okay, let's continue. We know we're not the only ones interested in Tagget. In fact, MI-6 is the first to send a man to take him out and their man winds up all over the sidewalk. We also know that the Russians have turned up, either out of their usual curiosity or because they want something from Tagget. And the Company doesn't want to risk that happening . . . According to what one specialist told Howell, Tagget will continue to experience certain episodes which will make it increasingly difficult for us to deal with him."

"So far," one of the men said, "we—or at least most of us—haven't got any idea why Tagget has become so important, or why his file was coded red by the Bureau in the first place."

Reynolds shook his head. "Just get him. Do that and you'll have done your job."

By the time Reynolds called an end to the meeting, it was 7:30 P.M. He was tired but he was also concerned that Tagget be nailed before Howell started making loud noises from Langley, so he asked Smith to join him in his office for a few minutes.

When they were alone he said, "I don't have all the information on this flap yet, but I do know that Howell thinks Tagget is a danger to a major joint Company–MI-6 operation. I mean something current. He didn't go into details with me, but it's one of those top secret operations run by our people and theirs for a third entity."

Smith nodded. "If Langley would open up to their field offices a bit more, we might be able to get something done," he said.

Reynolds gestured with open hands. "That's what I keep telling them but they only want to hear what they want to hear."

"How are you going to handle Singer?" Smith asked.

"We don't have time to play games," Reynolds said. "Straight down the line. Rough if necessary."

"If I can track him down tonight, do you want me to talk to him?"

Reynolds thought for a moment.

"It could save time," Smith added. "If he opens up, we might be able to get onto Tagget within the next twenty-four hours."

"Okay," Reynolds said. "Pay Singer a visit and get him to talk. The faster the better."

Tagget knew it was foolish to torture himself. Foolish, because the pain he had endured was nothing more than a memory, albeit a terribly real one. But the feelings came as much from the intense sense of loss as from the remembrance of the ordeal that had left him less than whole for the past thirty-five years. The war had taken more than his youth, it had taken a part of him, and mingled with his anguish was a growing rage, a long unrealized hatred of whoever had condemned him to living the life of half a man. *He was the one who had been betrayed*—in France, in the hospital after the war, in the setup at Schiller's home—and there could be no pleasure in the killing he had done until he had killed whoever had done this to his life—until he put out the eyes of the octopus.

He stood up, walked into the bathroom and splashed cold water on his face, then went back into the darkened room to stand at the window, looking down at Twenty-ninth Street.

The years just after he had come out of the hospital and married came rushing back to him. All the things he could not do then, including make love to his wife normally, or dance with her, or play ball with the other men he knew, or feel secure in crowds, or . . . it was a long list.

He was about to light a cigarette when there was

a knock on the door. Hentz was the only one who
knew where he was staying.

He slipped the snub-nose .38 out of his belt holster,
flicked off the safety and moved quietly away from
the door.

There was another knock on the door, then, "John?
It's me, Claudia."

Tagget unlocked the door and let Claudia into the
darkened room. He looked out into the empty hall,
then locked the door. Claudia watched as he put the
safety back on and replaced the revolver in its holster.

For a moment they said nothing. Then he took her
in his arms, kissing her, finding her tongue with his.
She hugged him back, letting his beard rasp against
her face. "Don't be angry with Albert. I got him to
tell me where you are . . . I told him that if you're
killed, he will be at least partially responsible. The
poor man is very upset over your situation and the
bizarre death of his partner. . . . I would have told
him anything to see you." She touched his bristly
cheek.

"In a few days it will hide the old me," he said,
holding her close. "Maybe good riddance."

"Do you mind if I put the lights on?" she asked.
"The dark makes me more uneasy than I already
am." She switched on one of the lamps. "Someone
wants to meet you. He says you might be able to help
each other."

Tagget looked at her closely. "Who? And how does
he know me, or that I need help?"

She took off her coat and sat down in a frayed
club chair. "A man . . . a Colonel Uri Chelenko, contacted me . . . I'm not sure what I'm trying to say
. . . none of it makes any sense." She took a deep
breath. "My husband Frank worked for him and for
the CIA, or so he says. According to Colonel Chelenko, the CIA killed him."

"I knew that," Tagget told her softly.

She stared at him.

"I was only told two nights ago," he said. "There wasn't any way for me to tell you until now."

"Would you have told me later?"

"Yes, when the time was right," he answered. "When all of this trouble was behind us."

"Isn't it remarkable? I lost my husband to the CIA and now I stand to lose you too."

"What did Chelenko want?"

"John, he claims to have the names of the men who operated out of Russell Square during the war. He very much wanted me to be sure to tell you that."

"Are you *sure* that's what he said?" he asked, beginning to pace back and forth.

"He says the Russians are as anxious to find them as you are . . . He wouldn't say why."

Tagget dug a pack of cigarettes out of his jacket pocket and half-smiled. "They'll be looking for a man who smokes a pipe."

Claudia sat on the bed. "Did you find out anything from Schiller?"

"I got to his house too late," he answered, blowing smoke through his nostrils. "I missed him. . . . This Colonel Chelenko, is he available?"

She opened her bag and took out Chelenko's card. "He said you can call him any hour of the day or night."

He took the card and slipped it into his pocket.

"John, are you sure this is what you want to do?"

He nodded and told her what had happened to him in the pet shop and later in the hotel room. "You have to try and understand," he said. "I've gone too far to stop now. Even if I wanted to, the CIA or MI-6 wouldn't let it alone. Ralph Singer had made it clear that I can't go to the police or the FBI. If Chelenko is telling the truth, then everything the Company and MI-6 has done to stop me begins to make some kind of sense."

"Well, I'm afraid I don't see it."

"They're trying to stop me from getting to the two men from Twenty-nine Russell Square," he said. "They don't want me to find out—or to remember and reveal—something about the past, something about the mission." He stubbed out the cigarette. "I hate these damn things."

"Do you think you can trust Chelenko?" she asked.

"Hell no, but I don't see that I have any other choice. With Schiller dead, no one else is in any position to help me."

"What about Detective Singer?"

"He's already gone way out on a limb for me . . . Besides, he's only a city cop and his sources of information are limited."

Claudia stood up. "So you're going to phone Chelenko?"

"Yes, I can't stay here forever."

She looked around and shook her head.

"What's that all about?"

"It's seedy looking and smells musty."

"Would it bother you to go to bed with me here?" he asked.

"No," she answered, and put her arms around his neck. "It would be the only way to brighten this place up."

He reached around her and turned off the light.

When Singer entered the inspector's office there was another man there, seated to the inspector's right—someone he recognized.

"Detective Sergeant Singer, Mr. Smith," the inspector said.

Smith stood up and shook Singer's hand.

The inspector told Singer to pull up another chair. "Mr. Smith wants to talk to us about a problem he has. Let me explain," he said as soon as Singer was settled, "that Mr. Smith is with a government agency and what is discussed here must be kept confidential."

"I know, he's CIA. We've met," Singer said, looking first at the inspector and then at Smith. "I've seen him outside the building where Pete—"

"That's right," Smith said. "I was one of the men assigned to watch John Tagget."

Singer rested against the back of the chair.

"I'll get straight to it," Smith said. "The CIA wants Tagget."

"Then they should get him," Singer answered.

"We hoped you would help us."

"Let me set *you* straight. The answer is no, because not too many days ago your people, maybe you, blew away my partner and dropped a cheap cover story on the press about him. I don't think I owe the Company any damned cooperation."

"Tagget has killed one MI-6 agent, one of our men and critically wounded two others."

"They were trying to kill him first."

"Then Tagget *has* been in touch with you since he returned to New York," Smith said, looking over at the inspector.

"He hasn't, but I do know something about this situation. I probably know as much as you—maybe more."

"Good, then you know how simple it is . . . the Company wants Tagget, he's too dangerous to—"

"That's your problem," Singer told him. "My problem is to deal with the criminals in New York."

"And Tagget is one of them," the inspector said. "He killed a man by throwing him off the terrace of his apartment, then in Maryland he—"

"Inspector," Singer stood up, "a man has the right to defend his own life."

"All right, you'd better sit down, sergeant," Smith said. "I had hoped to have your cooperation, but that obviously is not going to be. So I want you to know that I did a little digging before I came here. I had a brief but informative chat with your ex-wife."

"So what?"

Smith reached into his inside breast pocket and pulled out a small black leather notebook. "You're divorced from your wife."

"That's right—for the last year."

"And the reasons for the divorce were—"

"Inspector," Singer said, "he doesn't have the right to ask me any questions."

"You're absolutely right," Smith said. "I'll just make statements . . . Your wife divorced you because you were involved with, or rather indebted to, several bookmakers, loansharks and other elements of the underworld."

"My ex-wife forgot to tell you that the debts were hers, and that those that she couldn't pay off with her ass, she passed on to me . . . That's right, Mr. Smith, when she couldn't screw herself out of debt, she gave them to me to pay off . . . I divorced her because I didn't have any other choice if I wanted to stay sane."

"I'm afraid you don't have much of a choice now," Smith told him, "if you want to stay on the force . . . This information doesn't *have* to go to Internal Security. . . ."

"There's where you're wrong," Singer told him, standing up. "It does. I've already asked the chief for a full dress departmental investigation, inspector . . . Now if you'll excuse me, I'll get back to the reports he's requested."

Tagget's meeting with Chelenko was set for eleven o'clock in the morning at the Strand Bookstore. Tagget arrived five minutes early and went inside to the tables where the half-price review copies were displayed. From time to time he glanced toward the door.

At ten-forty-eight a well-dressed, oriental-looking man walked up to him and said, "Chelenko. Is there some place we can talk?"

Tagget had not seen him come in. He looked like the man Claudia had described.

"There's a bar across the street," Tagget answered. "I can't vouch for its security."

Chelenko shrugged. "You go there," he said. "I'll follow."

A few minutes later they were drinking vodka in a

booth of darkly stained wood. The place was dimly lit, smelled of sour beer and had an old-fashioned embossed sheet metal ceiling. "Luck," Chelenko said, lifting his glass.

Tagget echoed the toast.

"It seems," Chelenko said, leaning against the back to the booth, "that our paths have crossed at a most opportune time."

"You told a friend of mine you had certain information I might be able to use."

Chelenko nodded. "You obviously don't want to waste time on small talk—"

"I'm afraid I don't have time."

"I understand. I've been hunted several times in my life and know how difficult it is to think of anything else. But let me assure you that your people, though they think you are back in New York, are still unable to locate you . . . Anyway, to put it succinctly, I know the names of the two men who were in charge of operations out of Twenty-nine Russell Square during World War II. And I believe I know where they can be found."

There was a roaring sound in Tagget's ears. The Russian drank more of his vodka and watched him silently.

Tagget took several deep breaths before he said, "I'm all right . . . go on."

"The two men are doing essentially the same thing now that they were doing during the war . . . only now the men they are recruiting are being sent into various nations in Africa."

"Mercenaries?"

"Leaders of mercenaries. They operate with funds from Rhodesia, South Africa and others. But they are sanctioned by the CIA and MI-6. It's a joint operation."

Tagget took another deep breath and said, "That explains why MI-6 and the Company have been trying so hard to get rid of me. They were afraid I'd eventually find my way to their operation."

"That, and other reasons," Chelenko said. "But for the time being you need only concern yourself with the recruitment aspect."

"If I might venture a guess, you're offering me the names of the two men who were my control during the war and where I might find them . . . if I agree to kill them?"

"Essentially . . . yes."

"Why can't your own people do it?" Tagget asked, resting his elbows on the table.

"We made two attempts to get them and both our agents were killed before they came anywhere near their targets. We don't even have a positive visual identification of your two controls."

Tagget nodded and asked, "What makes you so sure that I will be successful?"

"I'm not. It's an economy measure, if you will . . . a gamble."

"With *my* life," Tagget said, looking at the Russian.

"Without my information you are at a dead end and cannot advance toward your goal."

"You make it sound like a game, but what you're talking about is murder, treason—"

"Revenge."

Tagget became silent, then finished his vodka and said, "Let's walk."

Chelenko dropped a five-dollar bill on the table and they left the bar.

Tagget headed down Broadway with Chelenko at his side. It was several minutes before he said, "If we come to any agreement, it must be for *all* the information, not just the names of the men and where they are . . . I want to know everything you know. I've suffered too much to walk off without all the answers I can get."

"It's possible," Chelenko answered with a nod. "But only the names and where you might find them—until your end of the agreement is fulfilled."

"And what recourse do I have if you change your mind afterward?"

Chelenko shrugged.

They did not speak for several minutes. Tagget understood clearly that his only bargaining point was his willingness to kill these men Chelenko told him had sent him into France.

"We will of course protect you while you work for us," Chelenko told him, "though I might say that you do very well without any help from outside sources."

Tagget ignored the compliment and said, "I want it understood that once my business is concluded, then our relationship is at an end too. I have nothing but contempt for your organization and an intense dislike for your government."

"I never imagined your feelings to be otherwise."

"Then I agree to your terms," Tagget said without facing him.

"It's a wise choice, I think you know that."

"Since I'm being hunted, I might as well do some hunting myself."

"How soon can you be ready to leave the country?"

"Right away. Within a couple of hours."

"Have you the necessary documents . . . passport, credit cards and the like?"

"Yes," Tagget said. "In the name of Henry Morrison . . . But if I go to an airport, I'm sure to be spotted."

"That will be avoided," Chelenko replied. "Where are you staying?"

Tagget hesitated.

"Some trust is necessary, even between the two of us," Chelenko said.

"The Hotel Seville . . . It's on Twenty-ninth, just off Lexington . . . Room 804."

"Twenty-nine does seem to be important in your life," Chelenko commented with a smile. "My grandmother would have made much of that. Anyway, I will send a cosmetician to your room. When you emerge you will not be recognizable. Do not check out or pay your bill. That will be taken care of in a day or so."

Tagget nodded.

"Be at the information desk of the International Building at Kennedy Airport at six o'clock this evening," Chelenko told him. "You will be met there by someone from our mission who will tell you where to go for your plane ticket . . . When you arrive at your destination you'll be met by another one of our people and escorted to your hotel."

"You mean that your colleagues intend to keep a close watch over me, isn't that right?"

"You'll have the same freedom as any other agent working for us."

Tagget smiled. "Where am I going?"

"You will be told everything on the way to the plane," Chelenko said. "Now you must excuse me, I have to return to my office."

Tagget continued as far as Canal Street, where he hailed a cab and went back to the hotel.

Tagget's beard was shaved to a neat goatee, dyed the same reddish brown color as his hair, and he was given beetle brows and a pair of horn-rimmed glasses. Pieces of skin-colored wax were used to give his face more roundness. Neither he or the cosmetician spoke while the changes were made in his appearance to conform to the description in the passport Hentz had given him. When the work was finished, the cosmetician said, "Look in the mirror."

Tagget stood up and went to the mirror that hung over the dresser.

"Good," Tagget said with a smile. "Good, I wouldn't know myself."

The man then took a Polaroid camera and a U.S. State Department embossing tool out of his brown leather attaché case and photographed Tagget in his shirt, without a tie. As soon as the print was dry he trimmed it and had Tagget sign the edge of it, "Henry Morrison." Then he cemented it in place on the third page of the passport and embossed it with a strip of what looked like red and blue typewritten ribbon. He seemed satisfied, gathered his paraphernalia into the attaché case, picked up his coat and said, "I was asked to remind you to be prompt for your appointment."

"Tell Mr. Chelenko I will be there on time. And thanks for getting rid of these," he said, handing over his revolver and holster.

The man went to the door, turned and said, "When you meet Mssrs. Ross and Fleming, please give them my regards."

Tagget went back to the mirror to look at his face; he didn't know what the man had been talking about. Then, suddenly, he understood. He ran out into the hallway, but it was deserted. He shut the door, repeating the names to himself, trying to find faces to match them.

They meant nothing to him. He had thought that he would have more of a reaction—to this information above all—something that would ignite in him and bring his full memory rushing back. Instead his heart sank at the lack of response. He saw nothing, remembered nothing.

Or perhaps, he thought, they just buried this part deeper in me than anything else. . . .

At six o'clock Tagget walked toward the information desk in the International Building. A man with a coat draped across his shoulders fell in with him and put on an effusive demonstration of greeting to show that they were friends of long standing.

"I was so glad you called to tell me you're here for a few hours, Henry," the man said. "I'd have been very angry with you if you went off to London without having a drink with me . . . My, my, you haven't changed in years . . . You still look the same."

The man stretched his arm across Tagget's shoulder and whispered, "TWA, nine o'clock flight . . . in your name."

The charade continued as they made their way across the rotunda to a bar where they settled at a small table. The man continued to talk as if he and

Tagget had grown up together. Then he interjected, "Colonel Chelenko asked you be told that he wishes you well."

Tagget nodded.

"You will be paged at Heathrow by your new name and asked to go to the Intercontinental Auto Rental desk."

Tagget waited for more information and got nothing but a white envelope. "Your ticket," the man said. "First class."

"Tell Mr. Chelenko," Tagget said, as they got up and walked toward the doors of the building, "that so far the names mean nothing to me."

The man nodded, shook his hand and went across the roadway to the parking lot.

Tagget took the airport shuttle bus to the TWA terminal, walked directly to the ticket counter and found his flight number on the television monitor. He walked out to the gate with his small carry-on valise and was assigned a seat. Then he went to the newspaper stand, bought a paperback book and sat in the waiting area to read until boarding time. Now and then he looked up to see if anyone was watching him. He couldn't get past the first page of the book; Claudia and David were very much on his mind. He couldn't risk phoning either of them. If he survived, there would be no reason for him not to return in a few days, but if things went the other way . . . He took a deep breath and opened the book again.

Tagget waited for the final announcement before he boarded the plane. He walked up the drafty jetway and handed his boarding pass to the stewardess. To his left, the door to the cabin was open and he found himself looking at the co-pilot's seat.

It was empty.

He paused and stared at the vacant chair, feeling that he had forgotten something. He had an impulse to go through his suitcase one more time to see if everything was there. Then, for some reason, he thought of checking his gun to be sure that it worked.

The piece is German-made, Singer had said. . . .

He remembered that he had left the pistol with Chelenko's man to enable him to pass the airport security check. What was he thinking of? He stood looking at the co-pilot's seat. Other last-minute passengers were crowding into the vestibule, trying to get past him.

"Sir, you're in seat 6-E, right over here," the stewardess was saying.

He listened to the radios squawking in the cabin and the captain turned around in the pilot's seat to look at him. The stewardess had taken his arm and was trying to show him to his seat.

"What have you got back there?" the pilot said, sounding concerned.

A German machine-pistol answered the voice in Tagget's head.

"Sir, this way, please," the stewardess said. "As you see from the seatbelt sign here on the bulkhead we're about to take off. Please take your seat now."

"Where's the co-pilot tonight?" Tagget suddenly asked the captain.

"Right here," said a voice behind him. "Excuse me." The co-pilot squeezed past Tagget into the flight cabin carrying a cup of coffee.

The door to the cabin closed and Tagget went with the stewardess to his seat on the starboard side, just forward of the wing. "I'm an amateur pilot myself," he told her by way of excuse as she helped him fasten his seat belt.

"I see," was all she said.

He knew he was feeling a great deal of strain and realized that he needed some rest. He settled down with a pillow behind his head. Usually he was able to doze on long flights, but this one . . . Unlike the other passengers he would be crossing more than just five hours' worth of time zones. He was beginning a journey that would, he hoped, bring him face to face with the men he should have killed over half a lifetime ago . . .

Eventually the plane moved out to the runway and

the stewardesses made their usual announcements about the use of oxygen masks and the inflatable life preservers. He closed his eyes and let the familiar demonstration begin to put him to sleep. In another minute the engines turned up and the plane raced down the runway and was airborne, banking to the left over Jamaica Bay as it gained altitude for the long flight across the Atlantic.

A few minutes later, through a deep drowsiness, Tagget heard the captain's announcement to passengers over the intercom thanking them for flying TWA and reporting that their estimated flying time would be eight and one-quarter hours.

"We will be flying tonight at a cruising altitude of thirty-seven thousand feet," he said. . . . *We're going down to seven hundred feet,* said another voice . . . "and expect to arrive at Heathrow airport at approximately ten o'clock London time" . . . *They're behind us,* said the other voice, *one at five o'clock, the other at seven. Usually they stay about five hundred feet behind me. . . ."*

". . . —turbulence, but should we encounter any, please observe the 'fasten seat belts' sign on the bulkhead in front of you. Good evening, and have a pleasant flight." . . .

Drop zone said a voice to Tagget in his sleep.

XII

Ross PUT down the phone and immediately summoned Fleming to his office, then made a half turn in the swivel chair and looked through the large window at Great Ormond Street, which was wet with rain and glistened under the light from a street lamp across the street. He rubbed his chin and wondered whether Howell was unduly alarmed, or the situation as serious as the deputy director had made it sound.

Fleming entered the room without knocking.

Ross turned and said, "I just had a call from Howell in Washington . . . You remember John Tagget, don't you?"

"Yes, of course I do," Fleming answered, settling into a large leather chair in front of the desk. "Has he turned up again?"

"Howell said he might be on his way here to kill us," Ross said. "Now."

"How could that have happened?" Fleming had gotten to his feet again.

"I asked Howell the same question," Ross said, "and he hedged. Tagget, from what I could gather, managed to figure out his connection to the Twenty-nine Russell Square ops. He dredged up some residual association with the place, and then there was a series of incidents that enabled him to verify it—"

Fleming shook his head. "I thought that situation was taken care of years ago, when we turned him over to that special American unit—where was that hospital located?"

227

"Somewhere in Texas," Ross answered. "Howell thinks the KGB might try to get at Tagget, set him up and make this whole thing look like one of our agents has rebelled against oppressive Western intervention in indigenous movements within the Third World. Their typical bullshit, but in this case it would be most effective, considering who Tagget is and was."

"How the bloody hell do they know about *him?*" Fleming asked, now pacing back and forth. "Good God, does anything ever get by them?"

"It's only a guess on Howell's part," Ross said. "In any event, the man is worried. Tagget has already done a good deal of damage."

"What are we supposed to do?"

"There isn't much we can do," Ross said. "I suppose the Company and MI-6 can step up our security . . . But if the Russians couldn't get to us, I don't see how Tagget would manage. All the same, before we interview any of our prospective clients for the first time I think some of our people should visit them and do some screening."

Fleming nodded and said, "Tagget gave us a great deal of trouble. I don't even remember how we finally managed to have him captured, do you?"

"No," Ross answered. "I don't really remember what he looked like, at least not enough to recognize him now. But Howell is wiring facsimiles of some recent photos tonight."

"Perhaps we should close up shop here for a while and move to another location."

Ross frowned. "That won't be necessary. I suspect Howell was overreacting."

"The Russians no doubt know where we are and what we're doing. My guess is that if they wanted to take us out bad enough, they would have done it by now."

"That's my thinking," Ross said. "The loss of two men wouldn't have stopped them, especially since we've increased our activities in the last six weeks."

"I'll give our man at MI-6 a call and tell him

about your conversation with Howell," Fleming said, going to the door. "I'll suggest he arrange some sort of a schedule with your people in London to give us a bit more security."

"That should do it," Ross said.

The door closed and Ross was alone. He bent over the papers on the desk and after making a half-hearted attempt to read them, he leaned back in the chair, rubbed his eyes and thought why a man like Tagget would go to such extremes. He thought back to the war . . . he knew the real problem was that Tagget had never been a professional—Fleming, he had to admit, had seen that right away. But he himself hadn't realized how significant this was until he had become involved in cold war operations against Russia. Then he had to have professionals on his side or he wouldn't have survived.

The men he was recruiting now for various assignments in Africa were all professionals: They fought, died if they had to, because they did it better than they did anything else. They had no illusions about humanity or causes.

Tagget hadn't been cast in that mold. Even though he may have been a superb soldier, he always had been a civilian at heart . . .

Ross gave a quiet sigh. Some years back he had reached the conclusion that the Taggets of this world were better off dying gloriously than living to face the truth that they had been used, whether for an individual mission, as Tagget had been, or some larger, more routine operation like a battle.

Ross reached across the desk and switched off the lamp; then, taking his metal crutches from their stand behind his chair, he stood up and made his way slowly to the door. As far as he was concerned, Tagget had as much chance of ever getting to him and Fleming as a snowball in bloody hell.

Tagget put the paperback book down, reached up and switched off the reading light. The passenger next to him was a young woman who had watched the in-flight movie and was now asleep with a blanket wrapped around her shoulders. He envied her; he hadn't really had a restful night's sleep since . . . since when? He realized that no more than six, maybe seven days had passed since he had met with Hicks. No, that was wrong . . . it was more like eight days.

He wasn't really sure.

Tagget shifted his position and looked out the window. Far below, to the southwest, he saw the lights of a ship. He tried again to visualize Ross and Fleming but couldn't. Gradually the sky in the southeast became lighter and the clouds turned pink and then yellow with the on-coming dawn. Tagget closed his eyes and slipped into a light sleep. . . .

He awoke to the announcement that they were beginning their final descent into Heathrow. The young woman next to him gave him a cheery smile and said in a crisp Oxford accent, "I hope we're on time, I have another plane to catch."

"Where to?" Tagget asked, really looking at her for the first time. She was tall, slender and dark-eyed. Her hair was closer to light brown than to the dark blond he remembered seeing in the glow of his lamp.

"Moscow," she told him.

He looked at her questioningly.

She nodded and said, "I hope you enjoy your stay in London."

Tagget didn't know whether he was amused or annoyed. He apologized for staring at her. "It's just that I'm not used to being so well looked after," he told her. "First class, I mean."

She gave a small, light-sounding laugh and said, "I was on my way home anyway."

The plane dropped lower, banked and skimmed into a dense cloud mass. The FASTEN SEATBELTS sign came on, followed by the NO SMOKING sign as the plane passed through a little turbulence and did some violent jouncing for several minutes. Unexpectedly the plane dropped out of some low clouds and in less than a minute it touched down, sending a curtain of water flying from its wheels as it rushed down the rain-soaked runway, slowed and turned toward its unloading area.

Tagget and the young woman said good-by as they filed out of the plane. He checked through security and customs, then went into the main concourse of the passenger building where, as planned, he was paged over the public address system and asked to go to the desk of Intercontinental Auto Rentals.

"Nikolai Trusov," said the man there, offering his hand.

"I just left a charming comrade of yours," Tagget said. Trusov was a tall, good-looking man in his thirties with a black mustache and greenish eyes. "I have a car," he said. "Come."

A few minutes later they were in dark blue MG sedan heading toward London on A30.

"For tonight," Trusov said, "we have arranged for you to stay at Worsely House Hotel. Tomorrow you can take lodging anywhere. We want to make some changes in your appearance."

"That was already done in New York," Tagget said.

"Better if it is done again," Trusov said. "The room is in my name. It is a double. The cosmetician is waiting for us. And oh yes, you must limp again . . . Colonel Chelenko has informed us of the change and we think it would make it more difficult for any one from MI-6, or the CIA to identify you, if you limped but used your left hand in the normal manner."

"Anything else?" Tagget asked.

"Your hair and eyebrows will be dyed blond, you'll be given a beard of the same color, and your face—well, we'll leave it as it originally had been. Please, Mr. Tagget," Trusov told him, "open the glove compartment."

Tagget bent forward and unlatched the door to the glove compartment. There was a revolver and waist-band holster there. He took it out, keeping it below window level. "I left one similar to this in New York."

Trusov nodded.

Tagget opened his coat, lifted his jacket and clipped the holster to his belt.

"Now," Trusov said, "let me tell you some things about the men you're going to kill . . . You know of course what they are doing?"

"Recruiting mercenaries."

"That's right . . . Naturally we want to stop their operation . . . We had initially thought of having one of our men infiltrate their organization and expose it to the press—"

"I'm not in the least bit interested why you want them dead. Tell me where they are and I will do what I came to do."

"Colonel Chelenko warned me that you aren't much of a conversationalist."

"Do you know where they are?"

"Here in London, close to Russell Square . . . We were able to get a postal box number from the envelope in which they send their magazine, which by the way is sent to a select list of people who we think have been prescreened by MI-6 and the CIA as individuals who might be interested in mercenary assignments. Through the postal box number we were able to narrow the area down from the entire city to a street, then a house—not too far from Russell Square, as it turns out. We also have another problem; we don't really know what either one of them looks like."

Tagget started to laugh. "You mean to tell me that you've been able to find out their names, what they're doing and where they are, but you have no idea what either of them looks like?"

"We know that one of them uses crutches," Trusov said. "But many people do."

"I know all about crutches, Mr. Trusov. I'll keep that in mind."

Tagget lapsed into silence and looked out of the rain-spattered side window, hoping that he was on the verge of making a connection between the names and the faces that belonged to them.

"We were hoping that you would be able to identify them," Trusov said.

Tagget turned to him. "Maybe I will," he said. "So far they're just names."

"We'll talk about it later," Trusov said. "There are ways in which we might be able to help your memory."

London was a familiar city to Tagget. In recent years he had often made as many as five annual visits, and he always stayed at the Connaught, whose Victorian ambiance he preferred to the newer and flashier hotels.

Tagget had been idly watching the streets go by as they drove downtown and suddenly realized they were in the vicinity of the British Museum.

"Russell Square isn't far from here," he said, turning to Trusov. "It's just on the other side of the University of London."

"Then you have visited it before?"

"Yes . . . but not with any real purpose. I pass it all the time on my visits here . . . There's a very good Italian restaurant on Southampton Row, not far from the square."

"And you recalled nothing special during those visits?"

Tagget shook his head.

"We will drive there now . . . I would like you to have a chance to look at it again."

"I'm at your disposal, in a manner of speaking," Tagget said. He found himself wondering where Trusov carried *his* gun.

Trusov guided the car slowly around the British Museum to Montague Street, made the first right turn he could and then another right on Russell Square; then he stopped for a moment. "Twenty-nine is still there," he said, gesturing to a three-story brown sandstone building.

"Nothing," Tagget told him. "Absolutely nothing."

"I thought that perhaps under the influence of recent events, you might remember something about the house and the men you dealt with there."

"It was worth a try."

Trusov put the car in gear and within a half hour they were in the hotel room where the cosmetician, a slender gray-headed man, was waiting for them.

Trusov spoke to the man in Russian, then said to Tagget, "His name is Boris Yatsyna."

Tagget shook hands with him and glanced around the smallish room. There were two windows on one wall and a dresser and a mirror on the opposite side.

In English, with very little trace of an accent, Yatsyna said, "Please make yourself comfortable . . . Sit in front of the mirror."

Tagget loosened his tie and opened his collar as he looked at his face in the glass. He could see the strain of the last few days; his eyes were bloodshot from lack of sleep.

There was another exchange in Russian and it made Tagget uncomfortable to know they were talking about him. Trusov shook his head several times and Tagget suddenly sensed that Yatsyna outranked the other man.

Yatsyna said, "Comrade Trusov does not think you will agree to being hypnotized."

"And that was what the discussion was about? You're a hypnotist?"

"Yes."

"You're going to try and help me remember, is that it?"

"Yes, I would like to try."

"Go ahead, Mr. Yatsyna, hypnotize me." At this point, he would not be squeamish.

Yatsyna stepped in front of Tagget, while Trusov switched off the light and drew the shades on the two windows, steeping the room in gray.

"I want you to relax," Yatsyna told him in a pleasant tone. "Relax and look at the light." He took a pen light out of his pocket and moved it back and forth in front of Tagget. "Relax, and look at the light . . . Are you relaxed?"

"I don't know if I can."

"Tell yourself to relax," Yatsyna said. "Take several deep breaths and tell yourself to relax . . . Look at the light . . . You're beginning to feel much more relaxed . . . Much more relaxed . . . Tell me what you are thinking about, John."

"A sky full of clouds."

"Very good . . . Continue to look at the light . . . You are so relaxed, John, that you want to close your eyes and sleep . . . Your lids are very heavy . . . Close your eyes, John . . . Yes, John, you are now . . . relaxed . . . Can you hear me?" He could see Tagget responding well, as though he had been hypnotized before, he thought.

"Yes."

"John, I want to know about the men you met at Twenty-nine Russell Square."

Tagget nodded.

"I would like to know what they looked like."

Tagget took several deep ragged breaths. "In a plane," he said. "Night." He was perspiring.

"Who put you in the plane?"

"Ross and Fleming . . . Plans for an invasion . . . plans to give to Cordez."

"Where is Ross?"

"Ross is behind a desk . . . Fleming is to one side . . . There is a table with plans for the . . . invasion."

"Was Ross an Englishman?"

"An American," Tagget answered, shaking his head. "Walked with crutches. Fleming had long face with bad teeth."

"Tell me what Ross looked like?"

"Chunky man, barrel-chested." Tagget stopped, then jerked his head and made some guttural sounds. He began speaking in French and frantically waving his arms.

"John," Yatsyna said, "we are still in London. Tell me more about Ross . . . what did he look like?"

"Ross sat behind a desk . . . Fleming stood off to one side . . . He had a red face."

"Who had a red face, Ross or Fleming?"

"Ross . . . Ross had a red face," Tagget said.

"Can you see his face?"

"Yes."

"Can you remember Ross's face, and Fleming's face?"

A pause, then, "Yes, I can remember."

"John, when I count to three you will open your eyes. You will feel rested and you will remember very clearly what Ross and Fleming looked like." Yatsyna repeated his instructions twice before he began to count.

At three Tagget opened his eyes and sat quietly for a moment, then said as if on cue, "Ross was a chunky man with a barrel-chest and red face. Fleming was tall and slender, with a long face and gap teeth."

Trusov switched on the lights.

"How do you feel?" Yatsyna asked.

"Rested," Tagget answered, excited. "And I have a *good* picture now of what they looked like."

"Fine," Yatsyna said, "and now I will change your disguise."

Tagget asked if he had revealed anything else about his past.

"Nothing of any consequence," Yatsyna assured him. "You spoke in French, and mentioned a Cordez."

"I was sent in to find him," Tagget said. "But I never did. Strange, I don't even remember why I was supposed to find him."

"You said you were to give him the plans for the invasion, of Europe, I assume." Yatsyna said, removing the pieces of wax that had been placed on Tagget's face to make it appear fuller.

"Is *that* what I said?"

"Yes."

"Could you help me recover my memory of what those plans were?"

"I could," Yatsyna said, busying himself with the makeup, "but it's not within the scope of my orders."

"I don't understand," Tagget said.

"I was to hypnotize you solely to provide you with access to a description of Ross and Fleming . . . No other information is to be pursued. I am sorry, I cannot do what you ask."

Tagget was about to object but Yatsyna bent down next to him and looked at him in the mirror. "You are a very special case, and you must be treated with great care. We do not want to risk any sort of emotional trauma." Yatsyna began to color the beard. "You might wind up killing someone other than your targets, or perhaps go temporarily insane . . . I'm afraid that unless reasonable precautions are taken, you could find yourself in great difficulty."

Tagget was becoming more uneasy.

"What I am telling you," Yatsyna said, "is true . . . I have certain medication that I could have administered if you had reacted adversely to the things you remembered." He reached across the dresser and tipped his black bag toward them so that Tagget could see the various ampules it contained.

"Suppose I remembered the information on my own —would I still have a violent reaction to it?"

"I cannot answer that," Yatsyna said.

Tagget said nothing more. He was beginning to feel as if he were a walking time bomb. . . .

When Yatsyna was finished, Tagget's hair and beard were completely gray and his eyebrows were spotted with gray hairs. He was another man entirely. Trusov handed him a highly polished thornwood walking stick and suggested that the three of them go to lunch.

The next morning Tagget changed hotels, returning to the Connaught, where he registered as Mr. H. Morrison. His disguise was a success and he went completely unrecognized, even though he knew the manager, the desk clerk and several other employees from his previous stays.

He spent two hours before lunch shopping for some additional clothing. The shops and large stores were decorated for the coming holiday season and crowded with shoppers. He passed a window where a large illuminated calendar reminded the shoppers that there were only ten shopping days left until Christmas, and he reflected that he couldn't think of anything as remote as ten days away. The largest span of time he could project ahead was an hour, and even that seemed a generous amount. He spent time in Harrod's and walked along Oxford Street, stopping in a men's store to buy a serviceable trenchcoat and an Irish all-weather hat.

When he returned to the hotel he found Trusov in his room. Tagget was almost amused by the situation —Trusov obviously expected some sort of reaction, and when he didn't get one he seemed almost put out. He sat in one of the easy chairs, still in his coat and hat. He said nothing.

Tagget went about the business of opening the packages he had brought back to the room, then announced, "I'm going to lunch." He put on his new trenchcoat.

"We've located them," Trusov said finally.

Tagget stopped buttoning the coat. "Where?"

"A building on Great Ormond Street," Trusov said, as he stood up. "Here are several photographs for you to identify." He reached into his breast pocket and pulled out a small envelope.

Tagget crossed the room, took the envelope and moved to the desk where he could spread out the photographs. "How did you manage these?" he asked.

"This has been an ongoing investigation for some time now . . . You have come on the scene at the end . . . we hope. They publish a magazine *New Wars and Weapons* . . . I told you that we knew where they were receiving their mail . . . We simply had their people followed."

"And the photographs?"

"Once we located the house, we photographed everyone who went in and out of the place. We've been doing it for the last three months . . . But until you gave us the description of Ross and Fleming we had no idea who they were, or whether they were actually in the London office. Once we knew what they looked like, we went through the photographs. These are the best ones."

Tagget's hands trembled but he managed to open the envelope and take out the photographs. "Fleming," he said in a tight voice and set the first photograph down. "Fleming again," he told Trusov, putting a second photo next to the first. "Ross . . . I told you he walked with crutches."

One by one he went through the dozen photographs. "I can see them in that room at Twenty-nine Russell Square . . . I can see them as clearly as if I were there now. Ross has grown heavier and grayer, but Fleming hasn't changed that much."

"They're heavily guarded at the offices of the magazine," Trusov said.

"Is there a way for me to get to them?" Tagget asked.

"There always is. It is simply going to take some time."

"I don't have time," Tagget told him, almost shouting. "Any day now someone from MI-6, or the CIA is going to find me . . . I have to act within the next forty-eight hours. . . . Don't you think by now the CIA knows I left New York? And it wouldn't take any great genius to guess that I'm in London . . . They probably already know that I've teamed up with you people."

"We will do the very best we can," Trusov said defensively.

"If you don't do it, I'll try it myself."

"And get yourself killed in the attempt."

"I can't afford to wait for an ideal situation. I have to move now." He was pacing back and forth.

Trusov said nothing.

"Can you tap their phone lines?" Tagget asked, stopping suddenly.

"Yes . . . We've already done that. But they no doubt assume we have. We haven't picked anything up."

"Suppose I phone one or the other of them, posing as a potential recruit and explain their number was given to me by a mutual friend . . ." The plan quickly came full-blown into his head. "I call and say I'm a Frenchman . . . I speak the language well enough to pass for one . . . I can say I was given their unlisted number by a mutual friend . . . I hope you have the name of someone they recruited."

"We have a roster of all the mercenaries killed or captured by revolutionary forces in several African countries. It is by no means a complete list, but it is virtually certain that most of the men on it were recruited out of London, by Ross and Fleming . . ."

"Well, then forget it. They probably have records of some of those deaths and captures too. It leaves too much for them to check on, to verify—too much to go wrong. I need a journalistic cover, something on the same order as the cover they're using. You'll have to supply me with the name of a fairly obscure right-wing French journalist, someone likely to be interested in *New Wars and Weapons*, maybe someone who would want to do a story on the magazine, something like that."

"But the magazine is not just a cover; it is more properly what you call a front for the recruitment of these counter-revolutionaries. I think they will be exceptionally alert, even in their publisher roles—and especially now. What if they don't take this bait?"

"It's a chance we'll have to take."

"I will present your plan to my superiors," Trusov told him.

"Do that," Tagget said. "And tell them I want an answer by four o'clock this afternoon."

"And if they reject it?"

Tagget pretended not to hear the question and turned to the desk to gather up the photographs. "Here, I don't need these anymore . . . I know what they look like." He handed the envelope to Trusov. "Tell your people that four o'clock is my deadline." Literally, he thought.

Trusov went to the door, turned and said, "I will be back."

Tagget knew he had not left Trusov any room to move. He had given him a simple ultimatum because he planned to use the Russians to help him draw the British security people away from the house on Great Ormond Street and bring them in force to the area around the Cheshire Cheese restaurant. He would set it all in motion with his phone call and get the Russians and British out of his way.

He went to the window. The snow was as heavy here as it had been in New York, he thought, and traffic in the street below was just as snarled. You're close, he said to himself, very close, but not there yet. . . . He took a deep breath and left the room. Despite the snow, he couldn't bear the thought of waiting in a hotel room until four o'clock.

Tagget made the call to the offices of *New Wars and Weapons* just before five P.M. from the rear of a small pub on Doughty Street not far from where Charles Dickens had lived. He used the name of Gene Touret, a senior editor of the Paris-based monthly, *The Word of Truth*. Trusov had managed to come up with a copy of the French magazine from an archive somewhere and Tagget took the name from the masthead, hoping that Fleming, if he checked at all, would look into it no more deeply than he had.

He spoke with Fleming . . . feeling curiously calm . . . and arranged to meet him at eight that night at the bar of the Cheshire Cheese, explaining he had some business in the meantime with one of the publications on Fleet Street. It went so smoothly that he immediately began to wonder why.

He came out of the pub and walked over to pick up Trusov and Yatsyna, who were waiting inside the Dickens house.

"Fleming will meet me at eight tonight," Tagget told them. "He liked the idea that a French publication wanted to tell the story of his magazine's commitment to a free world."

"Where will you meet?" Yatsyna asked. Tagget told him as the three of them left Dickens house.

"Fleming will no doubt be guarded," Trusov said, "by two men, possibly more."

"I realize that," Tagget answered. "But if I get to Fleming, his guards won't be able to do anything."

"You don't mean you intend to shoot him at the restaurant?" Yatsyna said.

"Not if I can help it. The restaurant is on the right hand side of an alleyway . . . Some distance away, on the other side, is Doctor Johnson's house. Between the two, there's a large poorly lighted area, and just beyond the archway that leads into the street there are several more places that are also dark and big enough to hide me . . . If I get in to Fleming quickly, whoever is with him won't see it coming until it's over. You can't convincingly maintain a cover like theirs and at the same time have real security in the middle of London—you'd need to take ten men with you everywhere you went." He paused to see what the two Russians would think of his plan. He had certainly researched it carefully enough. It almost sounded workable to him; if he wasn't careful he'd be tempted to try it.

"There is one more thing," Tagget told them, playing it big. "I'll need a car and driver."

"But you never mentioned that before." Trusov had stopped walking. "We've less than three hours. We will not supply—"

Tagget cut him off. "Do I have the car?" he asked. "I'm not going to wait around to sign autographs on the street when this is over."

"It will be there," Yatsyna said, taking Trusov by the arm.

The three of them continued to walk, and to Tagget's relief there was no further discussion.

"We don't know that it *is* Tagget," Fleming said across the conference table to Allen Bisby, the MI-6 agent in charge of security for the operation. Fleming looked to Ross for concurrence as he spoke. "The man on the phone was certainly French . . . I know *that* when I hear it. Besides, he gave the name of Paul Duval, which checked out by our records as a fellow we did indeed recruit from L'Orient for the Ugandan project."

Bisby was a tall, angular man with a boyish face and limpid brown eyes. He was shaking his head. "George, this time it's an easy decision. My orders take the fun out of your burgeoning publishing business, I know, but they're explicit . . . I couldn't possibly allow you or Harry to expose yourselves to anything that in my judgment is such a potentially dangerous situation. I can handle things smoothly either way, just as long as you're not there."

"Harry," Fleming said in a tone that clearly indicated his exasperation, "will you please say something to this man to stop him from interfering."

Ross stubbed out a cigarette and said, "This time I'm afraid Allen is right. If this Gene Touret fellow really lives up to his magazine's name and was telling the truth, Allen could simply bring him back here and we could do the interview. Allen, we could make you a contributing editor for the evening."

"Good God, man, I can take care of myself," Fleming sulked.

"Yes, George, I'm quite sure you can," Bisby said, putting his hands in his pockets, "but this Tagget is by all accounts something of a kamikaze, isn't he? He's unstable. He's working entirely on his own, as far as we know. And he has already killed several men . . . all of them trained agents and I daresay fitter than any of the three of us." He smiled, but then caught sight of Ross's crutches. "Ah, well, look here, I've arranged for some of our people to pick him up at the Cheshire Cheese . . . If it's your French editor, then fine, we'll bring him here. If it's Tagget, we'll roll him up. The CIA want him, but if he gives my chaps too much of a fight—well, that's just why I don't want either of you about. Now the best thing you both can do is go about your normal routine . . . There is nothing further either of you can do until we've vetted this fellow."

"I'm going home," Ross said. "It's going to keep on snowing and I'd rather not have to move about in it. Are you coming?" he asked Fleming.

"I'll be along later . . . I have some editing to do."

Ross pulled himself up on his crutches and said to Bisby, "Give me a ring at home when you settle with Tagget—"

Fleming looked at him sourly.

"—if that's who he is, I mean," he added.

For the remainder of the evening Tagget had to contend with the watchful eyes of Trusov and Yatsyna in the hotel room. There was very little conversation among the three of them, though now and then Trusov and Yatsyna spoke to each other in Russian. He couldn't understand why Trusov was still so unhappy about providing a car and driver.

He turned on the TV set and pretended to settle down to watch a film. The two Russians pulled up chairs and joined him. After fifteen minutes he went into the bathroom, where he waited for a minute, then flushed the toilet and ran water in the sink. Then he drew his revolver from the holster and quietly opened the door.

Trusov and Yatsyna had changed the channel and were watching the evening news.

Tagget stepped back into the room and said in an ordinary voice, "Gentlemen, do not make any sudden moves . . . stand up slowly, hands on your heads."

When they turned and looked at him, Trusov started to speak in Russian—

"Put your guns on the chairs in front of you," Tagget told them. "One at a time. Use your little finger only."

Each man placed his weapon on the chair.

"Now take off your belts and ties."

"This will not go well with—"

"Your superiors," Tagget said, finishing the sentence for Trusov. "I don't really care all that much about them . . . I can do what I came to do better without the two of you following me around like nervous apartment dogs . . . Trusov, turn around. Yatsyna, you bind your comrade's hands behind him with a tie and his legs with the belt. And do it well. I'm sure you learned how in the Pioneers."

"What about the car and the driver?" Yatsyna asked.

Tagget shrugged and answered, "He'll probably be picked up by Fleming's men at the restaurant and sent out of the country . . . Yatsyna, come over here next to me . . . Closer. Come on, get over here." Suddenly Tagget raised his free hand and delivered a short chop to the back of Yatsyna's neck that dropped him to the floor. Tagget picked up the other tie and belt and bound Yatsyna's hands and feet.

"I thought we trusted one another," Trusov said, looking at his partner lying unconscious on the rug, and thought to himself, if Tagget became linked to the KGB his whole assignment would have been defeated.

"I wouldn't have to be doing this," Tagget answered, "if your superiors trusted me." Then, using his own neckties, he gagged first Trusov, then Yatsyna, and tied their necks to the iron bedstead. When he was satisfied that they were securely bound, he left his room, rode the elevator to the lobby and asked the doorman to hail a cab for him. It was still snowing.

By 7:30 P.M. Tagget was on the southeast end of Great Ormond Street. Number 16 was a third of the

way up the block, on the north side. He had left the
cab on Theobalds Road and walked to where he was
now standing. He was counting on at least one of
them being in the office, if for no other reason than
to hear the outcome of the operation that he hoped
was now in progress. If he found them both, they
could go as a team and his task would be that much
easier—and more rewarding. He could finish it quickly.
He also suddenly realized that the nest might be
empty and wondered if he should have burned his
bridges with the KGB so thoroughly. He had reacted
emotionally, angrily, he knew. Well, he was tired of
waiting.

He crossed the street and went directly to Number
16. There was a watchman seated on the other side of
the glass door.

Tagget went up the steps and knocked at the door.
The watchman waved him away. Tagget continued
knocking with his left hand, keeping his right hand in
his coat pocket, holding the .38.

The man came to the door and motioned to indicate
the building was closed.

Tagget pointed down the street, and the man finally
unlocked the door to ask, "What is it?"

"My car has run—" He pushed his way inside and
pulled the revolver out of his pocket. "The offices of
the magazine?"

The watchman pointed to the upper floors.

"Where?"

"One flight up."

"Anyone there now?" Tagget asked.

The man hesitated, then nodded.

Tagget ordered the watchman into the broom closet
off the hallway and tied him to the pipes of the deep
sink using the cord of a floor polisher. He moved up
the steps to where the editorial offices of *New Wars
and Weapons* were located. They appeared to be
closed for the night, but there was a sliver of light
coming from under one door.

Tagget placed his hand on the knob, listened to the

boom of his heart for a moment, then shoved the door open. He cocked the revolver; in the small room it made a sound like knuckles cracking.

Fleming was at his desk. As he looked up, astonishment filled his face, then disappeared as he asserted the old control.

"Do I need an introduction?" Tagget said.

"How did you get inside?"

"I just followed my nose. It took me thirty-five years."

"What are you doing here?"

"I want to report back to you, at long last."

"You've altered your appearance, but you haven't changed that much . . ."

"Oh yes, I have. There's a whole new side to me." Tagget reached out with his left hand and swept the large globe from the table beside him. It crashed to the floor.

"Look here, I can appreciate—"

"We're going to have a debriefing session." Tagget stepped closer, breathing hard. For an instant he remembered the office at 29 Russell Square. Before, Fleming had always stood off to the side of the room, where the fireplace had been.

"Why was I sent into France?"

"You were on a unique and highly sensitive mission. At that time—"

"Stop it! I want you to tell me *why I was sent in.*"

"Well, you went in to deceive the Germans . . . It was arranged with Gunner, one of our men. It was one of the most difficult things I have ever . . . good lord—"

Tagget stiffened. He had put both hands on the pistol to steady it, and Fleming had stopped in midsentence. The memory of the pain he had suffered filled his brain and made it difficult for him to speak. He was afraid he was going to empty his gun into this man's face without stopping to learn what he had come to find out. Finally he managed to ask, "What information did I have?"

"You don't remember?" Fleming was talking to him like a priest to someone on the ledge of a sky-scraper, calmly, soothingly, the way Yatsyna had spoken during the hypnosis. Tagget shook it off.

"Would I ask if I did?"

"All right. You were to tell them that the invasion would take place in Brittany, with the city of Brest as its central objective. You were to give them the right date but the wrong place. Our hope was that the Germans would believe you and shift their armor south."

"They did, didn't they? I mean, they believed me . . ."

"Yes, and they shifted the panzer divisions. It was one of our most successful operations—"

"Why did they believe me?"

For several moments neither of them spoke; then Fleming said, "The war simply had to be won . . . many things were done to make that possible. Your sacrifice, then—"

"I remember my sacrifice. I asked you why the SS believed me. How was I able to persuade them that my information was true?"

Fleming's composure began to drain away. "You were highly trained, very highly motivated. Even under interrogation you were able to—"

"I wasn't able to do anything except beg for it to stop—that I do remember. And I gave the Germans everything I had, I spilled it all to them finally, I remember that too. I lived with the guilt of that betrayal . . . never mind that I wasn't consciously aware of it . . . twisting inside of me for thirty-five years. Whatever you two gave me, the Germans got. So why would they still believe my story about an invasion at Brest?"

Tagget watched real fear spread across Fleming's face, and suddenly he understood. "Oh Jesus"—he almost choked on it—*"that's all I had. That's all you gave me, wasn't it?"*

"All I can tell you is that your mission was one of

several coordinated efforts—successful ones—to facil-
itate the invasion of Fortress Europe, and that in the
context of those who did not even survive, your sacrifice was a very grave one but still short of what many
others suffered—"

"What about the things being done to me now,
these last two weeks? How much longer did you plan
to let me pay for failing to yield up the 'ultimate
sacrifice' and just die in that stinking Nazi cell?"

"The work we're doing is important," he said. "It
has to continue." He spoke in a dead monotone.

"You're sweating," Tagget told him.

Fleming used his hand to wipe the perspiration from
his face.

"I want Ross's address," Tagget said, suddenly
calmer. "You can give it to me and spare yourself
some pain, as they say, or—"

"No matter what I do you're going to kill me."

"Yes."

"Then do it and get it over with."

"I won't make you wait thirty-five years . . ." He
couldn't manage even a grudging admiration for the
man, though he wondered if Ross would make the
same show of courage—

Fleming moved. Somehow there was an automatic
in his hand and he was trying to pull the slide back
to get a round into the chamber.

Tagget squeezed the trigger of his revolver. The
explosion filled the room, and blood spurted from
Fleming's neck.

Tagget pulled the trigger again. He imagined he
saw the bullet hit Fleming in the chest. Fleming
slumped over the desk with the automatic still in his
hand.

Tagget went to the desk and found a sheet of paper.
With Fleming's blue editing pencil he printed a large
T—he couldn't think of anything else—then started
out of the room.

The phone rang.

Tagget went back to the desk and lifted the receiver, instinctively staying away from the window.

"George," the voice on the other end said, "Tagget wasn't at the Cheshire Cheese. No one was. Bisby is on his way back to the office, so stay there until he shows up. Something went wrong."

Tagget looked down at Fleming's body.

"George?"

"George is dead, Ross," he said into the phone.

"Who is this?"

"George is dead . . . you'll be next . . ."

"You're mad . . ."

"I suppose we both are, in a way . . . except you're blind to yours . . . To you and the people with you, everything is still a game. It isn't, though. It never was. The war I remember was a fight for survival, and I did survive . . . I will survive, Ross. You won't. . . . Sooner or later I, or someone like me, will get to you. The Russians know who you are. Just hide, Ross. Find some rock and crawl under it."

Tagget put down the phone and walked out of the room, down the steps and out into the street. All he wanted to think about was somehow going back to New York, getting his story to the President's aide, Nathan Pierce, and marrying Claudia. He had seen his past, and like most men, he looked forward to forgetting it. Someone he once had been had ceased to exist somewhere in France during 1944, only it took the better part of his life for him to hear about it. . . .

London, May 25, 1944

Fleming put his head into Ross's office. "It's confirmed. Tagget was taken prisoner last night at the town of Monteneuf. A member from his own group set the capture up."

"Your man?"

"Yes," Fleming said.

"Now we just have to wait and see how much the

Germans believe of what Tagget tells them," Ross said.

"At least the bloody beggar is no longer a threat to us."

"Yes, that's something," Ross answered, going back to work on the papers on his desk. Fleming went to the map on the wall to see exactly where the town of Monteneuf was located.

"We should hear from Ultra within seventy-two hours," Ross said without looking up, "whether von Rundstedt will be moving anything south to defend Brittany."

"I think generals Menzies and Donovan should be notified of Tagget's capture and alerted to the possible redeployment of enemy tank units."

Ross smiled, nodded, and reaching for the phone said, "I think this calls for something of a modest celebration."

"I couldn't agree more," Fleming answered, allowing himself a pleased little laugh. . . .

Bestsellers

from

BALLANTINE BOOKS

20   AL-39